ZODIAC TACTICAL
RESCUE UNIT

CODE NAME:

LIBRA

USA TODAY BESTSELLING AUTHOR

JANIE CROUCH

CODE NAME: LIBRA - ZODIAC TACTICAL

To all Libras out there…
Thanks for keeping the scales balanced and trying to make the world a better place.

Chapter 1

Landon Black

Taking a bullet to the chest sucked.

Taking a bullet to the chest from someone who was your friend *really* sucked.

But worse than either of those were the side-eyed glances you got from everyone around you as you recovered.

The *whoa, is he going to topple over?* side glances and winces after people slapped you on the shoulder, worried they'd hurt you with the friendly gesture.

I'd become way too familiar with those over the past six months.

Worse than the bullet hole itself—and that had been pretty damned painful—was the fear that no one was ever going to treat you normally again. That you were never going to remember you were once a deadly Navy SEAL, then had become an agent for one of the top security firms in the world.

Because that person felt pretty long gone.

But smiling through it all? *That* was the absolute worst.

Smiling was what I did. It was what I was known for. I was the charmer, the peacemaker. The one who made everyone laugh and was tactful and charismatic.

The *Libra*.

It was my code name here at Zodiac for that very reason. I was all of those things.

And now I was expected to be all of those things with a bullet scar on my chest only a few centimeters from my heart.

Honestly, the scar I didn't mind so much. It could've been worse. I knew that every single day.

But I'd been relegated to desk duty for the past six months since "the incident." *That* was driving me nearly insane.

Zodiac Tactical was a world-renowned private security contractor started by my best friend and former SEAL teammate, Ian DeRose. The company provided expertise in tactical work of all types: risk consulting, intelligence gathering, private and corporate guarding, international hostage negotiation and rescue.

If the law couldn't—or wouldn't—handle it, Zodiac Tactical could.

And *did*, on a regular basis.

But we'd taken some hits of our own over the past year: kidnapped employees and loved ones, criminal masterminds attempting to take us down, bullet holes to the chest.

We were only now finally finding our footing again, putting Zodiac back on track and stronger than ever. The threat was over, eliminated by us. Everyone was free to return to their regularly scheduled programming.

Except me.

Every time I looked at the active mission calendar, my

name wasn't on it. For the past four months, I'd been traveling around to the different Zodiac offices, helping rebuild morale and take the emotional temperature of each group of people.

Flashing 'em the famous *Landon Black smile*, complete with dimples I knew how to use to my advantage.

Hopefully, no one noticed if it was a bit frayed around the edges.

Today, I'd been called into the Los Angeles office by Ian. Until "the incident," I'd mainly worked in the Denver office. But since that was where I'd gotten shot in the chest by the woman my best friend loved, it had made the place a little haunted for both of us. Neither of us had spent much time there since.

It was Saturday, which meant none of the regular staff was around the office. But when Ian had asked me to come in and meet with Callum Webb, I'd agreed. Callum was a federal law enforcement agent with the Omega Sector task force, or he had been until he'd been fired for helping Zodiac rescue one of our own a few months ago.

"Anybody here?" The empty reception area didn't answer me. "Yo, Ian?"

"Conference room," he called.

Even though he was the owner of the company, Ian didn't keep a real office here. He'd been spending most of his time in New York, wanting to be near Wavy and her newly prosperous art career.

The conference room at the end of the hall held a big, shiny mahogany table and expensive leather chairs.

"Morning." I walked into the conference room and smiled at the coffee and pastries on the table. "Nice."

"Help yourself." Ian motioned for the food. "Callum stepped out to take a phone call."

"What's going on?" I stuffed an icing-coated cinnamon

something in my mouth and moaned in pleasure. I tried to eat healthy as much as possible, but damn I had a sweet tooth.

"He wanted to wait for you to explain it all." Ian cracked a grin as he watched me eat. "You need some time alone with that?"

I laughed and washed the pastry down with the coffee —black, hot, perfect. "No, but you knew bringing anything cinnamon in here would tempt me."

He nodded. "I did, indeed."

Before I could press him more about that, the door at the back of the conference room opened, and Callum walked in. He looked the very picture of a federal agent: hair cropped short, tie wrung to the side where he'd pulled at it, exhaustion bracketing his mouth.

Ian and I both stood, and I held out my hand to greet our friend.

"How's it going, Webb? You here to ask for a job?"

We'd both give him one in a heartbeat. He may not have been a SEAL like Ian and me, but he was someone I would trust at my back during a fight.

"No, I've thankfully been reemployed by Uncle Sam, at least for the time being. The fact that we put Mosaic away for good helped get me out of the doghouse."

Mosaic—a pretty name for an ugly group of scumbags —had been the bane of our existence for nearly a year. They were the reason I'd been shot and the reason why Ian now had a little gray in his dark hair.

I reached for my coffee cup and held it up as a toast. "To doing what we can to stop the bad guys."

"I'm hoping maybe you'll be interested in stopping some more bad guys." Callum fixed his serious gaze on me as we sat down around the conference table. "You specifically, Landon. Some undercover work on a tropical island."

I glanced at Ian out of the corner of my eye. He didn't look surprised as he took another sip from his mug. Which meant he knew from the beginning Callum had been here to see me.

I ran a hand through my hair and let out a sigh. "No need for a pity fuck, you guys."

Callum laughed as Ian spewed his coffee. "I'm pretty sure Wavy wouldn't approve of me fucking you in any way, pity included."

I leaned back in my chair and kept my eyes pinned on Ian. "Did you offer me to the Feds because you know I'm going crazy on desk duty?"

Callum held out a hand in a gesture of peace. "Hang on. Ian didn't contact me. I gave him the mission parameters and asked him who he thought was the best fit."

I raised one eyebrow so high I was afraid it might get stuck there. "And surprise, surprise, Ian thought of his friend Landon for a gig on a tropical island. Sounds like a way to get me to take a paid vacation."

I'd had enough vacation sitting in that hospital a few months ago. I was tired of feeling useless.

Ian crossed his arms over his chest. "Why don't you hear Webb out, then you can decide if you're interested in this particular fuck. Which, I can promise you, is not pity."

Ian and I stared each other down. We'd known each other for nearly twenty years. Had saved each other's lives more times than either of us kept track of.

But the last few months had been hard for both of us.

"You don't owe me anything, Aries," I muttered, calling him by his Zodiac code name. "Wavy doesn't either. What happened, happened."

He gave me a short nod. "I'm not sure she sees it that way, but I'm not trying to babysit you. Callum came to me, and you're the best fit for the mission. If you don't want to take it, that's no problem."

I stared at Ian a couple more seconds before turning to Callum and flashing him a full-dimple smile. "Woo me."

Callum chuckled. "Imagine the beautiful sandy beaches of a private Channel Island…"

Off the coast of California. Known for their beauty and privacy—particularly catering to the rich and famous. "Sounds good so far."

"Now imagine a high-level member of the Frey Cartel being there, ripe for giving up information to us."

I sat up straighter in my seat. He was talking about one of the biggest organized crime syndicates in California, probably in the entire United States. "Seriously?"

"Yeah. The Frey Cartel was in bed with Mosaic. We didn't have enough intel to make arrests, but they've been on federal law enforcement's watch list for a while."

"And they're going to be hanging out in the Channel Islands?" I asked.

"Vincent Frey, third-highest member of the cartel, is going to a wedding there. Oliver Thornton, father of the bride, was connected to him in the past."

"Is Thornton a criminal also?"

"Not as far as we know. He's a financial investment guru. In the past, he's offered financial advice to the Frey Cartel for their freshly laundered money. Ethically questionable, maybe, but not illegal."

Callum opened a folder on the table in front of him and slid several pictures toward us. "Thornton's daughter Christiana is getting married. They're doing an over-the-top, weeklong celebration on the island, and our intel tells us Vincent Frey is on the guest list."

"Do you have enough to arrest him?"

"We could arrest him at any time, but not for anything

significant, and it wouldn't bring down the cartel. So what we need you for is an info-gathering mission. The main objective is to put a nano transmitter on either Frey's phone or computer."

Ian and I exchanged a glance. Nano transmitters were virtually untraceable once placed and would allow Callum and his team to gather important intel—track locations, record calls, access any apps or websites that were opened on the electronic device to which it was attached.

But Frey wasn't just going to offer up his phone to a stranger. Computer would be even more difficult. "Good idea. But that's not going to be an easy task."

Callum rubbed the back of his neck. "Very true. If it were easy, we'd have already done it. We're hoping the wedding will put everyone a little more at ease. Thornton has rented out the entire island for the event, which is, of course, invitation-only. And security will be top-notch. Nobody is getting on that island if they're not part of the wedding."

Ian slid the tablet to me, and I flipped through the pictures. The first few were various angles of Vincent Frey. The last one was of a family. I focused on it.

The caption said the man in the center was the financial adviser and host of the wedding, Oliver Thornton. To his right were two women who looked like they'd stepped out of a trophy wife catalog—identical younger and older versions of each other. Perfectly coiffed blond hair, pencil-thin figures, heels that had to be nearly impossible to walk in. Their clothes were tailored to fit them, and the perfection in their faces screamed expensive spas and high-end cosmetics.

To Oliver's left was another woman, not quite as impeccable as the other two. Her hair wasn't truly blond, but it wasn't brown. It was pulled back and over one shoulder in messy curls. She wore a tailored dress as well, but where the other two women's were deep blue, hers was a cheery, pale yellow. She also had several more pounds on her than the other two—not fat by any means, but...*softer*.

While the whole appearance worked well for her, she looked out of place in a photo obviously meant to show off the family's level of wealth and prestige.

"Meet the Thornton family," Callum said. "The one with curly hair is Elizabeth. She goes by Bethany and is who you'll be focusing on. The other daughter is Christiana, the bride, and next to her is Thornton's wife, Angelique."

"Why are we focusing on Bethany?" And why did she look like the odd man out in her own family photo?

Callum shrugged. "Intel suggests Bethany is not close to her family. She owns a bakery about an hour north of here."

I slid the tablet back to Callum. "Why aren't you handling this in-house?"

He leaned back in his chair and ran a hand down his face. "We have a mole—someone in the department is leaking intel. I know it's not me and am certain about my direct supervisor, but that's it. He gave me permission to outsource this and is securing funding our department won't be able to trace."

Callum glanced quickly at Ian then back to me. That probably meant Ian wasn't charging Callum anywhere near what Zodiac would normally charge for a mission like this. Ian was a billionaire and could afford to take the loss. He also knew I'd work for free if it meant helping take down the Frey Cartel.

They were all sorts of bad news—weapons and information sales, drugs, backing terrorists. It would be my pleasure to do this small part in helping to shut them down.

"How are we going to get invited to this high-society wedding?"

Callum tapped the picture on the screen again. "Bethany."

I raised an eyebrow. "I'm not interested in some sort of Romeo seduction mission."

Ian smiled. "Speaking of pity fuck…"

Callum shook his head. "No, romance is not our in, but Bethany's business is. She's a baker. While investigating the family, I found that one of her employees has a record. And, conveniently enough, a bench warrant for unpaid child support."

I hissed. "Asshole."

Callum waved it off. "Best I can tell, he paid it. But the idiot didn't do it through the courts, so the ex is claiming he never did. I've already talked to him and got him on board. The bench warrant goes away and his record will be cleared if he helps us get someone inside Bethany's baking business."

"That doesn't get us to the island."

"It does if she's doubling as both the bride's sister and as the primary dessert-provider for all the week's events. Christiana hired Bethany's Slice of Heaven to cater."

I frowned. "Why would someone with so much family money open a bakery?"

Callum shrugged. "The family has millions, so I don't know why the elder Thornton sister opened her tiny bakery at all. All I know is we're going to use it if we can."

"How? I may love to eat sweets, but I'm never going to pass for a professional baker."

"You don't need to be. The employee of Bethany's we're putting pressure on, Harley Winterfield, is an older guy who assembles her intricate cake stands and towers—

something that will definitely be needed for the wedding. It involves carpentry and basic mechanics."

I looked over at Ian. "This is why you suggested me."

Ian had known me long enough to know that carpentry was a side passion of mine. I loved tinkering—putting things together, figuring out how they best fit, making them beautiful. It was something I'd done since back in the Navy. It was a great hobby for when my insomnia kicked in and I wasn't getting much sleep.

"See?" Ian raised an eyebrow. "Not a pity fuck, asshole. Your skills are needed."

Callum smiled. "So, you'll do it?"

No mention of my injury. No questions about whether I was up to it. I wasn't sure if Ian had coached him on what to say or if Callum had faith I could handle it.

To be honest, I didn't want to know the answer.

It was a real mission, it was important, and it involved my expertise. I would take it.

"Hell yeah, I'm in."

"Bethany was due to fly out with Harley in two days." Callum pulled some papers out of his folder. "Here's the address of the bakery and a few small details about Harley that will help prove you know him. As soon as I give the go-ahead, Harley is going to call Bethany with some excuse about why he can't go to the island, but explain you're willing to step in."

I nodded and looked over the info. It said Harley and I had met at a home improvement store in the Valley and had traded a few jobs over the years, more acquaintances than anything.

Callum pulled a small jewelry box out of his suit pocket.

I already knew what it was, but I allowed my eyes to get wide anyway. "Callum, oh my God, don't you make me remember this cinnamon roll forever by proposing to me."

Ian laughed and coughed over words that sounded suspiciously like *pity fuck*.

Callum took it in stride and dropped down on one knee next to me. "Libra, would you do me the honor of" —he popped open the jewelry box to reveal the nano transmitters—"helping us catch some real dickheads and making sure they go to prison for a long time?"

I put my hand up to my mouth and batted my eyes at him. "I'd thought you'd never ask. This is the happiest day of my life."

Callum snickered and handed the box to me before dropping back into his chair. It contained three clear pieces of what looked like tiny strips of tape with a wire in them that was just as translucent.

"Phone is best, followed by a computer," Callum said.

I studied the transmitters more closely. "Getting close to Frey isn't going to be easy. These cartel guys are well guarded, wedding or not."

Callum waggled his eyebrows. "That's why we came to you. My fiancé is good with people. If anyone can get close to Frey, it'll be you."

Before being shot, I would've said that was true. Now it felt like my people skills were as rusty as my smile. "Yeah, that's me. People person extraordinaire."

"You're going to have to be," Ian put in. "Because if you get caught, Frey won't hesitate to take you out—and I don't mean on a date—and you're not going to have any backup that can get to you quickly."

Callum flinched. Ian knew what it was to work under-cover—for the very law enforcement team Callum was a part of—and for them not be able to get to him in time to stop him from going through hell.

I didn't want Ian's past to spiral into me needing a babysitter. "I can handle it."

For just a second, it looked like Ian was going to argue, but he nodded instead.

"Once you get on the island, before you get anywhere near Frey, you'll need to hack into the resort's security feed," Callum said. "Frey's people will be watching it, and we don't want to make them suspicious. I'll talk you through it once you're on the island."

Didn't sound too hard. "Okay."

"But first, you need to get Bethany Thornton to agree to take you with her. Her employee was sure she knows nothing about any cartels when we explained Oliver Thornton's connections. Says she's one hundred percent on the up-and-up."

"You concur?" Ian asked.

Callum shrugged. "It's hard to say with these kinds of people. Don't assume anything." He slid the whole file over to me and stood. "Everything I know that could help you is in there. Memorize it. Don't take it with you."

I made a face as I stood also. "Not a rookie, asshole."

He shot me a grin. "That's fiancé asshole to you, lover."

"Bigger problem is that you're pairing sweet tooth here with a baker," Ian said. "He may weigh three hundred pounds by the time this is over."

Callum shot me a smile. "Fine with me as long as we take down the bad guys."

Chapter 2

Bethany Thornton

"Bethany, you there?" Harley's voice came over the answering machine and filled the kitchen. "Pick up if you are."

I hurried toward the landline on the wall, mixing spoon in one hand, spatula in the other, and hit the speaker button with my elbow. "I'm here."

"Sorry to call you like this. I didn't know if you'd answer."

Harley knew I usually came in for prep and to freeze cakes for the week on Sunday mornings before we opened. "Only for you. What's up?"

Sunday was the only day we kept reduced store hours, and I never answered the phone if the shop was closed. I'd learned that lesson quickly—keep regular hours and stick to them. Everyone deserved downtime, even store owners.

Maybe especially store owners.

"Bethie…"

I knew right away I was in trouble. Harley and my other employee, Michele, only called me Bethie if they were about to break bad news.

"I'm really sorry to do this so last minute," he continued, "but I'm not going to be able to go with you to the wedding. I've got a family emergency I just can't get out of."

I nearly dropped the spoon as I stared at the phone.

No. *No, no, no.*

Any time one of us wasn't able to work unexpectedly, it threw a kink into our well-oiled machine. Slice of Heaven required Michele, Harley, and me to do our individual parts at the required times. One of us not being able to do it put undue pressure on the other two—made life hard.

But this was much worse. *This* was a disaster.

I brought my hand up to my forehead to rub at the stress pooling there already, then snatched it back down when I realized I still had the spatula in it. I tossed both utensils into the sink.

"Harley, no. Please. I can't pull this off alone."

Especially not this. Arguably the most important event of my career.

"Bethie, I know. I'm so sorry. I…I can't get out of this. Believe me, if I could, I would. I wouldn't do this to you if it wasn't a noose around my neck."

He sounded so contrite I couldn't get angry with him, but I couldn't stop the dismay washing over me. What Harley did with the cake stands was beyond my expertise. I was a baker, not a carpenter. The complicated cake stands he put together took more than just understanding of how to use a drill.

I turned on the sink to wash the flour off my hands. Harley had worked for me for the past year, and every time he went on a job and did his magic with the cake stands, I wondered what I'd done without him for the year before when he hadn't been around.

Actually, I knew exactly how I'd done it. My cakes, while still delicious, hadn't been showcased well, and they had sold accordingly. My business had increased considerably over the last twelve months, and Harley's contributions were no small part of that.

I let out a sigh. "There's nothing you can do?"

"Family emergency. Believe me, I wish I could do something about it."

The word *family* almost seemed like a curse. *That* I understood, even though I'd never even heard Harley mention having one. He'd taken a few days off for fishing trips over the past year, but never for family.

He was a good employee overall. But this was leaving me hanging in the worst possible way. My own family emergency.

I dried my hands and rubbed my forehead again. "I don't know what I'll do."

"It's not total bad news. I've got a carpenter friend." He paused for a second, then continued. "He's available and needs the work. He'll be coming by later to introduce himself."

"One of your fishing buddies?" That was the last thing I needed.

"No, definitely not. His name is Landon Black. I'm sure he'll do just as well as I do."

"I doubt that. But I don't have much of a choice, do I?"

"I'm so sorry, kiddo. I was looking forward to heading to the island too. I'll see you when you get back."

"Yeah, Harley. Talk to you later."

I hit the button on the phone to disconnect the call and

pressed my forehead into the cool kitchen wall, fighting the urge to bang it instead.

Harley knew this job would put Slice of Heaven in the black, finally.

Yes, it was my sister's wedding. And yes, my relationship with my family left something to be desired. But the connections I would make by providing the most delicious of desserts all week would hopefully catapult the bakery to the next level.

Harley knew that. But he didn't know the bad part. That Christiana was marrying my ex-boyfriend.

It wasn't as seedy as it sounded. Simon and I had dated years ago and discovered pretty quickly we weren't meant for each other romantically. I hadn't cared when the two of them started dating. Their getting married wouldn't have been my first preference, but overall, it didn't bug me too much.

But oh, how the gossipmongers loved to make it into a *thing*. I was already the black sheep of the family because I'd done something as squalid as actually *working* for a living. Then my younger, thinner, more attractive, more exotically named sister *stole my one true love*.

Eye roll. It wasn't like that at all; Simon was very definitely not someone I was pining over. But nobody cared because...never let the truth in the way of a good story.

But it was critical nothing go wrong with the desserts I was providing. Harley not being there meant we were off to a banging start.

Christiana and I may not be close, but we were still sisters. She'd done me a huge service by hiring me to create the multiple cakes for her wedding reception, as well as the baked desserts for a number of events throughout the wedding week.

There would be so many wealthy, influential people in attendance, most of them from here in California. If I did this right, word of mouth from this particular group of people would propel Slice of Heaven to an entirely new level.

So, I'd accepted the job when she'd asked behind our mother's back. I wasn't sure I'd wanted to, but I couldn't turn down the exposure. I needed Slice of Heaven to grow.

There was no way I would ever go back and ask my family for money, no matter how much of it they had. No matter how many eighteen-hour days I had to work in a row to make Slice of Heaven successful.

For two years, I'd been chipping away at my personal savings, not taking any sort of salary, to get the bakery off the ground. And now, this was my chance.

I knew the exact point my mother had found out about Christiana's choice of me as baker. Three weeks ago, a friend of mine from culinary school had called to tell me Mother tried to hire her to provide the cakes for the wedding.

I'd expected it to happen sooner, if I was honest. Christiana must have done a spectacular job keeping me a secret. And three weeks out from the wedding, Mother hadn't been able to find someone of caliber who could fill in.

She'd thrown a fit that Christiana had hired me. I hadn't lost any sleep over it. Just like I hadn't lost any sleep over my parents partially disinheriting me when I'd gone this route.

The commoner's route. Mother had had the actual gall to use those words, as if we were the Bridgertons or something.

As if me pursuing my passion for baking—*owning my own damned business*—rather than marrying and playing tennis at the club brought embarrassment onto our family.

For shame. For shame.

With a sigh, I turned back to my cakes and got busy. I couldn't truly be mad at Harley. He'd been far too good to me. He'd worked insane hours helping me, and he hadn't stopped with carpentry. He'd done dishes, watched the front of the shop, and once had even helped me bake, though he hadn't liked it.

And when our business was at its leanest, he'd let me pay him late. I'd vowed then that I'd never forget that, and I never planned to.

I couldn't pretend to be happy now, though. Harley's announcement was just the, pardon the pun, icing on the cake. Things had been steadily going downhill for the past three weeks since Mother found out I was providing the wedding desserts.

First that, then my boyfriend had dumped me. He'd decided he was tired of always coming in second place to my business. He didn't like the hours I had to put in there.

There was no point in reminding him that I'd said no to going out with him six months ago because I'd known it would be unfair to any relationship to have to play second fiddle to my business. But Brad had insisted it wouldn't always be that way and that I was worth the wait.

Evidently, I was only worth six months of a wait.

I hadn't even cried. I'd honestly been more upset that I'd lost my date for the wedding than that our relationship was over. I'd envisioned myself standing proudly on Brad's arm while everyone oohed and aahed over my delicious creations.

Everyone, including my mother and father, bride and ex-boyfriend groom, would make their way over to me to show their amazement. They'd gush about how I was not only a fantastic baker, but a savvy businesswoman and someone who obviously had her personal life together.

I'd graciously accept their praise and smile up at Brad, who would stand supportively beside me, stating he'd never doubted this was how it would all turn out.

And...*scene*.

Yeah, maybe Brad had been more of a prop than an actual boyfriend.

But now, I was going to show up at the wedding not only as the hired help, but without my *plus-one*.

Mother would revel in it.

She'd already tried a power play. When Christiana wouldn't let her fire me, she'd decided to change the entire concept of the wedding cake design.

Every single bit of it. From size to tiers to structure to flavors. Then she'd announced she and Christiana would be coming to the bakery three days later to taste and see the conceptual design.

Brad should be glad he had broken up with me, because I didn't leave the bakery for a full seventy-two hours, working my ass off to get everything ready for their visit. By the time they'd walked through the door, I'd had a completely new design and several prototypes.

Mother hadn't said one nice thing about it, but I knew she loved it because she'd also not said one negative thing.

Not about the cake, anyway. My shop, my hair, and my hips were another story.

Story of my life. Always closer to a size twelve than a size two.

But hey, never trust a skinny baker.

I sighed and got back to work making cakes for this week. My other part-time employee, Michele, would be keeping the shop open while I was gone. No way could we afford to close for a solid week, even with the new business the wedding would hopefully bring in.

If this carpenter friend of Harley's worked out and the entire event didn't fall apart.

My mother would have a field day if it did.

I heard the back door unlocking. "Morning," Michele called as she walked through. "How was your weekend?"

I worked weekends whenever possible to give Michele that time off. I winced. Maybe if I'd saved a couple of weekends for Brad, he wouldn't have broken up with me.

"Well, there's good news and bad news." I grimaced at my friend and employee.

"Oh shit. How bad is the bad news?" She hung her purse on the hook by the door with mine. "On a scale of dang-it to jump-off-the-nearest-bridge?"

"Closer to bridge than dang-it."

She shook her head and grabbed a clean apron with *Slice of Heaven* embroidered on the breast. "That doesn't sound promising. Start with the good news."

"I got a lot baked and frozen for this week."

"You didn't have to do that." She bumped me with her hip. "I'm capable of baking everything on our menu. It's the fancy cakes I'm no good at."

"I know," I said. "But you're going to be working more hours than normal this week, so I wanted to do what I could."

"You do too much. Okay, bad news?"

I returned to the mixer and added a few spices, following the recipe exactly. "Harley called."

Michele was busily wiping down the glass fronts of our display cases. I glanced at the clock on the wall and realized it was time to open. Good grief. I finished the mix and got the cake in the oven, setting one of the many timers.

"Is he okay? I thought he would be here so you guys could finish your prep for tomorrow."

"No. He's got some sort of family emergency and can't come with me to the wedding."

She froze and looked up at me with her jaw hanging open. "You're joking."

I shook my head slowly. "Nope. He said he's going to send someone to talk to me who can do the job for him, but I don't know. A stranger?" I rubbed my eyes again, headache creeping back. "And I can't afford to close the shop and take you with me, even if you could do the stands."

Michele rounded the counter and put the cleaning supplies away as I stared at the front window, running possibilities through my head.

A car pulled into the parking lot. Usually I was happy to see the first customers right as we opened, but today, I could use a little more time to figure out exactly how I was going to handle this situation.

"First customer," I muttered, then plopped down onto the stool behind the counter. "Maybe I should cancel entirely."

Michele snorted. "You know you're not going to do that. One, your cakes are fucking awesome, and it's time for you to show both your family and all their bougie friends that. Two, there is no way you're going to give your mother a reason to say I told you so."

I straightened my spine. Michele was right. Well, sort of. If I canceled now, Mother would never say a thing. But her smug silence would be so much louder than her screaming *I knew it!* over a loudspeaker.

But I was really in a lot of trouble. The stands Harley was responsible for were elaborate and a huge part of the floating design Christiana and Mother had approved. I could probably do it myself, but it would take me five times as long. I was going to need that time for dessert preparation and decor.

The elaborate floating design with multiple arms and moving parts... I wouldn't even know where to begin.

The pain in my head was back with a vengeance. "I could go with a different design and just deal with my mother's fury afterward."

Michele wasn't listening to me; she was studying the man who'd gotten out of the car and was walking toward the door. "Damn. He's freaking hot. Ten bucks says he wants a red velvet cupcake to put an engagement ring in."

It happened at least once a month. A guy wanted to be original, and nothing said love more than decadent chocolate cake with cream cheese icing. We usually helped by providing a heart-shaped box.

I glanced in hot guy's direction, but I couldn't even force myself to focus on him or his engagement needs. What was I going to do? What if Harley's carpenter friend wasn't as talented as Harley was? Or what if he didn't show up at all?

I hunkered down on the stool behind the back of our display, hidden from the door. I didn't care about a hot guy. I was about to show up at my sister's wedding as both a personal and professional disaster.

The bell on the door rang as it opened, and I could hear the smile in Michele's voice as she called out her greeting. "Welcome to Slice of Heaven. Have you been in here before?"

"No. This is my first time." A smooth, deep voice washed over me like a blanket of soft silk, almost making me forget my misery for a second.

Almost.

"Let me guess, you're looking for a red velvet cupcake."

"That sounds delicious. But actually, I'm looking for Bethany."

I froze and hunkered down farther. What did he want with me? Why did he know my name?

"Harley sent me."

Holy shit. The gorgeous man with the equally sexy voice was Harley's replacement?

Chapter 3

Bethany

Sliding off my stool, I peeked through the crack in the cardboard display to get a truly good look at him, knowing he couldn't see me. He definitely was not one of Harley's fishing buddies as I'd been expecting.

Brownish hair with some gold highlights. Eyes streaked with gold and green. One of those fascinating granite jaws, covered with just a little bit of stubble, that made you want to scratch your nails gently down it. A mouth spread into a wide, handsome smile. Complete with dimples.

If those weren't overkill, I didn't know what was.

And that wasn't even taking into consideration his broad shoulders and long legs. His long-sleeved shirt was rolled up to expose the muscles in his forearms, wrists, and long, trim hands.

"Uh, Bethany was just here," Michele said. "Let me see if I can track her down."

He shot her another smile and turned to look around

the shop. So, I did what any reasonable woman would do when faced with handsome charm personified.

I dropped to the floor and crawled into the back room so he wouldn't see me.

Once the door shut behind me, I straightened up and tried to look normal.

Michele busted through the door. "Did you become a magician? How the heck did you get back here without us seeing you? I turned around, and you were gone."

"I cannot deal with a man like that," I declared. "Tell him to go away. I'll figure something else out."

How could someone who looked like him be willing to take a short-term carpentry gig that didn't even pay that much?

Michele looked at me like I'd lost the last bit of sense I had to begin with. "A man like what? Drop-dead gorgeous? That's his crime? You're telling me if he had a dad bod and adult-onset acne, you wouldn't have a problem with him working for you?"

I crossed my arms defensively. I did not need Michele pointing out how unreasonable I was being. "Might as well be. Bad things always happen in threes. First Brad, then Harley. Now this dude? No thanks. One look at him and I know he's bad news."

"You are being utterly ridiculous." Michele put her hands on her hips and stared at me. "Stop it right now."

I sucked in a deep breath. "I swear, Michele, this is too much."

All of it was too much. It was bad enough I had to deal with my family all week, maintaining the highest level of professionalism. But add Mr. September to the mix and I could smell the fiasco coming a mile away.

I could not show up to the wedding dateless, with a

gorgeous assistant in tow who may or may not know how to do his job.

Michele grabbed my upper arms. I had her in height by about four inches, but she wasn't about to let go. "Get out of your own head. I know you think of yourself as the ugly duckling, but enough is enough. He's hot, yes. But he's just a guy, and if Harley sent him, you need to give him a chance."

She glared at me until I squirmed. Who was the boss here anyway?

But damn it, she was right. I'd judged him in the way I didn't want people to judge me: on looks alone. Appearances could be very deceiving. I knew that better than anyone. Looking at me, nobody would've ever guessed I came from a wealthy and prominent Los Angeles family.

I let out a sigh. "I guess insanely hot is better than nothing."

"That's the spirit!" She gave me a thumbs-up and an eager grin before pushing me toward the door. "Now get out there before he thinks you're insane."

"I am," I grumbled as I pushed the door outward to go into the front.

The man was staring at our different desserts like he'd like to take his sweet time savoring each one.

What would that sort of intensity mean if it was focused on a woman?

I resisted the urge to fan myself. *Business. Focus on business.* Jeez.

I stayed on my side of the counter. There was no way I was walking around to his side. I needed to keep an expanse of glass and metal between us. "Hello," I said. "I'm Bethany."

He held out his hand across the counter. "Nice to meet

you. Harley told me you needed some help this week with carpentry."

I shook his hand, trying not to be distracted by his broad shoulders, deep hazel eyes, or those damned dimples. Tried and failed.

I cleared my throat. *Business.* "Yes, I do need some help. Do you have carpentry experience?"

He ducked his head. "I'm not a professional, but yes, I believe I have the experience you need. Since I left the Navy, I've been trying to figure out where I want to land in the civilian world. This job would help me out a lot, let me get a feel for carpentry work again."

I winced. "I'd hoped for a professional carpenter."

"I've always been very good with my hands." Was that a double entendre? Did I want it to be? I schooled my features and didn't acknowledge his choice of wording.

He'd been a service member. Now I had to deal with my imagination trying to conjure up an image of him in his uniform.

His *well-fitting* uniform.

My brain easily succeeded in imagining it. Then it changed, conjuring up a Navy uniform from days past, white with blue accents. A blush crept up my neck, but I ignored how hot he was in my imaginary uniform. This was going to be a lot of trouble.

Business. Business. Business.

And it wasn't as if I could say no. What kind of heartless bitch would I have been if I didn't give him a chance? A man who had defended our country. He was a veteran. A hero. He deserved at least the opportunity to prove his abilities.

"Would you mind giving me a demonstration of your carpentry skills?" I asked in the politest voice I could muster. My mother would've been proud of my cool tone.

"It's important that I don't head off to the event without being certain you can do the job."

"I'd be happy to," he exclaimed. "What do you have in mind?"

I turned to discover Michele behind me with an enormous shit-eating grin on her face. "Shut up," I hissed as I walked through the door and held it open for the mystery sailor carpenter. Turning my attention to him, I tried to smile, even though I knew it had to be coming across like a drunken grimace. "I didn't get your name."

To get between Michele and me at the door, he ended up sliding very close to me. I could've sworn I felt heat coming off his body.

As I tried to convince myself it was all my imagination, he stopped and looked down at me. His dark hazel eyes twinkled, and his gaze lingered on my mouth. "You've got a bit of flour there on your lip," he murmured. "And my name is Landon."

My breath caught in my throat as he moved farther into the kitchen. I released it and swiped at my lip, pushing the door closed in Michele's face so I wouldn't have to keep looking at her goofy smile.

"Through here," I said, motioning to the left to the large supply closet. All of Harley's tools and equipment were in here.

He seemed at ease as he followed me, looking around in interest. "I've never done any work at a bakery," he said. "If I worked here all the time, I'd have to spend every other moment in the gym."

"Oh?" I asked. I didn't look at him as I pulled out one of our simpler stands, and I forced my mind *not* to imagine him at the gym.

Too late.

"Yeah, I have a major sweet tooth. Especially for cinnamon."

I grabbed the small toolbox that Harley had put together and set it on the table in the middle of the room. "We have a delicious cinnamon roll cake you'll have to avoid, then."

He let out a groan that sounded actually pained.

Straightening, I spun around with my arm out. "The instructions are there on the table." The timer I'd set in the kitchen went off. "I've got to get some stuff out of the oven. If you could put this stand together, that would be great."

He saluted and turned toward the stand.

I wasn't sure I was meant to see that part, so I high-tailed it out the door and focused on my cakes. I needed to get a couple more in the oven before calling it a day, as well as frost a few I'd baked yesterday.

I didn't even get all my ingredients out before Landon walked into the kitchen. "All done."

He couldn't have been. That had been faster than Harley even, and Harley had a year's worth of experience with these stands. I followed him back into the storeroom and looked at the stand in shock. It was perfect.

"Did you use the instructions?" They didn't look like they'd been moved at all.

He shook his head. "No. This was fairly simple."

I tried to contain my amazement. "Wow. Okay. Yeah, that was one of our simpler stands, but you still did it really quickly. Interested in trying a more complex one?"

I wanted him to show me what he could do, but I didn't want to seem like a jerk.

"Sure." Dimples beamed. "Point it out. You don't have to get the materials. I know you have things to do."

I pointed to the shelf with our most complex stand,

one I'd be taking to my sister's wedding. "And, I hate to ask, but if you could dismantle this one?"

"No problem." Landon turned to get to work, so I stammered a quiet thanks and made my exit.

As I measured ingredients, I fully expected him to come to ask for a helping hand. There were intricate parts that Harley said needed two people.

But after a few minutes, I lost myself in my baking. That was what almost always happened. It was what had drawn me into the business in the first place. Mixing and measuring, focused only on what was in front of me, was like my therapy. Nothing existed but my ideas for treats, the ingredients, and making it all come together.

Everything else—pardon the pun—melted away.

I was well into frosting the mini-cakes the shop would be highlighting tomorrow when Landon stuck his head in.

"Bethany? I'm ready."

I set down my spatula. "You're finished? You didn't need help with the second level?"

He shook his head. "No. I developed a work-around."

A work-around. I was staring at him. "How long has it been?"

He gave me a half smile. "About an hour."

An hour. It would've taken Harley at least twice that, even with my help. Not that I'd ever complained about Harley's work. But Landon was faster by far.

Which was good. He'd need to set up nearly a dozen of these stands, and a couple much larger ones, while at the wedding.

"Let's have a look at it." I had a sneaking suspicion I didn't even need to check. I'd walk into the room and find it perfect. I wasn't sure if that reassured me or made me more nervous.

Michele walked through the door from the front. "Landon, we've got a couple cupcakes that we have to throw out today. Would you like one?"

His eyes lit up. Then he glanced at me and shook his head. "Not right now, but I appreciate it."

I laughed and took pity on him. He'd said he had a sweet tooth. "Go eat a cupcake. I'll come out when I'm done." I glanced at Michele. "That mix should be ready. Can you throw it in the oven?"

"Of course." She still had that giddy look on her face —like she knew if I hadn't thrown Landon out by now, I wasn't going to do it.

I hated that she was right.

Landon had erected the complex stand perfectly. I had no reason to deny him the position. He'd done an exemplary job, was utterly polite, and he'd look amazing in a suit setting up at the parties.

I wanted to bang my head against the wall.

"You have to hire him," Michele hissed as she walked back in. "He's perfect."

"Simmer down over there. Perfect is pretty extreme." I rolled my eyes at her. "But yeah, he did a great job."

"I know how important this wedding is to you. Impressing your family. Getting our name out there." Michele bent over and studied the underside of the stand. "This thing is exactly right, isn't it?"

"Yes." Of course it was exactly right. Was there anything about Landon Black not exactly right? "And yeah, this wedding is important."

"So, you're going to hire him?" Michele stood up and clasped her hands together. "C'mon, hire the hottie."

"You've got to stop." But a little laugh escaped despite myself. "You're going to get me sued for sexual harassment."

She giggled and grabbed my hand. "Come on, live a

little, Bethie. Give yourself some eye candy while you're having to deal with your stressful family."

"This is my chance to prove to my family that I made the right choice in opening my bakery," I said. "I'll hire him because he did a good job. Not because he's gorgeous."

"But you do think he's hot?" she asked.

I rolled my eyes. "Of course, I think Mr. September is hot." I made a sizzling sound as I pressed my finger against my hip, and Michele laughed.

A throat cleared in the doorway.

Aw hell.

"Sorry, I finished my cupcake and wanted to make sure you didn't need me for anything else."

There was no way he hadn't heard what I'd just said. I wanted to melt into the floor. Instead, I squared my shoulders and turned to face him as if I hadn't just made a completely inappropriate statement.

And lawd, he really was attractive. I gave him a brisk nod as I got my hormones on a tighter leash. "If you want the job, you're hired. We leave for the Channel Islands tomorrow."

He nodded back, all sexy hazel eyes and dimples. "I want the job."

"Michele will get you the info you need for this week." With that, I turned and walked with whatever scraps of dignity I had left back into the prep kitchen.

Crisis averted. I had a skilled carpenter who was going to help me make sure my desserts were nothing less than showstoppers at the wedding events this week.

What could possibly go wrong?

Everything.

And then some.

Chapter 4

Landon

Bethany Thornton was not what I had expected.

She'd looked a little out of place in the picture Callum had shown me—a little less glamorous and a little more sunny than the rest of her family. But she was coming from a lot of money, at least some of it gained illegally, so I'd been expecting someone at least partially closed off or defensive.

Bethany hadn't been either of those things. She'd been stressed by my presence and a little flustered, but she definitely hadn't come across as criminal in anything she'd done or said.

Of course, that didn't necessarily mean she was innocent. The last time I'd hung around a woman who'd seemed lively and creative and innocent, she'd shot me in the chest.

Things weren't always what they seemed.

But they weren't always what they didn't seem to be either. I could wax poetic about that for a while.

After she'd hired me yesterday, I'd taken the stands down and loaded a van with them and several more, along with a host of supplies. Evidently, Bethany didn't trust the island would have the specific ingredients and materials she needed to make her desserts. It seemed like she was taking most of her shop with her.

After we'd loaded everything nonperishable, she'd thanked me—still not quite making eye contact—and paid me cash. It had been my instinct to refuse since I was making a lot more money to infiltrate her company, but that would've been a dead giveaway. In the end, I thanked her graciously and promised to meet her here at the airport bright and early this morning.

She touched my arm as I turned to leave. "Don't be late. This wedding is…important."

Her voice was soft, a little hesitant, very un-criminal. She seemed quite young and unsure, and all I wanted to do was what came naturally to me: pull her in for a hug and let her know she could trust me.

Which she could. Sort of. At the very least, she could trust I was going to show up.

"I'll be there."

She nodded and attempted to tuck a strand of that riotous mess of curls into a braid behind one ear. She turned away, then glanced back at me over her shoulder. "Thank you. For showing up tomorrow. For your service to our country. For diving in and helping me out of a tight spot."

And didn't I feel like an ass?

I spent all last night studying the files Callum had given me. I knew more than I ever wanted to about Vincent Frey and the Frey Cartel. I read up on the Thornton family and Santa Catalina Island.

The information about Bethany herself hadn't been very thorough. She hadn't visited her parents in a couple of years, so obviously, they weren't close. There didn't seem to be much of a financial connection between them either.

Slice of Heaven was barely making it. Her parents could've helped out and at least eased the burden of the start-up loans Bethany was paying, but they either hadn't offered or she'd turned them down.

I saw her as my cab pulled up to the private jet section of the Long Beach airport. This airport was nowhere near as big as LAX, but it was definitely bigger than most regional airports in the country. Regular flights took off from here daily, but this section was reserved for private flights. No long-term parking that required a shuttle. No TSA security lines.

I'd gotten used to using Zodiac's private jet for a lot of my travel, although it was set up for meetings and strategy while getting from one place to the next. So, private jets weren't new to me. But they would be new to Landon the carpenter—I'd have to act the part.

Bethany stood beside a white van, checking things off a list on a clipboard while two men in yellow vests unloaded the van and loaded the items onto the plane. She shaded her eyes and turned to watch me step out of the cab, giving me a little wave. Relief was clear in her features. She'd been worried about whether I would show.

I grabbed my duffel and garment bag and looked around before pretending to notice her and returning her wave. The bay bustled with activity, boxes being loaded onto the plane, flight attendants and people in uniforms walking on and off the private jet.

Bethany walked toward me. I widened my eyes and nodded toward the plane. "We're flying on a private jet?"

She grimaced. "I may not have mentioned that the wedding we're catering is my sister's. And my family is…" She trailed off and turned to look at the jet with a lost expression on her face.

"Wealthy?" I supplied.

"Yeah. *Wealthy*. I'm not, but they are, and since I'm doing all the desserts for the whole week and technically a part of the family, we get the jet."

I whistled through my teeth. "You won't see me complaining."

One of the workers called over to Bethany.

"Go find a seat," she said. "We'll be taking off in a few minutes, but I want to personally make sure everything we need from the bakery is on board."

I boarded the plane and sat in the back, where I'd be able to observe everyone coming and going. The jet wasn't that big and had been built for luxury more than function. There were only a handful of seats in the passenger area. I wondered how large the cargo area was.

My answer came when the men in vests began loading boxes into the passenger area. Bethany came in and directed them while I sat back quietly watching.

With every second she worked, I could see why Harley had been convinced she was innocent. Why would someone put this much effort into a front? She obviously loved her bakery and took it seriously. Thankfully nothing about this mission should affect her business. I would be in and out without her ever being any wiser.

If it all went as planned.

I rubbed my chest over the bullet scar. It was a reminder that sometimes things went the complete fucking opposite of *as planned*.

It wasn't long before Bethany collapsed into the chair across from me. I grinned to cover my surprise that she sat with me instead of across the cabin.

"It's not even ten, and I'm already exhausted," she complained.

"You should've let me help."

As she rubbed her eyes, she smiled behind her hands. "This was more supervisory. I needed to make sure we have everything. But don't worry, there won't be as large of a staff at the island airport to help unload. I'll need your assistance there."

Which was unfortunately where I would need to get to my real work as quickly as possible, but I wasn't going to leave her in the lurch. "I'll be ready."

It wasn't long before the plane began to move, and I pretended to be excited to build my cover. "I'm used to flights on big Navy planes, strapped in and crammed next to my buddies."

Bethany peered out the window closest to her, then shut the shade. "This was the only way I traveled until I was eighteen and moved away from home to go to school."

"Are you excited to be catering the wedding?" I asked.

She sighed. "That's a loaded question. We're not catering the whole thing. Just the desserts, but…yes, I'm eager to show what I can do."

"Your family must be so proud and excited to have you serve your delicious treats—if they're anything like the cupcakes I tried yesterday."

She crinkled her cute little nose. "My family wasn't exactly supportive of my choice in career. My sister hired me without telling them."

"Your sister obviously has more sense than the rest of them." I gave her an encouraging smile. "This will be your chance to show them what you can do. And probably bring in more business from word of mouth."

Her eyes lit up. "Exactly. My parents have booked the whole island for Christiana's wedding. There will be so many potential clients there, I knew I had to get in on it."

"Are you in the wedding also?"

"No, Christiana isn't doing a traditional wedding party. But I'll be part of the multiple events. There's going to be a luau as a welcome reception, a masquerade ball in place of the rehearsal dinner, and various other events."

I already knew about those from the file.

"Are you and your sister close?"

Bethany turned toward the window. "Not really. She and I are very different. I…" She trailed off with a sad shrug. "We're just very different. You'll understand when you meet her."

"I'm looking forward to it."

If anything, her eyes got a little sadder. "Christiana never disappoints. I'm sure you'll be charmed by her."

So, definitely tension between the siblings. That could possibly be used to my advantage later. But, looking into Bethany's green eyes, those thoughts made me feel less strategic and more like an ass.

So I shot her a smile. "If she's anything like her sister, I'm sure I will be."

The words were more real than my smile. Everything about Bethany seemed authentic and likable. I wished I were sitting here under different circumstances. I'd seen Christiana in the photos. She was beautiful, thin, with perfect…everything.

Under different circumstances, I'd assure Bethany that I would take her *real* over Christiana's *perfect* any day of the week.

Not the mission, asshole. Focus.

Bethany pulled out a pad of paper and read over it. A small wrinkle appeared between her eyes. "I hope I didn't forget anything."

"You didn't."

Her brows furrowed deeper as she continued to study the list. Her fingers were gripping it tighter as each moment passed.

"Hey," I said. "It's going to be perfect."

She bit her lip, drawing my attention there.

Her lips are definitely not the fucking mission, Black.

"It has to be perfect. It has to be. It has to be."

She was working herself into a panic. The least I could do was help head it off.

"Hey, you've got it all ready. You're prepared."

She looked up from her list. "What if I forgot something? What if it all falls apart? What if—"

I poked her gently on the knee to stop the escalation. "Can I give you some sailor advice?" Actually, it was Navy SEAL advice, but that wasn't part of my cover.

"Sure."

"You prepare as much as you can for the mission at hand, but then roll with the changes when that mission inevitably alters. You've already prepped to the fullest. Now, you'll work the problems as they come."

She set her pad next to her in the seat. "I guess you're right."

I winked at her. A wink I'd used hundreds of times with both men and women to make them feel comfortable, let them know I liked them, help them feel at ease.

This was the first time I'd ever felt like shit using it.

"Tell me more about your family. That'll take your mind off the catering."

She laughed. "Sort of like how a beautiful woman

takes your mind off your headache by lighting your bed on fire?"

Surprised, I laughed out loud. This woman was so genuinely real. "Wow. Is your family that bad?"

"My family basically disowned me because I started a *commoner's* business." She rolled her eyes. "And not only is my sister—gasp, the younger daughter—getting married first, she's also marrying my ex-boyfriend."

Oh shit. That hadn't been in the report. "Wow," I repeated, genuinely at a loss for what else to say. "Is that a problem for you?"

"Nah. Simon and I weren't a thing for long, and we were never serious. But still, you know, I've kissed my sister's fiancé." She made a gagging sound.

I chuckled again. "Speaking of lighting the bed on fire."

But at least she was relaxing into her seat. Family stress wasn't as overwhelming as family stress *plus* business stress.

"Then, a couple weeks ago, I lost my plus-one. My boyfriend and I…"

My phone buzzed in the middle of her sentence, and I glanced down to find a text from Callum.

Package One confirmed on island.

Good. Vincent Frey had arrived. If he'd changed his mind at the last minute, this would've been for nothing.

I looked back up at Bethany. She'd been saying something about her boyfriend, but she'd stopped when I'd turned my attention away.

"What were you saying?"

"Nothing." She shook her head. "Nothing important."

I could press. I wanted to press. I wanted to know more about her. This friendly, hardworking woman who'd turned her back on extravagant wealth to follow her dreams.

She was soft and sexy and alluring. And seemed to be as sweet as the desserts she made.

But ultimately, getting close to her wasn't good for either of us. I needed to keep things professional and keep my distance. So, I gave her a brisk nod and looked down at my phone rather than encouraging her to talk.

I had a feeling I was just one more person in her life who'd done that to her.

Chapter 5

Landon

By the time we landed less than an hour later, Bethany was clutching that checklist in her hand again. After I'd shut down our friendly banter, she'd gone back to it. She hadn't freaked out anymore, but neither had she tried to engage me in conversation.

As soon as the plane stopped, she jumped to her feet and rushed toward the door. The attendant barely had time to get it open before Bethany hurried outside. I shrugged at the attendant and followed. Bethany was ready to work—as tense as she'd been before.

I could've helped her relax more on the plane and get her mind off it, but I hadn't.

Focus on the mission.

Bethany's emotional well-being and stress levels were not my problem. But it still went against my nature to see someone carry such a big burden on their own when I could help.

She was heading toward where the cargo was being unloaded when she was stopped by a woman waiting on the tarmac under an umbrella held by a man in a blue uniform. Her clothes seemed far too formal for island life.

"Bethany, darling," she called out.

I recognized her as the groom's mother from the files I'd studied. It paid to know as many faces and names as possible in a mission like this.

"I noticed your plane was scheduled for this morning. I thought I'd say hello." She walked over and blew air-kisses on either side of Bethany's cheeks.

"Hello, Patricia." Bethany's smile was forced, nothing like what I'd seen from her earlier, and she held out her arm toward me. "This is Landon, he's helping me. Landon, this is the groom's mother and a longtime family friend, Patricia Carter."

I held out my hand. "Pleased to meet you, ma'am."

She shook it with a limp wrist, then ignored me. I was the help, obviously not even worth speaking to. She turned back to Bethany.

"I'm so pleased you were able to find it in yourself to support the wedding, darling. You know I had hoped things would turn out differently, but it's so big of you, despite everything."

Bethany's smile got even stiffer but stayed in place. "Simon and I were never that close. So think nothing of it."

"I know." She grabbed Bethany's hand. "But it still has to be hard for you, Christiana being the younger sister and all."

This woman was just trying to stir the pot. Fortunately, Bethany recognized it too. "I promise I'll be fine. Now, I need to oversee the unloading of my supplies. You go have a nice drink for me. I'll see you at the brunch."

Patricia made a distressed face. "You're sure you'll have everything you need for the desserts you're providing? I would hate to think of anything going wrong. Accidentally or…otherwise."

Bethany stiffened, smile barely hanging on to her face. Patricia had basically accused her of sabotaging the event. "Nothing is going to go wrong. I'm sure you'll be impressed, Patricia. I'll see you later."

Bethany turned and walked toward the back of the plane, leaving me standing with Patricia. The older woman was obviously not used to being dismissed. She glared at me, as if daring me to say something.

I was tempted. Lord, was I tempted. But the help didn't get the luxury of telling the uber-rich that they were fake and crass and that Bethany had more work integrity in her little finger than Patricia had ever had.

Patricia spun on her too-formal heels and walked toward the main building, the uniformed umbrella-holder struggling to keep up with her. Good riddance.

I needed to get to the resort's security building. Callum would be sending instructions on how to hack into the feed soon. But instead, I hustled over to catch up with Bethany.

She nodded at me as boxes were unloaded from the plane. "I'd prefer we'd carry these cakes ourselves. The crew can help with the other stuff, but the prebaked cakes are the most critical element. We have to get them in the freezer at the main lodge auxiliary kitchen."

She stepped up and took over from the hotel staff and jet crew members. They all fell in line with her commanding voice. I stood at her side, and when the cakes were uncovered, she and I moved them to a waiting, air-conditioned van.

"The fondant too," she muttered and pointed to

another series of boxes. "It's too important to leave to just anyone."

I hurried over and began moving those boxes one at a time. The rest of the staff loaded the other items, and we had two vans full of cakes and supplies in no time.

We split up then, each of us riding in the passenger seat of the vans driven by men in hotel security uniforms. I watched out my window, getting my bearings against the map of the property I'd studied.

Santa Catalina wasn't very large, and the entire island was owned by the resort. The main lodge housed thirty rooms and suites, and cottages were scattered all over. The northern end of the island was higher, with cliff views of the Pacific. The southern half had been made into more traditional beaches…white sand with lots of beach chairs, umbrellas, and cabanas.

Some of the cottages had their own pools or hot tubs. Then outside the main lodge was a huge pool/hot tub combination with views of the ocean. It was the primary gathering place on the island and where the resort hosted most of their activities.

According to Callum, the entire main lodge and over half the cottages would be occupied with wedding guests. Thornton had gone ahead and rented the rest of the rooms for the week to ensure the only people on the island were either resort employees or guests who'd been invited.

And me.

As soon as I broke into the resort's security building and finished my tasks there, my first order of business would be to figure out where Vincent Frey was. I needed to get on that immediately. I knew how quickly a week would go by.

But damn it, first I had to help Bethany. There was no

way I could just bail on her right now, despite my *focus on the mission* mantra bullshit.

The vans stopped at the back of a large building, in front of a cargo door. Bethany jumped out of the lead van and didn't even wait for the driver to open the back. She did it herself and began unloading.

The woman definitely wasn't afraid of hard work. And I was sure Patricia's comments suggesting sabotage were not helping Bethany's peace of mind.

I grabbed more cake and followed her inside. The cargo door opened into the main resort kitchen. She quickly found someone who directed us to the auxiliary kitchen where we'd be working this week, so I followed her.

She looked around as she walked it, taking stock of the equipment and space. She nodded. "This will work fine. I can do everything I need to here."

She set her box down on one of the metal counters then opened the door to the walk-in fridge.

"To the left." She pointed to a shelf with her elbow. "The resort's in-house catering company gets the right side."

"They didn't leave you much room."

"Yeah. The resort wasn't thrilled that Christiana was bringing in an outside vendor. This is one of their ways of making that known."

"We'll make it work. I'll be happy to start stacking some of their boxes somewhere else if you want me to." I looked closer at some of the labels. "Some of this doesn't even need to be refrigerated."

She shot me a smile even through her stress. "I like how you think. Let's see if we can make it all fit."

I went back out and got more boxes. When I came back in, she was checking that damned list of hers. "This one is for in here." She took the box from me and walked it into the non-refrigerated storage. "I've got them marked based on when we'll need them."

When we exited the storage room, a couple of young men and a young woman in a starched white uniform approached Bethany. They each had a box in their hands. "Ma'am, where do you want these?"

Bethany's face tightened. She'd only wanted us to handle these particular boxes. I expected a meltdown, but it didn't come.

"Thank you," she said. She sent one of the boxes into the refrigeration unit and the other two into the freezer.

"You stay here and supervise." I told her. "I'll grab the important stuff and try to direct the staff to non-critical elements."

It took over an hour to get everything unpacked and situated to Bethany's liking. She was polite to everyone, but more than once, I found her moving things herself because she didn't like where or how it had been positioned.

Once all the freezer and refrigerated items were placed, I thought she might relax a little. But then she started rearranging everything in the nonperishable storage room, once again checking things off against her precious list.

I couldn't wait any longer. I needed to get to the opposite side of the island. Bethany didn't need me anymore. I'd come back and work on the stands after I got my real job started.

The kitchen bustled around us. Guests had already arrived on the island, and multiple waiters were bringing out drinks and hors d'oeuvres to people lounging by the pool. That would give me the opportunity to—

A server, obviously not aware that we had occupied the auxiliary kitchen, decided to cut through on her way out to the pool. She looked away from where she was going and ran straight into Bethany—lurching forward, drinks flying off the tray. Orange juice and champagne soaked Bethany's white shirt.

And, even worse, ruined her list.

"No, I'm so sorry!" the server exclaimed, eyes big. "Oh no."

Bethany was staring at her ruined list as it lost its shape and folded over her hand. Now I'd get to see that rich-lady ire that was sure to come out of her.

But she kept her cool, wiping off the paper as best she could, before trying to do the same with her blouse so it wasn't clinging to her chest. My eyes shot to the lacy bra exposed by the liquid before quickly jerking back to her face.

Then, to my utter shock, she crouched down with the server to help pick up the larger pieces of glass. "Are you okay?"

The woman looked over at Bethany in shock, tears rolling down her cheeks. "I'm fine. I'm so sorry. I'll get fired. They told us not to cut through here this week, but I forgot. They don't tolerate mistakes like this."

Bethany offered the younger woman a smile. "Then we'll tell them I ran into you. Accidents happen."

I belatedly realized I was standing there doing nothing, so I grabbed the broom from the closet. I reached down and offered Bethany a hand so she could stand. "You guys step out of the way. Let me sweep this."

Bethany gave me a grateful smile as she took my hand. The server was still in tears.

"Please don't worry on my account," Bethany said. "I've got plenty of shirts, and these drinks can be remade, okay? We're fine. Go get back to your work."

The poor server nodded and swiped away her tears. I finished sweeping and dumped the pieces. When I came back, Bethany was studying her ruined list, almost in her own tears.

I was going to get a special spot in heaven for not looking at her breasts, even knowing that lace—my second biggest weakness after sweets—was clearly visible.

I gently pried the list from her fingers. "This paper has done its job. You know you have what you need. You've planned well, everything is here, you know what you're doing."

"If the mission alters, I work the problems as they come," she repeated my words from the jet back to me.

My phone chimed in my pocket again, but this time, I ignored it. Mission be damned.

"Exactly." She bit that plump bottom lip, and *that* I couldn't keep my eyes from.

"You're right. I can do this." She tossed the paper in the trash. "Plus, I've got to get ready for the welcome reception."

Shit. "Are we baking for that?"

"No. It's the only wedding event I'm not doing any work for. But I've got to change and get ready." She straightened her shoulders.

"Uh-oh. Family?"

She rubbed her eyes. "Yeah. Might as well take them all on at once. I guess you're free to get checked in and hang out. You have a room assigned, and really, there's nothing you need to do until later this afternoon to get ready for the welcome reception setup tonight."

My phone chimed in my pocket again.

She looked down at her shirt and realized its state. She quickly pulled it from her chest, cheeks burning. "I'll see you later. I can't go to the brunch looking like this. Thanks for your help."

She turned away, but I grabbed her elbow gently,

immediately aware of her soft skin under my fingers. I didn't turn her to face me, but I stepped closer so I could lean down to speak softly into her ear. "How you treated that server a few minutes ago makes you richer than anyone else on this island. You don't forget that."

I was holding her way too close to be considered professional, but I didn't care. She was obviously about to go into the lion's den, and if I could offer her some support, I wanted to do so.

She nodded, and I let her go, watching as she walked briskly through the busy kitchen, making sure to keep out of everyone's way.

My phone dinged again, and I pulled it out of my pocket. Callum.

Change of plans. More details forthcoming. Proceed to security building.

I'd been on the ground less than an hour, and already things had changed. I shouldn't be surprised.

If the mission alters…work the problems as they come.

Chapter 6

Landon

The resort on Santa Catalina had been developed for the famous and uber-rich. Every whim could be catered to for the right price, and the security on the island reflected the clientele that visited here.

I strolled along the path of the guest section, nodding and smiling at other people who were walking with drinks in their hands. Once past them, I took a sharp turn to the north, along a road obviously not meant for guests.

As soon as I did, I dropped all pretense of leisurely wandering and began a fast jog toward the north side of the island. Half a mile later, I cut back into the treed section and made my way toward the resort's security building.

I came at the building from the east, stopping so I could observe. There were staff everywhere at the resort, but none of them carried semiautomatic weapons like the man guarding this building. Not to mention the other two guys, not in the resort security uniforms, standing over to the side, who also were carrying. Those had to be Frey's men.

I definitely wasn't going to be able to walk through the front door. Even playing lost tourist wouldn't work—I didn't want to do anything that was going to make me more memorable to security.

Despite his *change of plans* message, I knew Callum would be providing instructions soon. I hoped they would be pretty thorough. I'd spent my pre-mission time memorizing the info in the file rather than worrying about getting into this building—leaving that to him.

But now, looking at the security measures surrounding Fort Knox here, it seemed like the whole mission could be over before it started. From here, I couldn't see a single entry point.

A message came through on my phone, but not from Callum. It was an unlisted number.

Present for you at the bottom of the south side cliff.

I hoped it was a bazooka or a full SEAL team because that's what it was going to take to get me inside this building.

I eased back from my observation post and headed down to the bottom of the south side cliff as instructed. What awaited me there wasn't what I'd wished for, but it was close enough.

"You lost, sailor?"

Tristan Zimmerman grinned up at me from where he was removing objects from a waterproof bag at the bottom of the cliff-side wall. His hair was dripping, and a wet suit was piled on the ground next to him.

"What are you even doing here, Pisces?"

Tristan was the head of the Zodiac Tactical Guardian

Unit, leading the bodyguarding and protection jobs. He worked out of Los Angeles.

He was taking rappelling equipment out of his bag. So that was going to be our plan. We would go up this cliff no one in their right mind would try.

"Callum sent me," Tristan said. "Evidently, the mole situation in his office took a turn for the worse yesterday, and he is not sure if he can trust anyone. He didn't want to have any more contact with you while this was going down in case it tipped off the mole. Ian had to leave to take care of some stuff with Wavy."

I nodded. Wavy still sometimes struggled with what Mosaic had done to her and then what she had done to me in the process.

"I had a couple days off," Tristan continued. "So, I volunteered to help sit on the beach, drinking mai tais and eating cake. Sadly, getting you into this building was the closest Callum could come up with."

"Looks like I'm going to need all the help I can get. Security at the front door is no joke."

"From the water too. Evidently, the Santa Catalina resort monitors all ships, no matter how small, that come closer than two miles." He grinned at me. "Couple-mile swim hauling gear through icy waters reminded me of the good old days at Coronado."

I chuckled. The BUD/S training he was referring to was considered the *good old days* by absolutely no one who'd done it. We were mostly glad to have just survived the Navy SEAL conditioning. "Your code name is Pisces, so you can be forgiven for loving the water so much."

He winked at me. "What's not to love?"

Tristan was in nearly as good of shape now as he'd been when he was a SEAL. As with everyone at Zodiac, just because we weren't active duty anymore didn't mean we weren't in fighting form.

Or, in my case, attempting to get back to it.

"Thanks for taking a break from your job of babysitting the rich and famous to help me out."

We both knew that wasn't anywhere close to what his job was like. Heading a security team involved a lot of long, uncomfortable hours and focus, often for people not much fun to be around. Glamorous, it was not. But Tristan was one of the best in the business.

And I'd trust him with my back any day.

"What's the plan?" I set out rings, anchors, and carabiners.

"I'll free-climb up and set up the rappelling equipment, in case a fast getaway is necessary. Then once you're up, we'll both go in through the ventilation system at the back of the building."

I looked up at the cliff wall. I was glad I wasn't free-climbing that. Unlike Tristan, I hadn't grown up in the mountains of Wyoming, and I didn't have nearly the experience he did.

"Please don't die. I don't want to have to make a trip to the Wyoming governor's office to explain."

He grinned over at me. "Dad is used to my shit. Or, if I'm taking a break from giving him more gray hairs, Andrew or Gavin take over."

Yeah, the Zimmerman brothers were...*active* when it came to danger. Even baby sister Lyn had nearly gotten herself killed a couple times.

"Just don't cut yourself. That'll draw the sharks on the swim back out." I was only half kidding.

He grimaced and handed me a comm device so we could communicate. I slipped it in my ear.

"Once I'm up and we're through the vents, I'll tranq

the guard in the observation room. When he's out, you can hack the feed from the server room and get everything set up. Instructions are on your phone, study them while I'm playing Spider-Man."

"Roger that. Be careful."

He winked. "Catch me if I fall."

"Uh, no can do, buddy. You may have heard Callum got down on one knee with me the other day."

"Damn it, missed my chance." He laughed and took off up the cliff walk like he had, in fact, been bitten by a radioactive spider and had the superpowers to show for it.

I watched him for a few seconds before turning to my phone to study what I needed to do once I was in the server room. Tristan would make it. I needed to be ready for my part once he did.

"I'm up." Tristan's voice came through the comm device a few minutes later. "Give me a second to secure the anchor, then you'll have your ride."

It wasn't long before the rappelling rope lowered down to me. I clipped myself in and started hoisting myself up. A *ride* it definitely wasn't. But this was why I'd pushed myself well beyond what my doctors and physical therapists had wanted me to over the past few months.

So that when the time came, I'd be ready.

Granted, hoisting myself up a cliff wall on an island that catered to extravagantly rich people hadn't been what I'd been envisioning when I'd worked myself to exhaustion in the gym so many nights.

Regardless, I made it. A little more winded than I wanted to be, but within acceptable limits.

Tristan and I crawled into the vent and scooted ourselves forward silently. Our shoulders barely fit in the square metal tube, making progress slow. I was glad Ian wasn't here with us. This would play hell with his claustrophobia.

He'd force it down and inch his way forward with us, but it would definitely take a toll. He'd earned his phobia the hard way, and sometimes even riding in an elevator was difficult for him.

By the time we made it to the server room, Tristan and I were both sweaty. I used a battery-powered screwdriver to remove the vent covering to the room and lowered myself into it.

"Watch your time," he said from above me. "Window is pretty narrow. I'll tranq the guard, which will buy us about five minutes before he wakes up, thinking he fell asleep in his chair. But if you're in the system for more than ninety seconds, it'll set off alarms."

"Roger."

Tristan took off farther into the vent, and I dashed through the server room to find the panel I needed.

Tristan and I would have to time this perfectly in order for it to work. We'd both have to trust each other to do our parts, or it would all be for naught.

And it felt fucking good to be part of a team again. This part of me had definitely been dormant for far too long.

I used my screwdriver again to release the computer panel from the wall of servers. The resort here truly did take its security seriously to have so much in place. Hosting its own server room meant no one could hack into it from off-site.

And would have to do some pretty death-defying feats to hack it from on-site. Like, climb up a cliff wall and muscle through ventilation shafts.

"Guard is night-night." Tristan's voice came through

the comm in my ear a few minutes later. "You're clear, Libra."

"Starting now. Count me down."

"Roger. Ninety seconds."

I blew out a breath and focused on steadying my hands and connecting the wires I needed in order to break in to their system. This override would allow Tristan to monitor the resort's internal system.

Once the wires were attached, I hooked up my portable keyboard and followed the instructions I'd been given to link the resort's system with ours.

"System patch complete," I muttered.

"Roger. Thirty-five seconds remaining."

"Going in for security camera override." I glanced at my phone for the info I needed then typed rapidly on the keyboard. Once this was done, no one would have any proof I'd been here, even if they came back to look at the security footage afterward.

The first override attempt failed, so I switched to the second.

"Twenty seconds."

Shit. I was running out of time.

I typed in the code, but a shaky hand caused me to enter one of the digits incorrectly. If this didn't work, the mission would be over before it even started. I needed to pull myself together.

I closed my eyes, sucked in a breath, then blew it back out.

Focus, Black.

"Ten seconds. Shut it down, Landon. We'll find another way."

I ignored Tristan and typed the code a second time. This was it. If I screwed up here, I'd not only fail to override the security cameras, I'd be sending out a red flag that someone was in their server room.

"Five, four…"

I finished the code, hit enter, and yanked the wire so the panel was no longer attached to my keyboard.

"I'm out."

"Hold for confirmation."

I packed the equipment back into the small backpack then jumped up to the air vent, grabbing the edge and pulling myself up. Regardless of whether the patch was successful or not, I had to get out. The guard monitoring the room would be awake before I could try it again.

Now we would see if my fuckup had blown the whole mission.

Maybe Callum should've sent someone else.

"Patch successful. We're a go," Tristan said. "Nice work, Libra."

"Roger that."

I lay back in the vent shaft and blew out a breath. I just hoped I didn't screw up the rest of the mission like I nearly had this.

Chapter 7

Bethany

I checked into my room and rushed to get cleaned up before the brunch. I'd spent so much time making sure my supplies were organized I had no time now to take a shower.

Of course, I hadn't expected to be wearing mimosas and what smelled like gin and tonics. My curly hair needed a lot of love after being washed, so showering would have to wait.

I wiped off my chest, cringing at the sight of my bra shining proudly through my now-transparent blouse. Great. I'd been standing in front of Landon half naked.

After getting as much stickiness off me as possible, I changed into a knee-length dusty-blue chiffon cocktail dress the porters had delivered to the room and hung while I was getting my supplies situated. Looking in the mirror, I realized the sleeveless cut of the dress probably wasn't the best look for my pudgy arms. But I liked its cascading ruffles, so I was going to wear it.

Twenty bucks said Mother pointed out how my arms looked. Or that she offered to send me her personal trainer or something.

My hair… I grimaced. It was relatively decent in my messy bun, so I wasn't about to fool with it. I'd be getting it straightened at the resort salon for the wedding itself, but until then, it would do its own thing, as always.

I blew out a breath as I stared at my reflection. "You can do this."

I wasn't sure if I was talking about the brunch, the catering, or spending the whole week working with my charming, gorgeous new assistant.

Probably D, all of the above.

But right now, I would concentrate on the brunch. It was the only wedding event at which I wasn't responsible for providing any desserts. The hotel was taking care of this one since I was arriving today. I'd offered, but Mother had put her foot down, arguing I wouldn't have enough time. That I would be too rushed getting in and trying to get everything ready.

My phone buzzed on the counter.

Where are you?

Mother. She'd been right; I wouldn't have had enough time to set up anything for the brunch. I was already late. This was going to give her more ammunition.

I brushed on a little lip gloss then rushed out the door, not worrying about anything else. No amount of makeup was going to turn me into someone who looked like Christiana, so why bother trying?

I left my one-bedroom suite then cut through the lobby, taking a right as I got outside. I was glad I was already familiar with the resort. We'd spent multiple vacations here as I was growing up. I'd wanted to go to Disneyland, but Dad had said that place was a nightmare.

It wasn't until I was in college that I realized he'd meant *security* nightmare. And that some of the people Dad worked with were quite a bit less than upstanding.

That knowledge had made the choice of separating myself from the family and starting my own business easier to make. Mother had acted like I'd joined some sort of cult that sacrificed kittens on a regular basis. Dad hadn't supported me, but he hadn't been that upset either. Christiana had done what she was told—cut me off. That had hurt most of all.

But I was here now. That was all that mattered.

As I passed the resort's massive pool, I half expected to see Landon lounging and chatting, all easy smile and laughter. He didn't seem like the type to stay in his room if there were people he could charm, just by his very presence.

He was good with his hands. Good with people. Landon Black was a pretty dangerous package.

And heck if *package* didn't send my mind spiraling in all sorts of salacious directions.

With a sigh, I turned and cut over to the glass-enclosed conservatory where the family brunch was being held. I wanted to stop for a moment, take a breath, get myself together. But I knew another more-frantic text would be hitting my phone any moment if I wasted more time.

My mother spotted me the moment I walked in. She hurried over, smile on her face but eyes traveling up and down the length of my body. "Bethany, dear, there you are! Are you sure you won't need a light sweater or shawl?"

In eighty-five-degree weather? Probably not.

I owed myself twenty dollars.

"No, Mother, I'll be fine. Thank you."

She leaned in and pressed her cheek to mine. "It's wonderful to see you, sweetheart."

She meant well. She just couldn't help criticizing with one breath as she gave affection with the other. She'd done it all my life. At least it wasn't reserved for only me. Christiana got it just as much.

"You should've let me hire someone else so you could enjoy yourself this week. You deserve a break." She fiddled with my hair. I took the opportunity to study her face. It was as unlined as I ever remembered it. She'd probably had more Botox.

She said it all as if we were perfect mother and daughter. As if we hadn't barely talked to each other for the past two years. Appearances were everything to my mother.

"I didn't want a break. I wanted the job," I said through a forced smile.

"Oh, you and your little cake shop." She waved her hand in dismissal of my *silly hobby*. "I'll never understand why you can't use your talents for charity work or to make a husband happy."

I nearly bit off my tongue in an effort not to respond. This was not the time to get into it with her again. My mother had never worked a day in her life. She'd been wealthy before she got married and even more so afterward.

She turned and hooked an arm in mine. "Come on, you were supposed to be here early to help us greet the guests. This brunch is for close friends and family only."

Fantastic. All the people who would feel close enough to me to comment on my life, flabby arms, and lack of a date. Maybe I'd get lucky and a tidal wave would hit the island.

"Well, you at least could've opened your shop in Beverly Hills instead of all the way out in the boonies of

Carpinteria. You might as well be in Minnesota," she complained.

Right. Because an hour outside of LA was the same as being halfway across the country. Actually, to my mother, that was probably true.

"And where is your boyfriend?" she continued. "I told everyone you were bringing him. I was hoping he would be here for the brunch."

I stiffened, about to explain, when Christiana and Simon made their way around one of the huge hanging flower arrangements, and I was able to see them for the first time.

Patricia was beside her son, but he stared down at my sister as if the sun and stars aligned for her very pleasure.

I hadn't seen them together much while they'd dated. Mother had been so upset about the bakery that it had been easier to ignore Christiana also. She'd chosen Mother and Father over me.

It had hurt, but I shouldn't have let it come between us. Christiana was younger than me, only twenty-two. And she'd only ever wanted this life. She wanted the charity work and luncheons with friends.

And just like I wished my family had not rejected my choices, I should not have rejected Christiana's. She was my sister, and I loved her.

And Simon did too. The devotion on his face made something click inside me. He and I, in the short time we'd dated, had never had anything close to the feelings he had for her now.

Christiana turned to respond to whatever he'd said, and her face changed when she looked at him. It softened, and her mouth tipped up in a smile. She could be as much of an ice queen bitch as Mother when she wanted to, but this was the *real* Christiana.

She loved him just as much as he did her.

I was happy for her. So, so happy.

I was still a little concerned that the desserts I would provide wouldn't be perfect, and that people were going to pity me because Simon and I had history. Me not having a date was going to add fuel to that fire. And everyone always noticed that Mother and Christiana were a size two and I was more than quadruple that.

But my sister was marrying the man she loved, and ultimately, that was the most important thing. Tears welled in my eyes.

My mother grabbed my hand. "Are you all right? I thought you were okay with Christiana marrying Simon."

"I am. Even more so seeing them together right now." I turned to her. "I want you to help me squash any rumors. There was never anything serious between Simon and me, and if you hear anyone try to make that a thing, you shut it down. I know you can."

She tucked an escaped curl behind my ear. "I will."

I smiled at her. Mother and I were always going to have our differences, and until she learned to accept Slice of Heaven as part of me, we were never going to be close. But I knew she had my back on this.

My shoulders slumped in relief as Christiana's voice interrupted us. If my mother said she'd take care of it, she'd take care of it.

"Bethie!" Christiana exclaimed. "I'm so happy to see you." I rushed over, and she pulled me in for a hug. I was a little surprised she was showing this much emotion in front of everyone, but then decided I didn't care and wrapped my arms around her tighter.

"Simon," I said when I pulled back. "Congratulations."

I gave him a genuine hug with one hand still in Christiana's. She beamed at us over Simon's shoulder.

"I'm so happy for you both," I whispered to my friend.

"I'm glad to hear that," he said. "I was worried it would be awkward."

"Not at all." I pulled back, stiffening as his mother joined us. "Hello again, Patricia. Good to see you."

"Darling." Completely inauthentic air-kisses. "You look…pretty. Did you get your…work finished?"

Her pauses said so much more than her actual words. I kept a smile plastered on my face. "I did. Thank you for asking."

A member of the hotel staff came to ask Patricia and Mother a question just as Simon was called across the room by his cousin, leaving me a few precious moments alone with my sister.

She still clutched my hand tightly. I gave her a concerned look. "What is it?"

She shook her head. "Nothing. Just nerves."

"You don't want to marry Simon?"

Her eyes shot over to him, and she gave a soft smile. "No, I definitely want to marry Simon."

"But the rest of it?" I asked.

She blanched. "Wedding jitters. That's the problem."

I laughed and put my arm around her. "I'm sorry I didn't check in on you these last few months. I could've helped more."

Christiana bumped the side of her head to mine. "No, stop it. You've been working at your amazing bakery. I'm the one who should've been more supportive of you. I'm just no good at standing up to Mother."

I kissed her forehead. "Don't you worry about it. Especially not this week. You focus on getting married."

She looked over at Mother and Patricia, who were both

speaking in low, angry tones to the staff member who'd requested an audience. I felt sorry for the woman. "I'm just worried about everything going perfectly this week. Normal Bridezilla stuff."

I snorted. "Don't pretend it's not Mother who's the Bridezilla."

"Patricia isn't helping. The two of them are such frenemies. Always wanting to outdo each other, but also willing to help the other tear someone else apart."

We walked toward the table of mimosas. "It means so much to me that you hired me for the desserts. It's going to do wonders for my business. Plus, I can't wait to show you what I can do."

"I know, Bethie, but…" Her hand shook as she reached for a flute.

"What?"

"Patricia thinks you're going to sabotage the wedding. You know how Mother was upset when she found out I'd hired you? Patricia was so much worse. She's convinced you took the job to ruin this week and the wedding."

"Because you're marrying Simon? That seems like overkill."

Christiana shrugged both shoulders. "That. The fact that the family cut you off financially when you opened the bakery. The fact that I'm getting married even though I'm younger."

I rubbed my eyes. "You realize how ridiculous and paranoid that sounds."

"Yes. *I* do."

But not Patricia. She loved drama.

I grabbed a mimosa and sucked half of it down in just a few seconds. Definitely tasted better than wearing it. "What about Mother? Does she think I'm out to sabotage?"

Christiana took a glass and sipped it at a much more appropriate rate. "I'm not sure. She never really contradicted Patricia, but she didn't agree that you would try to make trouble. Don't get me wrong, she still didn't want me to hire you. But for her, I think it was a status thing."

"Didn't want me to sully the family name by having a blue-collar job?"

She gave me a sheepish look and shrugged one delicate shoulder. "You know Mother."

"Well, don't worry." I drank down the rest of my mimosa, before placing the flute on a well-trained waiter's tray as he came by. "I have no plans whatsoever to sabotage any part of your wedding. I'm truly happy for you two."

I wanted to grab another drink, but resisted. As soon as this event was over, I had work to do to get desserts ready for the welcome reception tonight. It would be my first chance to prove what Slice of Heaven could do.

But I had to survive this brunch first.

I shouldn't have been surprised Patricia wanted someone else as the dessert caterer. If anything, the Carter family had even more money than ours. She would've wanted someone who had catered for celebrities so she could boast about it.

But to think I'd sabotage the wedding? She'd known our family for over a decade. That was pretty low, even for her.

Christiana slipped her arm through mine. "I know you would never do something like that. I'm so excited to taste your treats. I know they'll be wonderful!"

Mother and Patricia joined us and grabbed glasses of their own before I could respond. Both of them were looking quite pleased with themselves. Meanwhile, the staff member they'd been talking with looked close to tears.

"Darling, when is that handsome boyfriend of yours going to join us?" Patricia asked me. "Your mother showed us your pictures on social media. It's so nice that you... have someone."

That fucking pause again.

Worse, as Simon rejoined us along with some of his extended family, I realized everyone was staring at me, waiting for my response.

I couldn't do it. No matter how strongly I believed a woman didn't need a man to complete her, and that it was a practical and even noble choice not to pursue a relationship while getting a business off the ground, I could not stand here and make that announcement in front of everyone.

Patricia would probably suggest if I'd worn a light sweater over my chubby arms, I'd probably still have a boyfriend. Mother would nod and say I was always welcome back at home where I belonged.

Every second I stood in silence, the worse it got.

"Oh, he's going to—" I cut myself off and grabbed my phone out of my clutch as if I'd felt it vibrate. "Oh dear."

I stepped back a little so no one could see it and looked down, pretending to have a message. "I'm so sorry. I've got to deal with this. Work emergency. It's about the icing. I'll see everyone later at the welcome reception."

I kissed Christiana on the cheek, gave everyone else an awkward little wave, and hurried for the door.

I didn't move fast enough to miss Patricia's words. "See, Angelique? I told you you should've insisted on using another bakery. The...*problems* are starting already."

I didn't stop walking, but I strained to hear how Mother would respond.

"I'm sure it will be fine," she said. "But I did put the hotel on alert. So don't worry, we have a backup."

My heart sank. Mother didn't trust me to do the job. Maybe even thought I was sabotaging also.

I blinked back tears as I reached the door and pushed into the warmer air outside.

According to these people, I was the pitiful, unmarried elder sister of the bride.

I was the hired help who probably couldn't be trusted.

And I was the guest who'd RSVP'd plus-one, but wouldn't have a date. There was no way in hell that would go unnoticed, even when I made up some excuse why my boyfriend wasn't here.

I straightened my shoulders. I'd walked away from this life because it wasn't what I wanted. And although I couldn't deny that what they thought of me mattered, I wasn't going to let it derail me.

They might think I was personally pitiful, but by the end of this week, they would damned well know, professionally, I was someone to take seriously.

Chapter 8

Landon

Thirty minutes after sending Tristan back out into the Pacific, I was at the main pool area of the resort. I'd sprinted back, then gotten checked in. I needed to blend in with everyone else.

The hotel security feeds were no longer an issue. If things went sideways and someone from the Frey Cartel decided to search the hotel security footage from any of the public areas or hallways, they'd get nothing. My face wouldn't be traceable, and more importantly, they wouldn't be able to connect me to Bethany in any way.

But things weren't going to go sideways.

I'd wanted to be in the lobby to make sure I saw Frey and his entourage enter. I'd barely made it since I'd been roped into helping some woman carry items to her room, even after explaining I wasn't hotel staff.

Frey had arrived with three security guards, his

personal assistant I could identify from Callum's photographs, and his girlfriend.

Not his wife. Interesting. The file had a picture of both women. I would've thought the wife would accompany him to a society wedding like this.

I already knew which suite the hotel had placed Frey in since Tristan now had a direct feed into their computer system. He'd be providing me any intel updates if things changed. But I still took the next elevator up after he did. If I were in charge of Frey's security, I would've checked him in to one room, then actually placed him in another under a different name even the resort wasn't aware of.

Seeing if that was the case would give me a better understanding of what I was up against. But when my elevator opened on his floor, Frey was entering the room he'd been assigned. I took one look around and got back on the elevator.

"Oops. Wrong floor." I chuckled and studied my keycard. "I'm up one more." Both guards with him gave me a bored look. Only one even stiffened in the slightest.

Looked like Callum had been right; being on a tropical island for a wedding had everyone relaxing their guard.

After getting off on my floor, I went into my room and changed clothes, then headed back down toward the pool to look for the third guard who'd been missing from the hallway. He'd probably been sent to scope out the outside area to look for anything suspicious.

I smiled as I found him sitting at one of the smaller side bars, already nursing a beer. Maybe Frey kept his employees on a pretty loose leash and allowed them to drink on the job. But even if so, the beer in the security team member's hand told me things about him, just like what had happened earlier in the hallway.

Mainly that this security team wasn't in top form.

I slid into the seat two down from his and focused my attention on the game on the screen behind the bartender. When she turned her attention my way, I ordered the same brand beer the guard had in his hand but didn't otherwise acknowledge him at all. Then I waited.

When he cursed about a missed basket, I followed suit more quietly, but he noticed. "You a fan?"

"Yeah. I was stationed at a base for several months not far from there." That was true. I'd learned with undercover work to always provide as much truth as I could to my lies. I held out my hand. "Landon. Nice to meet you."

"Adams." He pointed at my drink. "Lemme buy you another."

I shook my head. "Naw, I'm technically on the clock. Just got away from my boss for a few."

"Security?"

"Sort of jack-of-all-trades for the bride's sister."

Adams nodded and looked back up at the screen. "This is a pretty sweet gig. Resort security takes care of most of our problems."

"I'm not complaining, that's for sure."

I knew not to rush. Fishing for info would only make Adams suspicious. Maybe after he got another drink in him, I could figure out a way to be chummier.

But he'd barely finished the one he had before catching something over my shoulder and stiffening. "Damn it. Fucking newbie."

I followed his gaze to see one of the two men who'd been assisting Frey into the hotel room when I'd been in the elevator. *Newbie* was also information I could use. I turned back to the TV and pretended not to be interested in their conversation.

"What is it, Fanshawe?" Adams asked the other man

tersely. "What part of stay upstairs and guard the door did you not understand?"

Out of the corner of my eye, I caught how Fanshawe's jaw tightened. He didn't like how Adams was talking to him. I didn't blame him. Fanshawe might be new, but he wasn't young. Early forties. Big guy—six foot, weighed probably two ten.

"Brammer and I were confused about Mr. Frey's schedule." Fanshawe crossed his arms over his chest. "Are we supposed to wake him up for the welcome event tonight?"

Shit. The event I still needed to get cake stands together for.

"By wake up, you mean pull him off his girlfriend?" Adams winked over at me. "I'll come up and go over it one more time with you, seeing as you couldn't quite get it right."

Fanshawe stiffened again. He might be the weak link… frustrated at being at the bottom. Adams treating him with disrespect wasn't helping. Adams himself was another option. He'd been around longer, but he was complacent and ran his mouth.

Maybe I could even pit both men against each other. Wouldn't take much. And while they were focused on each other, I would get closer to Frey's phone.

Adams stood from his stool and threw a twenty on the table. "Keep the change," he called to the bartender. "And I'm buying his." He clapped me on the shoulder as he walked away. "Good luck with your boss."

"Yeah, you too. And, uh"—I jerked my chin toward Fanshawe—"the rest of your headaches."

I stayed on my stool until I was sure they were gone. I hadn't even taken a sip of my beer. Drinking wasn't going to happen on this mission, not when I had to look for every possible available opening to get the transmitter placed.

Bethany caught my eye. She stormed out of a set of doors and took off across the other side of the pool. That wasn't good. She should still be at her brunch. And I didn't like how her arms were wrapped around herself protectively.

Definitely not good.

I threw a five on the bar for the bartender and high-tailed it after her. I thought I might lose her if she went to her room, but I saw her turn toward the auxiliary kitchen.

By the time I caught up to her, she was already wearing an apron over a blue dress and was securing her hair more firmly in a ponytail. She muttered to herself with her back to me as she started wiping down the metal preparation counter, but I couldn't quite make out the words.

"Everything okay?" I asked.

She whirled around, eyes narrowed at me. "Why wouldn't everything be okay? I'm starting the prep work for tonight's sweets. Something wrong with that?"

This was not my first day around women. I stuffed my hands in my pockets. "Absolutely not."

"I guess you think I'm an idiot for doing my work in my dress and heels."

Wasn't my second day around women either. "I think you should do your work in whatever you're most comfortable in."

"Damned right I should. Because I've built this business from the ground up, and I would never do anything to jeopardize it." She flung the cloth she'd been wiping with toward the sink. "I make desserts that are absolutely fantastic, no matter how unmarried, older, or flabby-armed I am."

Obviously, something had happened at the brunch. This conversation was a minefield. "Your desserts *are* fantastic, from what I've tasted."

"Damned right they are." She turned back toward the counter. "And now, if you'll excuse me, I have to make sure everything is absolutely perfect for tonight. There is no room for error."

She spun back around toward me so quickly my body tensed in preparation for an attack. "Speaking of error, have you got the dessert stands set up? That's what you're here for, not sitting around the bar looking sexy."

I raised an eyebrow. I'd skip the sexy comment altogether. "It should take about an hour to set up tonight's stands. I have two hours blocked off from three to five just in case more time is needed. If I set them up this early, they would be in the way of everyone else attempting to work."

Her jaw tightened at both my logic and reasonable tone. "Fine." She spun back around.

She needed…something, but I didn't know how to help her. Maybe the most help I could provide would be to get out of her way.

"I'll check back in with you later to see if you need any assistance."

"Yeah, do that."

This had been more the attitude I'd been expecting from her from the beginning. Maybe I'd been wrong and the kind Bethany was an act. I turned for the door.

"Landon, wait." I stopped but didn't turn back around.

"I'm sorry," she continued. "The brunch…didn't go so well. Like I explained on the plane, my relationship with my family is complicated. Some of it, I can't do anything about. The only thing I feel like I have control over is making these desserts awesome."

I turned. "Let me help. It'll give you more time, and you can make sure everything is exactly the way you want."

She rubbed her eyes. "You're only being paid for the carpentry and construction. And honestly, I can't afford much more than that."

I grinned and walked back toward her, hands held in front of me. "You get Mr. September's hands for free."

She let out a pained laugh. "I had hoped you didn't hear that."

I had heard it when she said it back at Slice of Heaven yesterday, and it had thrown me for a little loop since my code name at Zodiac Tactical was Libra. For just a second, I'd thought she'd somehow figured me out.

"Tell me what I can do."

"Are you sure? I did a bunch of the prep work at the bakery so that I would be able to handle everything here by myself. Wouldn't you rather go back out to the bar?"

It might have been smarter, but I'd honestly rather be in here helping her. "I was only out there to escape this lady who kept trying to put me to work carrying her bags. It was all very awkward."

Some of the tension fell from Bethany's face as she laughed and shook her head. "Lord. It was probably my mother."

"She said she was the groom's cousin. Lena or something?" I pretended to be confused, but I knew her name and profile from the file.

"Mina." Her eyes narrowed. "Yeah, I know her."

I grabbed an apron and put it on. "Put me to work."

"Wash your hands then start unloading those cupcakes onto the prep table. I'll start icing them." She handed me a box. "Thank you."

As we worked, she told me more about Mina. Definitely no love lost there, and based on Mina's behavior earlier, I wasn't surprised.

"Mina is an acquired taste. She and I have never gotten

along. I usually avoid her as much as possible. I'm sorry she made you do more work."

It wasn't even so much that as the fact that she'd hit on me the moment I'd brought her cases into her room. I appreciated a beautiful woman as much as the next guy, but this had been completely inappropriate and almost distasteful. I hadn't made a scene, but I'd gotten out of there as quickly as possible.

But I wasn't about to tell Bethany about that. I started unpacking the cupcakes. "No worries. I handled her."

Bethany laughed. "She hit on you, didn't she? Or flirted, at least."

I looked at her over my shoulder and raised my eyebrows. "How'd you know?"

"Mina is constantly on the lookout for her next fling. Always wants to be able to show off that she can get the best-looking guys. Has so much money that usually she's successful." She looked me up and down, waggling her eyebrows. "It's a miracle you made it out alive."

"It was touch and go there for a while," I said in a gravely serious voice. "Thought I might have to pull out some old Navy moves."

Her laugh filled the small prep kitchen and made me smile as I carefully lined up cupcake after cupcake.

Once she started icing, I probably could've run around naked and she wouldn't have noticed. She was completely focused on the tiny cakes in front of her.

When her phone beeped and lit up where it leaned against the wall the first time, she ignored it. When it happened again a half dozen more times, she cursed under her breath.

"Need to get that?"

She let out a sigh. "It's my mother. Or Patricia. Or at this point, maybe even my sister Christiana."

"Do they need you?"

"They're probably wondering if they need to get Plan B going. Evidently, Mother has the resort on standby to provide desserts just in case I can't get my shit together and I'm frantically icing cupcakes while still in a dress and heels as if it's my first day on the job."

She said it lightly like it was something she could laugh off, but I knew it stung.

I put my hand over hers on the icing bag and had her place it on the counter, then turned her toward me. "Hey. Stop for a second and look at what you've created here. We're surrounded by wildflowers."

And we were. She'd precut wraps for the cupcakes that resembled the paper that went around bunches of flowers. After attaching them, she'd begun icing the treats with tiny tips that made the tops look like flowers.

Each cupcake resembled a small, squat bouquet of wildflowers. It was elegant and quirky at the same time. When they were put together on the display structures, they would be stunning.

"Yeah. Christiana was always fascinated by wildflowers when we were young, much to Mother's dismay. She called them weeds."

I grinned down at her and winked. "Then I think this is a particularly nice, yet subtle, *fuck you* to your mom."

I couldn't help it; I tucked one of her wayward curls behind her ear. So soft. Her hair, her skin, this woman in general. My fingers trailed down her cheek of their own accord. "They're beautiful, Wildflower."

Those big green eyes stared up at me, and even though I knew I shouldn't, I wanted a taste of those sweet, plump lips.

That damned phone buzzed again and broke the

moment. I dropped my hand from her cheek, and we both stepped back.

"Text whoever it is back and tell them you've more than got it under control. In a few hours, they'll see what Slice of Heaven is truly about."

A smile brightened her face, and she nodded enthusiastically. "Damned right they will."

I kissed her forehead, unable to help myself, unable to stop cursing myself. She was just so fucking genuine. I wanted to bring a smile to her face as often and in as many ways as possible. Smiling was meant to be her natural state.

But I couldn't. I stepped even farther back. "I'm going to get the display stands together. Everything is going to be perfect."

Everything except for the fact that I needed to get my priorities straight and away from this woman who was way too distracting.

Slice of Heaven, indeed.

Chapter 9

Bethany

Because of Landon's help, or maybe more because he'd kept me from hurtling myself off the nearest cliff, I'd not only gotten the cupcakes finished on time, I'd had the opportunity to pamper myself a little while getting ready for tonight.

A soak in the tub and extra time to spend on my hair and makeup had me much more relaxed than I'd been at the brunch this morning.

Landon was right. People were about to get a taste—literally and figuratively—of what Slice of Heaven was about. The cupcakes looked fantastic, and their flavors were even better. The stand Landon had put together had worked perfectly. The finished product looked like a bouquet of cascading wildflowers.

Exactly how I'd planned.

Tonight's welcome reception wasn't a formal event. It was a chance for everyone to say hello, reconnect, make informal plans. The island was available for the entire week. Many of the people Christiana and Simon had invited were making use of that and staying the whole time. Others would be coming in closer to the wedding itself.

So tonight, there would be no sit-down dinner or assigned seating like at the actual reception after the wedding. Yet another reason why both wildflowers and cupcakes worked—casual and people could serve themselves. And hopefully be the source of smiles.

Everyone was walking around chatting when I arrived. Mother and Father were in conversation with some guests. Christiana and Simon were talking to some people we'd known at our private, exclusive high school.

And guests were already gathered around the elaborate cupcake display, studying and discussing it. It was all I could do to not break out in some sort of celebratory dance right there in the middle of the room.

Probably wouldn't go well with the gentle melodies coming from the string quartet in the corner.

I couldn't help myself; I walked toward the group. I wanted to hear what they were saying. At this point, almost no one would associate me with Slice of Heaven. So I could eavesdrop without being obvious.

I briefly greeted extended family members and business associates of my father's as I inched toward the display. But as soon as I got close enough to hear the comments, I wished I'd stayed away. It wasn't the words; it was the primary speaker: *Mina.*

As I'd told Landon earlier this afternoon, there had never been any love lost between her and me. We'd known each other in high school before Simon and I had dated. She hadn't liked him and me together, but we'd ended it before that could become an issue.

The fact that she hadn't wanted me to be a couple with Simon irritated me much less than the fact that she'd hit on Landon today. That was messed up on multiple levels I wasn't even going to think about now.

Mina's posse was hanging on her every word, just as they had in high school. Hell, some of them probably were the same girls from high school.

This was not a group I wanted to engage with. I turned to make my escape before they saw me but didn't get that lucky.

"Well hello, Bethany." The posse member who had outed me—Daniela? Desiree? She'd definitely gone to high school with us, but I couldn't remember her name—announced my presence with glee.

All five of the women turned in unison to face me.

"Bethany!" Mina blew air-kisses toward my face with as much practice as her aunt Patricia. "You over here to eavesdrop?"

Totally busted.

I forced a smile onto my face. "No, of course not. Just wanted to make sure everything was still looking as it should. I didn't realize it was you over here." *Because I would've lit myself on fire rather than come over if I had.*

"We were just discussing how you were providing the desserts this week with your little business. What is it called again? Slice of Pie?"

"Slice of Heaven."

Mina's laugh was high-pitched and nasal. "Right. Slice of Heaven. See, Diane? I told you it was something clever."

Diane. That was the woman's name. She muttered something about it not being so clever under her breath, but I ignored her, keeping my eyes on Mina. It was instinctual, like my body was aware that Mina was the most dangerous and taking my eyes off her would be a mistake.

"I see your sister hired you to make her…" She waved vaguely toward the dessert stand. "Cupcakes? So quaint. It's like a princess's birthday party."

Mina's posse did a poor job of smothering their snickers.

My balance shifted from one foot to the other as I tried to figure out what to say. I didn't want to justify my reasoning behind this particular dessert when I knew Mina didn't really care.

She went on before I could say anything anyway. "I mean, I like it. You've obviously got an artistic talent. These are lovely."

That was the thing with Mina; like Patricia and even Mother, she could offer such a blend of compliment and insult that the two were almost interchangeable.

This sort of social repartee was not my forte. It never had been, much to Mother's dismay. I hated playing these games. So I wouldn't.

"Thank you," I said simply. "I'm very proud of them."

Mina's eyes narrowed. She didn't like it when someone didn't do what she wanted, and she wanted us to fight. She forced a smile on her face.

"But the truth is in the taste, isn't it? We'll just have to see. Later, of course. Not while you're in front of everyone. Not trying to put you in the spotlight."

Maybe I did like to play the game a little bit. I couldn't resist this challenge. "Why don't you have one now?"

I knew I was taking a chance, that Mina might spit it out and call it disgusting here in front of everyone. But then she'd make herself a liar because I knew the cupcakes were good. *Better* than good.

Her lips pursed. "Since you insist."

She turned and picked out a cupcake. By this time, we had drawn in a small crowd. I hope this didn't detonate in my face.

I gritted my teeth when I saw that, instead of choosing a cupcake on an edge where it would have minimal effect on the overall presentation, Mina picked one right in the middle of the arrangement, leaving a small gap.

Bitch. I forced my smile not to slip.

She giggled and dipped her finger into the icing before placing it in her mouth delicately, sucking the small bit off the tip.

Her eyebrows went up. "Oh, that's delicious."

Damned right it is. "Take a bite."

She did, and a small moan of pleasure escaped before she realized it and stopped herself. But it was too late.

Now my smile was big and genuine. I knew my dark chocolate cupcakes with salted caramel frosting were, in fact, moan-worthy.

"Quite tasty," she said, placing the rest of the cupcake down on the small plate.

I knew that was all the positive I would get out of her. "Thank you."

Now I could leave.

"I'm not surprised," Mina said. "Truly. I mean, look at you. You can tell you're an excellent cook by looking at you."

I froze. I was already well aware that I was the only one in her entire circle who wore a size with two digits. Not fat, no. But not a size two either.

She put a friendly hand on my arm. "It's totally understandable, you putting on the pounds. With all that baking stuff, how could you not? You know, the best trainers in LA will make house calls."

I felt my face flush, and I jerked my arm out of Mina's grasp. "I haven't gained weight."

And it was true. I hadn't. I was very careful with what I ate and how much I exercised. I'd been this size before starting Slice of Heaven.

Once again, choked smirks surrounded us.

"You're right," she soothed. "I should never have insinuated otherwise. I just meant that your treats are so good, we may all be just as fat by the end of the week."

I stood there staring at her. Goddammit, why could I not think of a comeback? Where was my mother with all her venom when I needed her?

"But let's not talk about that." Mina had the audacity to link her arm through mine. "Where is this handsome boyfriend Aunt Patricia has been telling us all about? The one who reassures us you're not pining away after Simon."

Silence fell around us. Not just the posse but the crowd we'd drawn.

"Mina, stop this. This isn't the time," I said in a low voice, trying to keep the conversation private.

"We just want to meet him. He wasn't at the brunch this morning. But I know he's got to be here tonight." She made a big show of looking around.

I should've been honest this morning. As painful as that might have seemed, nothing could be as bad as having to admit this publicly. I spun back toward the cupcakes, trying to figure out anything I could do or say.

"He... We..."

Mina chuckled and swiped another bit of icing off her cupcake before slipping her finger into her mouth. "You what?"

"There you are, sweetheart. I've been looking all over for you." I turned toward Landon's voice behind me.

He looked amazing, in a well-tailored deep-blue suit

that fit his physique perfectly and played to every advantage he had. Which were *a lot.*

"I didn't think to look over here," he continued. "You promised me no working tonight—that you were going to enjoy yourself."

The crowd, when they realized Landon was talking to me, parted like the Red Sea. I tried not to let my jaw drop as he walked forward and put his hand on my waist, then bent to press a kiss to my cheek. "I'm sorry, I got held up on a phone call with the office," he said. "What did I miss?"

He looked around at the crowd expectantly, shooting that gorgeous smile—dimples out in full attack mode. Mina was the closest guest to me, so he held out his hand to her. "Landon Black. We met a little earlier today, I think? You mistook me for a hotel employee."

"You mistook *him* for a hotel employee?" Diane whispered a little too loudly. People chuckled, and Mina's back went ramrod straight.

"He was hanging out in the lobby like he was one." She crossed her arms over her chest. "You're Bethany's boyfriend?"

Each word of her question had a higher lilt, as if she couldn't figure out which word was most important to emphasize as ridiculous: *you're, Bethany's,* or *boyfriend.*

Hell, all of them worked.

"Bethany," Patricia chimed in as she walked over. "This isn't the man we saw on your social media a few weeks ago."

I felt like my face had frozen into that laugh-with-sweat-pooling-on-the-forehead emoji. "No, this is Landon, not Brad."

Landon shrugged and pulled me closer. "She and Brad broke up a while ago. He's old and tired news."

Mina was looking Landon up and down. Everyone was looking at him that way. He ignored them, smiling down at me.

I stared at his dimples to keep from hyperventilating.

Patricia finally spoke. "I thought you worked for Bethany."

"It's hard to be around Bethany without getting inspired by her work ethic. When her normal carpenter had a family emergency, how could I not offer to stand in as her Man Friday?" He chuckled and straightened his tie. "It makes a man feel good to work with his hands, if you know what I mean."

I couldn't get a word out. I wasn't sure if I was ever going to have the ability to speak again. But evidently, he didn't need my backup to continue this charade.

"Now, if you'll excuse me, I'd like to drag my sexy woman away from her work. Although, if you're all smart, you'll start with dessert. It's the best thing you'll have all night." He winked down at me. "I always like to start with dessert. And finish with it too."

The words dripped with sexual yumminess. Which, okay, wasn't a word, but Lord, nobody had any doubt what he was talking about.

He kept me pinned to his side with his arm around my waist as we walked away. "Want a drink?" he asked. "Or a hand grenade to lob over your shoulder? Though, it would be a shame to mess up your gorgeous display."

I tried to swallow past the huge lump in my throat, but it didn't work, so I just nodded—I wanted both. He steered us toward one of the less crowded bars and got me a white wine. After a few sips, I was finally able to speak.

"What just happened?"

"Sorry, I could not stand by and let Mina and her bot

crew do that to you. I probably could've handled it differently. Sorry," he repeated.

"Please don't apologize. You saved me."

"I know you would've preferred to keep things more low profile. This was the most direct way, but not the most subtle."

People were glancing at us in that *don't want to stare but want to get a closer look* sort of way. A few were sneaking cupcakes. That was good, at least.

Patricia and Mina had their heads together, phones in front of them. I was sure they were trying to find any details on Landon they could.

"Hope you don't have a wife or something on Instagram."

He chuckled. "No wife or girlfriend, don't worry. And no social media profiles at all."

I took another sip of my drink. "Smart."

People were still looking at us. Landon's hand still rested over mine. "You going to be okay?"

"Yeah. By tomorrow, they won't be talking about us anymore. Gossip will have blown over, and we can come up with excuses why you're not attending events or hanging out with me. Work emergencies or something."

He shifted slightly closer. "I don't mind attending, unless that's weird for you."

"No, it'll be great. Keep everyone off my back so I can focus on my desserts and the wedding itself. As long as you're sure you don't mind."

He smiled, but somehow, it didn't quite reach his eyes. "I'm happy to. It'll give me something to do. I can mingle with the guests."

It unsettled something inside me to see an inauthentic smile on his face. I stepped in closer and placed a hand on his chest, telling myself it was to sell the role.

"Are you sure? This goes way beyond the carpentry work and cake stand setup. I'm sure Harley sold you on helping me by telling you it was an easy week on a tropical island."

His hand covered mine, and he moved it in gentle circles, almost as if he were soothing a pain there. "I'm sure I want to be at as many events as possible. Now, how about if we go sell this little charade of ours?"

He stayed by my side for the next hour as we circulated. I saw Mother side-eyeing us as we talked to various people, but evidently, the gossip hadn't hit her yet. I would know when it did.

After my challenge to Mina to try the cupcakes, others had followed suit. Now I didn't have to eavesdrop to know what people thought. They were coming directly to me and telling me.

It was perfect.

Right up to the point when my mother tapped me on the shoulder. I knew immediately she'd heard the gossip and was not happy about it. My father stood by her side, not looking terribly pleased either. They'd waited until Landon had gone to get us drinks at one of the bars.

"How could you?" my mother hissed softly. "I can't believe you would do this!"

Her voice was low so no one could overhear. I kept mine low too. "Do what, Mother?"

She glared over at Landon.

I rolled my eyes. "You mean, bring a date?"

"It sounds like he's much more than just your date, isn't he?"

"Fine. Yes, he's my boyfriend, but I don't think that's any reason to get upset. I'm sure you'll like Landon once you get to know him."

Why was I defending my imaginary boyfriend? Once

we left this island, Mother would never see him again. Hell, *I* would never see him again.

If anything, my mother's stare got icier. "Boyfriend?"

Was this because she thought Landon was a carpenter? This was the last straw. I was about to tear into my mother when Landon joined us.

"Mr. and Mrs. Thornton," he said with one of his smiles as he handed me a glass of wine. "I'm sorry we're meeting this way. I'm Landon Black."

He shook my mother's hand then my father's.

"I hear congratulations are in order," Dad said.

Oh sweet Jesus. "I don't think dating really calls for congratulations." I tried to laugh lightly, but it came out pretty choked.

"No need to keep it a secret," Dad whispered. "We know."

"Know what?"

Mina stepped out from behind my father. "Oops, I might have let the truth slip. Sorry!"

There was nothing sorry in anything about her. If she were a cat, a canary would've been half hanging out of her mouth.

I narrowed my eyes at her. "You let the truth slip about Landon and me dating?"

Her smile got bigger. "About you two being secretly *engaged.*"

I stiffened, forcing myself not to fling the chardonnay in Mina's face. This was too far, even for her. She was deliberately trying to make Landon run for cover and publicly humiliate me.

I had no idea what to say. I could feel all the eyes on me.

Landon took it all in stride. "How did you know? It was supposed to be a secret."

Mina's face went from triumphant to shocked. Realizing I probably mirrored her expression, I tucked my face against his chest. His arm came around me, keeping me close.

Oh, bless him. I'd keep him in cupcakes for the rest of his life. He'd said something about cinnamon. Maybe I'd keep him in cinnamon rolls. Whatever he wanted.

Mina recovered quickly. "Well, show us the ring, you two lovebirds."

"We didn't even bring the ring. Bethany didn't want to take the focus away from Christiana and Simon." Landon pressed a kiss to the side of my head. "You're such a good sister, sweetheart."

For a second, all the drama around me disappeared, and I wanted that kiss to have been real. There was something truly special about kisses on the hair or forehead. They were a level of intimacy that transcended lust and moved into passion and true affection.

I wanted hair and forehead kisses. Every woman wanted hair and forehead kisses.

Too bad it was all a big lie, even if Landon had saved me from embarrassment twice in one night.

There were handshakes and hugs before I insisted we not discuss the engagement more. This was Christiana's week. Watching Mina skulk away, foiled, was the best part of this whole situation.

The worst part? Knowing I was eventually going to have to unravel this huge knot I was creating.

But that could wait until after this week. Right now, I was going to revel in the fact that my desserts were being enjoyed by everyone and my mother was actually beaming at me in approval for once.

I was going to float on a gorgeous, attentive man's arm.

I was going to smile up at him and pretend the sexy winks he gave me were real.

When we left the island after the wedding, Landon and I would have some dramatic breakup. I'd make Mother understand.

But for right now, I would pretend he was mine.

Chapter 10

Landon

Being Bethany's *significant other* opened way more doors for this mission last night than I could've opened on my own. I was grateful seduction hadn't been the plan ahead of time because I wasn't sure I could've done it.

Not because I wasn't attracted to Bethany, but because she was trusting me so completely.

Every time those pretty green eyes smiled up at me last night, I felt like shit. All I could do was keep repeating to myself that this fake-fiancé situation worked in Bethany's favor just as much as it did mine.

After Mina's little bombshell, we'd agreed with Bethany's parents to keep the *fiancé* thing under wraps. For this week, I'd merely be Bethany's boyfriend, so we weren't taking away from the bride and groom.

Fiancé or boyfriend didn't matter in terms of the mission. Instead of having to find a way to be invited to the events where Frey would be present, I'd been instantly included in the inner circle.

Hell, Thornton had even introduced me to Frey. I hadn't spent much time talking to him, not wanting to be too memorable. But I'd tried to gather as much detail as possible.

Frey was dressed casually—no jacket, just a black dress shirt with black tailored pants. As much as I didn't go around looking at other men's packages, I could tell his phone was in his front right pocket.

But knowing where his phone was didn't make it any more accessible. If I made a dive for that front pocket, I was going to get myself killed.

Bethany knew Frey by name but didn't seem any closer to him than she was with any of her father's business associates. I wanted to press her for any details she had—anything could give me an advantage—but knew that would seem odd. So instead, I kept my questions broad—asking about everyone, redirecting to Frey when I could.

Bethany may not have associated much with this crowd in the last couple of years, but her upbringing in wealthy circles was still evident. She could work a room like the best of them—conversing, smiling, remembering names and faces.

But even as she did it, she was totally different from most. She wasn't trying to impress anyone or get one up on them. She wasn't concerned with how they could help her climb the social ladder. She was authentically friendly. Most people were drawn to her for it.

That, and wanting to know a little more about the woman who had made such amazing cupcakes.

When anyone asked about me, I'd tried to keep with as much truth as possible. I told them I was former Navy—leaving out the SEAL part. I'd told them I'd wanted to be a carpenter as a kid, which made me perfect to help my sweet girlfriend with her cake stands.

All in all, being on Bethany's arm had been a great way to establish myself and make me less suspicious.

Now, to use it to my advantage.

I was back out at the pool. I had kept an eye on the area from my room, waiting for a chance to make a move.

When Fanshawe, Frey's pissed-off newbie security guard from yesterday, showed up at the bar, I had what I'd been waiting for.

He was alone at the same bar where I'd talked to Adams yesterday. Again, as I'd done with his boss, I sat one seat down and ignored him. This time, there was no television on, so I turned around to observe the hotel lobby.

Wedding guests milled about, enjoying the pool and beach. I hadn't seen Bethany since last night. She was supposed to be spending today with her sister and mother at the spa. She deserved to relax. There were no events today requiring effort from her.

Plus, her being at the spa meant I had uninterrupted time to work. After a few minutes, my plan worked. Fanshawe turned around and people watched alongside me.

"You're the guy who was talking to Adams yesterday," he finally said.

I glanced over. "Yeah, kind of. We were both watching the game. You work for him, right?"

His jaw got hard. "No, I work for Mr. Frey. Adams may act like I work for him, but I don't."

That's right, buddy. Get yourself wound up. "Sorry, man. That's hard to deal with."

He whistled to himself as a group of women walked up from the beach on the other side of the pool. Mina and her posse. She was leading them, as always.

"I wouldn't mind dealing hard with that one. Not an ounce of bounce anywhere on that body."

I didn't want to spend even one more second with this asshole, but that wasn't an option. "I prefer them with meat, myself."

He chuckled. "You're with the bride's sister, aren't you?"

I grunted. I wasn't sure how much he knew.

"She's definitely got some junk in the trunk."

Squaring my jaw, I looked over at him. "Careful. She's not just a job to me."

Hell if that wasn't becoming more and more true.

"Yeah, I heard you guys were together." He held up his hands. "I was just making an observation."

I reached over and slapped him on the arm even though I wanted to punch him in the face. "Just fucking with you. No harm." After clapping him on the bicep, I held out the same hand. "Name's Landon."

"Fanshawe." He shook my hand firmly, gripping too hard. Trying to prove something.

"Outside of people not giving you the respect you deserve, how's this gig going for you?" I asked him. "At least you're getting a little time off to enjoy yourself."

He rolled his eyes. "I mostly get shitty shifts off. You know, five a.m. to nine a.m. or something like that. Midafternoon like today. Nothing when there's any action."

"That sucks. Frey like to do anything interesting?"

"He likes to fuck his girlfriend and lie to his wife. Does that count as interesting?"

Making my chuckle sound authentic was tricky. "Anything that doesn't require you to guard his door?" Finding out Frey went for a dawn swim every morning would be nice. Or that he liked to go work out at two a.m.

"I wish. So far, it's either been at the room or standing near a table while he works. Fucking boring, especially here."

Dude was not going to make it long in security work. A lot of it wasn't interesting at all. It required you to stay focused and disciplined and ready for when the true action did happen.

Fanshawe would never be ready for real danger because he wasn't willing to put in the boring hours. We never would've hired him at Zodiac Tactical, no matter how big the guy was.

"Yeah, boring," I muttered.

"You would think they'd give me a little more respect, you know? This isn't my first job. I may be new with Mr. Frey, but I've got experience in the security world. Adams shouldn't be treating me like I'm some peon."

He started complaining about Adams again, but he cut off when Frey himself walked down to the bar and sat in a booth not far from us. He made no motion to join us or invite either of us to join him, but he was too close for Fanshawe to continue to speak freely.

I'd made my connection with Fanshawe, so I turned around in hopes of Frey saying something or doing something that would help.

I had one of the nano transmitters in my pocket. Maybe I'd get really lucky and Frey would go to the bathroom and leave his phone on the table.

Yeah, right.

I spent the better part of two hours sitting at that damn bar, listening while Fanshawe made obnoxiously sexist comments under his breath and Frey nursed a couple of drinks and read through papers. His other guards and personal assistant came and went, and the man didn't say or do anything that would help me.

When Frey left, Adams motioned to Fanshawe he needed to come too. Good. Let Adams continue to piss him off. Hopefully that could work to my advantage. But honestly, I didn't see Fanshawe remaining in Frey's employ for long.

I paid for the two drinks I hadn't done anything but swirl in my glass and stood.

"Here all alone? Where's your fiancée?"

I turned to find Mina right behind me.

"She's enjoying a spa day. She deserves it."

"Because she works so hard with her job. True." Her eyes narrowed. "I haven't been able to find much out about you. I'm somewhat of an expert at cybersleuthing. You don't seem very big on social media."

Because I worked for one of the best security companies on the planet and knew what a personal information sieve social media could be. "I'm not big on computers. If you'll excuse me, I've got to get going."

She didn't move. "I know you and Bethany aren't really together."

"Why would you say that?" I leaned my elbows back on the bar. The most important part about being undercover was not giving too much away.

She took a step closer, and I straightened. I didn't want this woman in my personal space. "Because someone like you doesn't go for someone like Bethany."

"Someone like *me*? Someone like *Bethany*?" I narrowed my eyes. "Do you know how elitist and conceited you sound right now?"

She shrugged one small shoulder. "I prefer the term realistic. And I'm not necessarily talking about her weight or her looks. Bethany has never really fit in."

"That doesn't necessarily seem like a bad thing, given

what I've seen." I stepped farther to the side, away from her.

"I used to think Bethany thought she was too good for us. Then I thought she wasn't aware of how our world worked. When she opened the bakery, her parents were shocked, but it made sense to me. Her mind had always been focused on different things than what we thought were important." She stepped closer. "But actually, it's neither. She doesn't care. Our opinions don't matter to her."

I wasn't going to discuss Bethany and her fears with Mina; that would only give the woman more ammunition.

"I think Bethany wants to enjoy her sister's wedding and provide the best desserts she can. Not a damned thing wrong with that."

"And what about you, Landon? What do you want?"

I straightened. "To help my fiancée in whatever way I can."

"That may be true, but that's not all. You're looking for something more than her. I can see it. Your focus is not fully on Bethany."

Shit. Mina had seen what everyone else had missed. She was misattributing the fact that my focus wasn't solely resting on Bethany, but she'd still seen it.

Mina placed her hand on my chest. "I can give you what you're looking for."

Oh, hell no. I picked her hand off my chest. "There is not any situation where you can give me what I'm looking for. And believe me, I would never choose you over Bethany. So, back off."

This conversation wasn't my normal way of dealing with people. I always tried for charm over rudeness. But this woman was a viper in very expensive clothing, and I wanted nothing to do with her.

I dropped her wrist and walked away. People like Mina didn't know how to handle the word no. She would either get pissy or take it as a challenge to further try to hit on me. I wasn't going to stick around to find out which.

I headed to the main lodge and got to my room. It was getting dark, and after spending the afternoon with Fanshawe and Mina, I needed a fucking shower.

I let out a curse when the keycard didn't work. I tried it again, but nothing. Gritting my teeth, I walked back to the lobby.

"How can I help you?"

My smile was forced even though the man at the counter was friendly and professional. "I'm Landon Black, room 306. My keycard isn't working, and I can't get into my room."

The guy's face brightened. "Mr. Black, oh yes. You've been moved into a suite. As per orders, the porter has already collected your belongings, and they should be at the new suite momentarily."

I stiffened. I'd gotten that corner room on purpose since it allowed me to see both the pool area and beach. Not to mention, it offered a second exit via fire escape if I needed it.

Did someone suspect I was undercover? I'd swept my room for any transmitting devices, and Tristan had eyes on the resort's security system. He would've notified me if something was off.

No news was good news, but someone had packed up my stuff. My weapons were hidden within my belongings, but if someone had searched systematically, they'd probably find them.

I shot the desk attendant a friendly smile. "I don't think I want to be upgraded. Any way I can get my previous room back?"

The guy's face crumpled like he was really upset. "The suite is a very nice one. Has an absolutely stunning view of the sunset from the balcony. As a matter of fact, the champagne should be delivered any moment."

"Champagne?"

"Mrs. Thornton was insistent that a bottle be delivered every night at sunset."

"The Thorntons are the ones who upgraded me?"

The guy's head bobbed up and down. "Yes! I'm sorry, she made it seem like you'd already agreed. I think she felt bad that their other daughter's"—his voice dipped lower, like he was in on the secret—"*fiancé* was in one of our smaller rooms. The suite is much nicer. So, she had us move your things."

I relaxed. I would still sweep the new room to make sure it wasn't under surveillance, but Angelique and Oliver upgrading me was much less suspicious.

"Yeah, she must've forgotten to mention it."

The guy programmed a new keycard and handed it to me. "I hope you enjoy yourself."

"I will. Thanks."

The suite was farther away from Frey's room, but that didn't matter much now. Fanshawe was my best bet. It was just a matter of figuring out how to use him.

My keycard worked fine at the new door. But as soon as it clicked, I froze. Someone was inside; I could hear voices. I reached down to my ankle holster and got my weapon as I slid the door silently open.

Chapter 11

Bethany

"So basically, everybody loved them."

I was curled up on the deep couch in my room, dressed in the fluffy white robe the spa had provided for Mother, Christiana, and me during our treatments today. This had been the first chance I'd had to check in with Michele since arriving on the island.

"And the tree motif worked like we planned? Landon didn't have any problem setting it up?"

"No, no problem. Landon has been...amazing." I winced at my pause, hoping Michele wouldn't pick up on it. I rushed on. "Everything going okay there? Any problems?"

"No, solid business for early week. Don't worry, Captain, your ship is sailing just fine without you. Now, let's go back to Landon being—dramatic pause—*amazing*. I know that means at more than building cake stands. Spill, sister."

Busted.

"He's been super supportive. Helped me defuse the whole dateless situation with my family." I wrapped one of my curls around my finger.

Mom and Christiana had asked me all sorts of questions about him today, but I'd deflected. Talking about him made it feel too real.

I'd spent the day reminding myself that none of this was real. Not the dimples, not the charm, not the forehead kisses.

Not. Real.

Fake.

Fake was a very clear term.

I just needed to remember it.

"Yay! See, I knew this would work out better than Harley. What did Landon do, pretend to be your boyfriend?"

Damn it. My silence answered her.

"He did!" I had to hold the phone away from my ear to keep from going deaf from Michele's squeal. "Oh my God, he pretended to be your boyfriend!"

I let out a sigh. "Even worse, when Simon's cousin tried to make it awkward, he told everyone he was my fiancé."

I had to hold the phone farther away.

"I love it! Did you kiss him? Lawd, I'll bet he's a good kisser."

I'd had the same thoughts myself. "No, I didn't kiss him. But I appreciate him helping me out."

"Girrrrl." Michele dragged out the r to an annoying length. "You need to run with this. Get as much out of this fake engagement as you can. Is he there with you in your room?"

I rolled my eyes. "Of course not, dumbass. First of all,

I wouldn't be talking about him if he were here, and second, *fake* engagement. *Faaaaake*."

She let out a dramatic sigh. "Whatever. I'm not saying the engagement needs to be real. I'm saying you need to get you some of those dimples since he offered and all. Invite him over. Make up an excuse to get him in your room and then jump his sexy bones."

I had to laugh. "I don't see that happening, but if he shows up, I'll see what I can do."

"Yeah, you do that. I don't want to hear that you—"

I heard the door rattle.

"Michele, hang on. Someone's at the door. Mother told me she was sending me a gift, so I guess it's arrived."

I stood and waited for the knock but didn't hear it. Then realized the door was *opening*. Oh shit.

Why hadn't I put the latch on? Who was trying to get into my room without announcing themselves? What should I do?

"Michele," I whispered. "I think someone is breaking in to my room."

"What? I can—"

I took a step toward the door as it opened farther, then let out a breath in relief when I saw it was Landon. My hand flew to my chest.

"Landon, oh my gosh, you scared me. What are you doing here?"

"Landon?" Michele screeched in my ear. "Landon is there? You just said if he showed up, you'd jump his bones. Get some! You—"

"I'll call you tomorrow." She was still making suggestions on what I should do with Landon when I ended the call.

Landon crouched down, messing with the hem of his

pants then tying his shoe. I took the opportunity to make sure my robe was securely tied.

"How'd you get a key to my room?" I asked once he stood and we were facing each other

"*Your* room. Of course it is." He scrubbed a hand down his face. "My key didn't work for my room, so I went to the lobby, where they notified me I'd been upgraded to a suite."

Oh my fucking God. "My mother."

He shrugged, face wry. "Yeah, seems that way. I guess she thought we should be together since we're…*together.*"

I nodded, big awkward smile on my face. Him sleeping in here was not a good idea, despite the fact that I could hear Michele screaming the opposite all the way from the mainland.

My suite had a bedroom and a living area with a couch, but still, it was too much. I didn't want him to have to sleep on a couch, and I didn't want him sleeping in the bed with me.

Even if I could still feel those kisses on the top of my head and forehead from last night.

"Let me call the front desk and sort this out."

Here I'd thought Mother was on her best behavior today at the spa. That she was actually honoring my wishes by not talking much about Landon, and keeping the conversation focused on Christiana.

I should've known she was up to something.

I picked up the phone by the bed that connected me to the front desk. "Hello, this is Bethany Thornton. My mother moved my fiancé into my room, but we'd actually prefer to keep separate rooms. Can we get one for him?"

"Sure," the receptionist said brightly. "One second."

I heard the sound of clacking keys on a keyboard, then

he came back. "I'm sorry, Ms. Thornton, but all the rooms are booked."

"That's not possible," I said. "We haven't used all the rooms in this resort. Perhaps you can discuss it with your supervisor, if that's okay. He or she may have insight you and I don't have."

"Of course. Hold one moment and let me get Ms. Hebron."

Jeez. I hated being the snob asking to talk to the manager, but what else could I do? I shot Landon an awkward smile as I waited.

He smiled back—not awkward. He never seemed awkward.

"Ms. Thornton, this is Nicola Hebron, resort manager. I am so sorry to say this, but Gregory was actually correct, we do not have any other rooms available."

"Are you sure?" I rubbed the tension building in the middle of my forehead. "I know my parents booked the whole island, but we don't have that many people attending."

"Right, that is correct." She said it with the practiced ease of someone used to customer service. "But the agreement the resort made with your parents was to give them a discount if they allowed us to do renovations on any unused rooms."

"I see." I rubbed my head harder. That made sense. My family had significant money, but renting out this entire island for a week was an extravagant event for them, especially when we were only using two-thirds of the rooms available.

"When your fiancé's room opened up, we were able to give it to one of the guests who had originally requested a second room for their teenagers. So, all of the available rooms are full."

"I see." I was aware I was repeating myself, but I wasn't sure what else to say.

She paused, then continued. "Your parents' suite does have an extra bedroom if one of you wanted to see about staying with them?"

It took all of my willpower not to laugh in the poor woman's ear. Staying with my parents wasn't an option. I'd sleep on the patio chairs first.

"No, that's not necessary. Thank you for your time." I put the phone receiver back on the base much more gently than I wanted to.

"No luck?"

I turned to face him with a shrug. "Doesn't look like it."

The knock on the door made me jump.

"Probably my stuff," Landon said then turned to answer it.

Sure enough, the porter pushed in a cart with Landon's duffel and hanging bag. "Mr. Black, I'll put these in the bedroom closet if it's okay?"

Landon looked over at me.

"Sure," I whispered.

The man worked quickly and efficiently, hanging Landon's shirts and pants next to mine, then setting up a suitcase rack and placing his case on it. He started to organize the contents of the duffel, but Landon stopped him.

"I've got it from here, man. Thanks." He tipped the porter as he left.

I was still staring at Landon's things next to mine in the closet. It was so domesticated. I'd never lived with a man, so it was a bit of a shock to my system.

Oh shit. I could feel panic bubbling up inside me.

"Okay, then," I said, trying to get myself under control. Perfect. Wittiest line since *I carried a watermelon.*

Landon walked back over from where he'd shut the door behind the porter. "You okay? Listen, why don't I go talk to the front desk? Nobody is working on the empty rooms at night. I can sleep on the floor."

I rubbed my hand over my eyes. "No. I'm being ridiculous. There's plenty of room for you to stay here. It's fine."

My phone buzzed in my hand, and I looked at the text from Michele.

Jump his sexy bones! Bow-chicka-wow-wow

Followed by what looked to be five hundred kissy emojis and a couple of highly inappropriate gifs.

The laugh that escaped me was tinged with hysteria.

He stepped toward me, concern evident in those hazel eyes. "It'll be okay. I'll sleep on the couch. We can make up a bathroom schedule."

He was still smiling. He obviously was not worried about the forced proximity like I was.

Because this relationship of ours wasn't real. I wasn't sure how many times I was going to need to remind myself of that. He obviously didn't need the reminder. He knew.

Not. Real.

Those dimples of his were staring me down like they wanted to start a fight. "We can do this, Wildflower."

Wildflower.

I snapped. "How can you be so calm?"

"About sleeping on a couch? I was in the Navy for over ten years. I've slept in much worse—"

"About it all! About my mother casually moving you in here without your consent! About pretending to be my boyfriend then my fiancé without even blinking an eye!" I walked over to the closet and gestured to the clothes. "About your clothes hanging right next to mine!"

He ran a hand through his brown hair, walking toward me. "Hey…"

"Why are you so calm? Why are you willing to do all this? Why don't you tell me and my family to go jump in a lake?"

"Calm is my superpower. That's how I operate. And thus far, nothing has happened that's too stressful. Pretending to be close to you is no hardship, Bethany. You're a beautiful person, inside and out."

I rolled my eyes. "You don't have to say stuff like that. There's nobody here to hear you."

He was next to me so fast I blinked. I'd never seen him move at anything more than a casual stroll.

"You're here to hear it, and you're who I'm talking to. You're beautiful."

I shook my head. "I know what I bring to the table. I'm smart and driven. But you don't have to look around this island for more than ten seconds to know that I'm not of the same caliber as them. You don't have to pretend to be attracted to me when we're in—"

His lips crashed against mine. Scorched air fled my lungs as he slid one of his hands into my hair at my neck to hold me in place as his lips devoured mine.

Holy hell, Michele had been right. Landon could kiss. His mouth was hot and wet and open against mine, and I was drawn under his spell. I wrapped my arms around him as he pulled me closer.

Then he slowed down, his teeth starting to nibble my lips, tease my tongue with his.

All I could do was hold on.

We were both breathing heavily by the time we pulled away. My fingers moved up to touch my lips of their own accord. His eyes flared a little as he watched.

"I'll have to pretend a lot of things while we're on this island, but being attracted to you isn't one of them. Get that straight."

"Okay," I whispered.

"Now, why don't you shower, or whatever, in the bathroom. I'll get the couch ready for me to sleep on."

I nodded, not sure whether to be disappointed or relieved. But I couldn't deny the heat in his eyes.

Fake had just become a lot more blurry.

Chapter 12

Landon

I'd never been a good sleeper. Home life for me as a kid hadn't been the greatest. Alcoholic dad with a temper meant I'd learned to sleep light. Or not at all.

My ability to cope with insomnia from an early age had given me a leg up when it came to SEAL training hell week. It was surprising how many guys rung out because of the exhaustion. Big, tough guys who could bench three hundred plus pounds without breaking a sweat cracked because their minds weren't tough enough to handle what lack of sleep did.

Hell, it was why it was such an effective torture method.

After getting out of the Navy a few years ago, my sleeping patterns had gotten a little better. Until I took that bullet to the chest. Almost dying had somehow thrown me neck-deep back into insomnia. I hadn't slept for more than a couple hours at a time in months.

I'd hidden it pretty well from my coworkers. Only those people closest to me—Ian, in particular—had recognized the symptoms and my coping mechanisms.

Insomnia was different for everyone, but for me, the key was not letting it get the best of me. I rarely lay awake in my bed, allowing my mind to wander. I got up and put my sleepless hours to good use: physical workouts, planning missions, research.

Not last night. Not after that kiss with Bethany. I shouldn't have done it, should never have given in to that instinct to cover those full lips with mine.

But not kissing her hadn't been an option.

She'd been standing there saying I wasn't attracted to her, and every instinct I'd ever had demanded I prove that wrong in the most visceral way possible.

It had only been through years of discipline and focus that I'd been able to pull myself back from what my body had really wanted to do—lay her down on that bed and fill her until we didn't know where one body ended and the other began.

Instead, I'd managed to get myself under control and say something non-caveman-like, although hell if I could remember what. She'd gone to bed, and I'd lain on that sofa, staring up at the ceiling.

I could've gotten out of the room without waking her. Hit the extensive resort gym or, hell, just walked the beach. I could've studied files I had on my laptop.

But this time when sleep wouldn't come, I'd let my mind wander. Straight to Bethany Thornton.

Everything about the woman was soft. In my line of work, soft was considered a weakness or insult. But her soft was a thing of beauty.

Soft lips, soft curves, soft soul.

And all I wanted to do was get as close as I could to that softness. Damn the mission.

I'd had respect for her before our lips touched. I'd been impressed by her work ethic, her kindness to others, the way she hadn't been hardened like the inner circle surrounding her seemed to be. I'd known she was attractive—big smile, riotous curls, cute freckles. And to be honest, I'd liked being her knight in shining armor. Being able to help her out by pretending to be her significant other made up for using her for the mission.

I'd *liked* her, but it had been in a sort of distanced way. Distance was necessary for undercover work.

But the moment our lips touched, that distance had been blown to hell.

It had been all I could do to stop. I had wanted nothing more than to place her on that bed and forget about everything else going on on this island.

But I couldn't. There was too much at stake. But when I hadn't been able to sleep, instead of getting up and doing something productive, I'd let my mind imagine all the things I'd like to do with Bethany. *To* her.

I hadn't held back—I'd put my insomnia to good use and gave my mind free rein. Positions, locations—kissing every inch of her from the crown of her head to the soles of her feet.

Knowing she was only a few feet away had been a beautiful sort of hell. Knowing that fantasizing about laying her out on that bed until she was crying my name was as close as I was ever going to get to being with Bethany was a *not-beautiful* sort of hell.

But I wasn't going to let this situation get out of control while on an active mission. No matter how much I wanted her.

No more mind-blowing kisses.

Focus on the mission.

~

Just before dawn, I'd cleared out of the room—not wanting to be there when Bethany woke up. If she wanted to talk about our kiss, I wouldn't shut her down, but there was so much I couldn't say that I wanted to avoid it.

But she didn't bring it up when we'd both found ourselves working side by side in the auxiliary kitchen. We'd both had a lot to do to prepare for the luau tonight. She'd spent the day putting together the various tropical-themed sweets being served. I'd gotten the stands set up and placed, then spent the afternoon trying to find a way close to Frey.

It was already Wednesday. I was running out of time. I needed to make a move tonight.

Tonight's theme was a luau, and everyone was dressed casually—sundresses for the women, khakis and Hawaiian shirts for the men. The drinks were mostly fruity, and a DJ was playing tropical-island-themed music.

I was on Bethany's arm again, doing boyfriend duty, when I spotted Frey at one of the bars. He was wearing a blazer tonight. He shifted, and I saw the outline of a shoulder holster.

Immediately, I went on high alert. No other time that I'd seen Frey had he had a shoulder holster. Why would he now?

Bethany was talking with one of the hotel staff who would be in charge of serving her desserts. I turned to excuse myself with a gentle squeeze at her waist. I wasn't sure what my plan was, but I needed to figure out what had changed that caused Frey to feel like he needed more security than just his team.

Before the words left my mouth, Bethany's father joined Frey at the bar. Oliver's features were pinched and body language stiffer than I'd seen this whole week.

Damn it, I needed to be over there for that conversation.

"I'm going to grab a drink. Want anything?" I whispered the words into Bethany's hair during a pause in her conversation. I tried to ignore the smell of it that made me want to pull her closer.

She looked up at me. "I'm sorry. I'm boring you."

I kissed her nose before I thought better of it. Damn it. "Not at all. I'll be right back."

By the time I made my way to the bar, Oliver was already leading Frey toward a man standing on the outskirts of the party near the shadows. *Fuck*. I couldn't go over there without being completely conspicuous.

Who was the man in the shadows? I continued to the bar then pulled out my phone, keeping it low, but pointing it in their direction, rapidly snapping pictures without looking like I was.

Oliver looked like he was introducing the two men, although neither of them offered to shake hands. I glanced down at my camera. One of my shots had gotten the mystery man's face.

I fired off a text to Tristan.

New guest at the party. Made Frey nervous enough to carry.

I tucked my phone back into my pocket as Oliver headed in my direction. He came to the bar next to me and ordered a scotch, neat. He drank it without saying anything then placed the glass back down for another.

"Everything okay, Mr. Thornton?"

He looked over at me like he wasn't sure who I was for

a moment, then nodded slowly. "Landon. Yes. Had an unexpected guest for the wedding."

"A friend of Mr. Frey's?"

Oliver's eyes narrowed. "You know Frey?"

"Met him here, making the rounds." I took a sip of my drink, hoping I hadn't made an error.

"Frey is part of a group of people I don't associate with much anymore. Evidently, he had some contacts with the groom's family, and that's how he got an invite. I would've vetoed if I'd known."

I was glad to hear that, if only for Bethany's sake.

"And the unexpected guest?"

Oliver took another sip of his drink. "Martinez is even worse than Frey."

Martinez. That didn't ring any bells for me.

"Do you want me to get resort security? If these people weren't invited, I'm sure security will escort them off the island."

Oliver shook his head rapidly. "No. No, just leave them be. Whatever is happening, I don't want to know. It has nothing to do with us."

"If you say so."

He turned more fully to me. "Look, I made some poor choices trying to get ahead when the girls were younger. I've spent a lot of time unraveling myself from people I should've never been connected with in the first place."

He sounded authentic. He leaned a little closer to me. "You were a soldier, so you may not understand, but the best way I can protect the people I love is to let those two men do whatever it is they're going to do and keep out of it."

I'd been in enough battles and fights to know that sometimes the only way to win was to walk away. So I respected what Oliver was attempting to do.

But I sure as hell wasn't going to stay out of it. Whoever Martinez was, he was scarier than Frey.

"I'll be sure to keep Bethany away from them." That was the truth.

"Thank you." Oliver seemed to relax just a little. "You're good for her. She smiles more when you're around."

Now I was back to feeling like shit. "She deserves to have every reason to smile." Truth again.

"I agree. I let Angelique convince me that not supporting Bethany in her business endeavor was the best thing. That was definitely incorrect, and I plan to rectify it. Those desserts of hers are amazing."

"Damned straight they are. And I'm sure she would appreciate your business advice so she can concentrate more on the aspects she's passionate about."

He finished the last of his drink and slid the glass to the side. "I plan to be as big a part of her business as she'll let me."

I snuck a look over at Martinez and Frey. They were still in the shadows closer to the beach. Adams and Fanshawe were staying discreetly to the sides. I spotted at least two other men who were probably Martinez's.

I looked back over at Oliver. "I think she would like that."

"Let me go find my wife before she hunts me down. Why aren't you with Bethany?"

"She was talking business with one of the hotel staff. I'll head back over in a second."

He slapped me on the shoulder and walked away just as my phone buzzed. Tristan.

"Can you talk?" he said without greeting.

"I'm here at a luau with about three hundred of my

closest friends, Mom." I smiled at the bartender who'd glanced in my direction.

"Fine, then just listen. I talked to Callum. That guy in the picture with Frey is Joaquin Martinez. He's pretty high in a terrorist organization that operates out of South America. Callum had no idea he'd be there."

"I'm pretty sure that's the case all the way around."

"You still have all three transmitters?"

"Yep, Mom. Sure do." Another couple came to stand at the bar. I gave them a friendly wave.

"Whatever Frey and Martinez are meeting about can't be good. Callum nearly wet himself at the thought of getting a transmitter on Martinez. Said it would be even more helpful than Frey. You can get it on his phone, computer, anything electronic."

"Sounds great, Mom. I'll do my best."

"Be careful. This Martinez guy sounds like bad news. Don't forget that you've got no safety net. I'm still only two miles offshore, but that's not going to help you if things get ugly. No transmitter is worth your life, Libra."

"Yeah, I love you too." I disconnected the call. There was only so long I could pretend to talk to my mother before it became weird. And I had the information I needed.

My mission had become twice as hard.

"Were you talking to your mom?"

Shit, Bethany. I forced a smile on my face as I turned toward her. "She doesn't always have the best timing."

Worry puckered her brow. "Is everything okay with her?"

I wrapped an arm around her shoulder. "Yeah, she gets a little worried sometimes. I might need to put a call in to her later." Better to go ahead and set up that excuse. I was going to need it soon. Having to call Mom was as good a reason as any to escape the party.

Bethany dipped her head against my chest. "You're a good son. A good man."

I gritted my teeth to keep my smile on my face. Then to make matters worse, Angelique spotted us and came fluttering our way.

"Speaking of mothers… Incoming," I whispered.

"Okay, you two. We're about to have family dances. You need to be out on the floor as a couple."

Bethany peeked up at me. "Is that okay?"

"Of course it's okay," Angelique interjected. "Why wouldn't it be okay? You do dance, don't you, Landon?"

"I do." But damn it, I didn't want to now when I needed to get closer to Martinez and Frey.

"Then it's settled." She grabbed my arm and urged us out to the floor.

Chapter 13

Bethany

I couldn't remember the last time I felt this free.

I was two for two when it came to the desserts. My tropical-themed goodies had been just as much of a success as the cupcakes had at the welcome reception. People were specifically starting to ask about the bakery. I'd given out over a dozen of my cards so far tonight. I wasn't sure things could be going better professionally.

Personally… Well, personally seemed to be going just as well.

I was dancing under the beautiful lights, surrounded by the crisp ocean breeze, in my fiancé's arms. I hadn't talked to him much today. I'd been busy making sure everything was ready for tonight. And besides, I wasn't sure what to say anyway. Despite Michele's three dozen texts asking for an update and coaching me—in unnerving detail—into putting the moves on Landon, I wasn't sure if that was what I really wanted. After all, what did I really know about him?

His thumb brushed down the middle of my forehead. "What's got you thinking so hard?" he asked.

I shrugged. Might as well be honest. "I don't know much about you. I've been fortunate so far that I've been able to deflect any questions."

He stiffened just slightly before relaxing. "What do you want to know?" he asked as we swayed to the music. He looked off to the side, but then back at me.

"You were just talking to your mom on the phone. Are you guys close? Do you have any siblings? Where are you from?"

He chuckled. "My mom and I are reasonably close. She's a recovering alcoholic, so we've become closer since she's gotten sober."

"Oh, I'm sorry."

"No, don't be. I'm happy for her. She is living a much better life than she did when I was a kid."

"Is your dad around?"

He shook his head. "No, he died when I was young."

"I'm sorry," I said again.

He looked like he was about to say more but stopped himself. "Thank you. My dad and I weren't close before he died."

Better to change the subject. "How about siblings?"

"None. It was just me. Well, that's not true, I guess," he continued. "I picked up quite a few brothers in the Navy. They may not be blood related to me, but I know they have my back and I have theirs no matter what."

He meant it. Sincerity was all but pouring from his hazel eyes.

"That's good," I said. "I believe in found families also. How long were you in the Navy?"

"I joined just after my seventeenth birthday. Forged my mom's signature. I was in for thirteen years then got out when some of my best friends did."

"How long ago was that?" I wasn't even sure how old he was.

"A while," he finally responded.

"I should stop prying." He obviously didn't want to talk about this.

"No, you're not prying." He pulled me a little closer. "I have a friend—Ian. He came into some money and started a business once he got out of the Navy. It's a sort of jack-of-all-trades company. We do lots of different things."

"Like carpentry?" I asked.

"Yeah, there's definitely some work like that involved. Ian hired a bunch of us that were in the Navy with him, so each of us takes on jobs based on whatever our strengths are. So, like this, with you, building the stands. That sort of mechanical work was right up my alley."

"And you like working for your friend?"

He nodded. "I never thought I would find a place where I fit in like I did in the Navy, but Ian's business, it's my home."

"That's good. I know some people struggle with finding their way once they get out of the service."

"Yes, definitely true," he responded.

I still felt like I was missing part of the information, but I really didn't want to pry.

"And truly, this gig with you has been great," Landon continued. "When I was growing up, I loved carpentry, loved to build things. I had a shed a couple miles from my house that was off on an empty lot, and I used to build all sorts of things in there. I'd forgotten how much I loved it until being back here with you. So, thank you."

He was *thanking* me. All I'd done was pay him a fair

wage for good work. He'd done so much more. "I'm glad it worked out for both of us."

The song shifted into something new, but Landon didn't miss a beat. We kept dancing.

"Now, let's talk about something important, like what do you do for fun?"

He was trying to get out of talking more about himself, but I would allow it. It was nice to have him focused on me.

"I'm not sure that I have done anything fun since I opened the bakery. It has taken up all my time. But I don't mean that in a bad way. I knew going in it would require all my time and effort to get the business off the ground. And I feel like we're almost there, especially after this week. If things go the way I expect, we'll need to hire a couple more full-time employees. Maybe then I'll get to take a day off."

His arm came a little more tightly around my waist. "What about if you took advantage of being on this island? You don't have any desserts you have to provide tomorrow, do you?"

I shook my head. "No, I don't have anything due now until the rehearsal dinner on Friday, so nothing tomorrow. But I'm not very good at relaxing." There was always so much to do even when I wasn't actively baking. Catching up on bills, emails, promotions.

He smiled, those dimples out in full force. "What if I help you with that? What if we spend part of the day tomorrow at the pool—relaxing, enjoying ourselves. Maybe a walk on the beach?"

I narrowed my eyes at him. "You don't have to babysit me."

His face turned wry. "Don't insult either of us. It would be my pleasure to spend time with you."

I stared down at his chest, not wanting to meet his eyes. I wasn't sure what was real and what was the part of him playing the role of my fiancé.

"Okay," I finally said, "the pool sounds great."

The DJ announced the end of the family dances, and the beat of the music picked up. Landon smiled at me as we broke away from each other.

"Okay, it's a date for tomorrow." He glanced at something over my shoulder and his brows pulled together, but Christiana rushed over and grabbed my arm before I could turn to see what it was.

"Can I borrow my sister?" She smiled at Landon.

"Absolutely." He gave her a little bow. "I'll grab a drink and entertain myself. Back in a few minutes."

I hooked arms with Christiana and walked in the other direction from Landon—he seemed to be going toward the ocean. I didn't think there was a bar in that direction, but he'd figure it out.

"You doing okay?" Yesterday at the spa, she'd seemed relaxed and perky, but now, her pinched features were back full force.

"Yeah, I just needed to escape Mom and Patricia. They made another hotel employee cry tonight because some of the seafood on the buffet tasted a little iffy."

I made a face. "The last thing we want is anyone getting sick from spoiled food."

She rolled her eyes. "It wasn't spoiled. They wanted something to complain about. I saw Patricia and Mina circling your desserts earlier. But I don't think they could find anything wrong with them, so Patricia moved on to easier targets."

"I'm sorry, sweetie." I bumped her with my hip. "But more sorry that you're marrying into that family."

"Don't remind me. I'm glad Simon's not like that."

I wrapped my arm around her shoulder. "Mom and Patricia aren't usually this bad either. It's how they handle stress. Some people drink, some people exercise, Mom and Patricia make themselves feel big by making other people feel small."

"God, it sounds so awful when you say it out loud like that."

I shrugged. "The best we can do is not follow in their footsteps."

She breathed in deeply and let it out before turning and grabbing both my arms. "Then don't assume I'm being like them when I ask you this. You're sure everything is good for Friday and the wedding, right?"

I kept my patience. Christiana was under a lot of stress. If it were any other bride freaking out a few days before her wedding, wanting reassurance I had everything under control, I wouldn't falter. I needed to treat Christiana with the same courtesy.

I tucked a strand of her hair back over her shoulders. Her hair was as curly as mine if she left it natural, but no one would ever know that. She kept it straight or, at best, in a gentle wave.

I smiled at her. "The groom's cake at the gala on Friday has so much chocolate, people might go into a coma. And your wedding cakes will be so beautiful, you might get mad that people are looking at them instead of you."

She let out a laugh that was more like a blubber. "We wouldn't want that."

I pulled her in for a hug. "I promise your wedding cakes will be absolutely perfect. You focus on getting through the ceremony, and don't worry about that at all."

"Okay. I wish Patricia would stop making offhanded suggestions that there might be problems."

I gritted my teeth. "What did she say?"

"Nothing to me directly, I overheard her. She found out Mother canceled having the hotel on standby as a backup since everything you've provided so far has been stellar. Patricia thought that was a bad idea, and the people she was talking with agreed."

People she was talking with. I rolled my eyes. "Let me guess. Mina."

Christiana bit her lip. "She was one of them. Suggested that if you were planning to make waves, you wouldn't do it at the beginning of the week. You'd wait until the end."

I cupped her face with my hands. "You know I would never do that. Although, if I could figure how to make sure only Mina and Patricia would eat it, I'd been tempted to put a ton of laxatives in their cake."

She smiled and leaned her forehead against mine. "I'm crazy. I'm sorry."

"Don't be sorry. But don't let them drive you insane. I can personally promise everything will be fine." There was no way I wasn't going to keep that promise.

"Thank you."

"Now, go find your fiancé and dance with him."

"Only if you promise to find yours and do the same."

I grimaced. "You heard?"

"You know how rumors fly. Once I get back from my honeymoon, I'm going to expect a full report."

By then, Landon would be out of my life. That made me sadder than it should. At that point, maybe I'd tell Christiana the whole truth. It could be something that bonded us—keeping the secret from Mother. "Full story once you get back. It's a deal."

She hugged me and rushed over to Simon, who immediately whisked her out onto the dance floor. I didn't see Landon anywhere around, so I went to check on the desserts. Everything looked fine; the serving staff was doing a good job. My babies were looking sexy and delicious as they should.

Speaking of sexy and delicious…

"Lose your fiancé?"

I didn't even justify Mina's comment with a response.

"I saw him leave right after you started talking to your sister. If I'm not mistaken, he was following a cute little blonde who started chatting with him. Just wanted to let you know he's not around, so you're not standing over here looking all pathetic."

I crossed my arms. "I know he left."

I didn't know he'd left. But it looked as if Mina was right. Landon was nowhere to be seen.

Why did that hurt? He didn't have to check in with me. He'd gone above and beyond with everything he'd done. Hell, even if he was flirting—or more—with some other woman, that shouldn't bother me.

Not. Real.

But somehow, it did hurt.

"Oh, and look, there's your mother and Aunt Patricia talking with another hotel employee."

"So?" I hoped they weren't about to make her cry.

"Oh, wait," Mina said with a smile. "I see who that is now. It's the pastry director for the resort. I wonder what they could possibly be talking about?"

As if Mina had choreographed the whole thing, at that very moment, my mother looked over at me, guilt blanketing her features. She turned and ushered the pastry director and Patricia in the opposite direction.

Mina bunched up her nose. "Yeah, that definitely has nothing to do with you."

I didn't know how to respond. It obviously did have something to do with me.

"Anyway, I'll leave you alone." She shot me a smile and turned. "That's your default setting when we strip it all down to the truth, isn't it? You being alone?"

Suddenly the lights and breeze I'd found so charming felt empty. Mina might be a bitch, but that didn't mean she was wrong.

I was alone.

Chapter 14

Landon

I left Bethany at the luau without a word. I felt like shit, but when I saw Frey and Martinez leave, I couldn't miss the chance.

They were using the wedding as an excuse for a face-to-face meeting. I might not be able to get the transmitter on them tonight, but I could at least try to gather as much intel as possible.

They'd headed toward the beach like they were going on a damned lovers' stroll, so I went in that direction too.

I never thought I'd use any of the tracking measures I'd learned in the SEALs while on a vacation island wearing a tropical-themed shirt and loafers. I'd much rather be attempting this in my camo and boots.

And with weapons and backup.

Good news was, Frey and Martinez and their teams weren't concerned about not leaving tracks. They didn't expect anyone to be following them. Why would anybody be when there was a great party going on?

And they had their guards, who wouldn't hesitate to put a bullet in my brain if they found me and realized I was undercover.

They'd walked far enough away from the festivities, so we were at the cliff beaches rather than the sandy ones. At some point, they'd cut uphill, still easy enough to follow since at least one of them was smoking. Once I pinpointed exactly where they were, I circled around so I was coming at them from the cliff side. Hopefully the guards would be paying more attention to the main path.

I had to lie flat just off the secondary path near the edge of the cliff to be able to hear Frey and Martinez at all. But the waves hitting against the rocks meant I was only able to capture every few words. I couldn't get any closer without them discovering me.

"…handoff is still a go for next week."

That was Frey. Whatever else he said was lost by the waves.

I pulled out my phone and opened the recording app. It was more sensitive than my hearing and would allow me to send the entire recorded conversation to Tristan. He could get it to Callum.

I kept the phone pointed at them from my awkward angle. The more I caught of the conversation, the more concerning it became. They were talking about deliveries and packages. I thought they were discussing drugs at first. Then maybe weapons.

Finally, I realized the *shipments* they were referring to were people.

Zodiac Tactical had already had a very up close and personal run-in with scumbags attempting human trafficking. Hell, that bullet wound in my chest was an indirect result of that.

Frey was on Callum's radar because of his connection with Mosaic, the above-mentioned scumbags. I shouldn't be surprised Frey and Martinez would be conducting similar sick business.

But it did make getting the nano transmitters placed even more critical. People's lives were at stake. If I wasn't able to—

A hand on my shoulder blew adrenaline through my body. "What are you—"

I reacted instinctively, not waiting for the whispered sentence to be completed. Reaching behind me, I yanked on the arm and twisted the person so that they'd be on the ground and I'd have the upper hand. If it was one of the guards, I had to get their weapon away from them and fast.

But as soon as I yanked the intruder down, I realized the body against me was soft, small.

Bethany.

Shit. *Shit.*

My brain raced. How not to blow my cover with her waged war with how not to get us both killed. Had we been heard?

Bethany's green eyes were huge in the soft moonlight. I placed a finger over her lips. I looked up and through the bushes, praying the guards hadn't noticed.

"Quiet," I mouthed. Her brows furrowed, but she nodded. I put my phone in my pocket and grabbed her hand, pulling her back along the cliff path. If I could get her out of this, I'd make up some story about a wild animal I hadn't wanted to interrupt.

We only made it a few yards before I realized they'd heard us. Frey and Martinez weren't talking anymore, and the guards were now all on high alert, barking quietly at each other. It wouldn't take long before they found us.

I needed a plan, right fucking now.

I stopped walking and yanked Bethany to me, wrapping one arm around her hips, the other cupping her nape. My mouth covered hers.

She stiffened. "Landon?"

I didn't let up. My lips nipped at hers and she opened them with a gasp, and I slipped my tongue inside, coaxing her, demanding a response.

She gave it. I felt the second she stopped fighting her confusion and gave herself over to the kiss.

God, she was so damned soft, so warm and giving. There was nothing I wanted more than for this to be real, for us to be alone where I could continue kissing her until neither of us could breathe.

Mission.

I forced the thought into my lust-hazed brain. This wasn't about a kiss; this was about preserving my cover— and getting us both out of here alive.

I didn't have long. Sweet Bethany didn't resist as I lowered us both to the ground, never moving my lips from hers. Her arms slipped around my neck, our tongues continuing to duel, as I laid her underneath me.

I slid my hand down the base of her thigh, coaxing it to wrap around my hips. The groan that escaped me as that lined up our bodies perfectly was only half fake. If it weren't for the clothes between us, I'd be sliding inside that delectable body.

Mission.

I moved my lips down to her neck, drawing a soft gasp from her. My hand covered her breast. Those guards were going to be on us any second. They had to believe that she and I were so wrapped up in each other that we'd decided to have a quickie right here in the sand.

Convincing my body that wasn't what was about to happen was pretty damned difficult. This might be a ploy, but I was rock hard against Bethany's soft curves.

And she was pressing up against me. Grinding. Low moans escaping her throat. Holy hell.

"What are you doing here?"

I heard Adams's voice and felt the muzzle of a gun pressed against the back of my neck. I immediately froze. A soft gasp left Bethany's lips.

I prayed my acting chops were enough to get us out of this.

"What the fuck, man? Do you have a gun to my head?" I wanted to roll off Bethany, but I didn't want that gun getting any closer to her. "Is a quickie under the stars a capital offense on this island?"

"Landon?" Adams took a step back, pulling his weapon with him. "You should not be out here. Neither of you."

I glanced at Bethany's face as I slid off her and stood, keeping myself between Adams and her. She looked well-kissed, disheveled, confused, scared. She was selling our cover story whether she wanted to or not. Thankfully, she kept quiet.

"Dude, we wanted a little alone time. I was showing her the cliffs."

Fanshawe came rushing into the clearing. "Everything okay? Mr. Frey wants a repor—" He saw me. "What are you doing here?"

Adams put his weapon away, but Fanshawe had his out. He was leering at Bethany where she still sat on the ground. I wanted to break the guy's nose.

"It's fine," Adams said.

"Oh, I see. Landon was getting himself some."

Fanshawe's grin was greasy. "Daddy's princess likes the wildlife, huh?"

"Shut the fuck up, Fanshawe." Adams pushed at the other man, able to see what Fanshawe couldn't.

That I was about to throw his ass over the side of the cliff.

"This isn't a good place to be, Landon," Adams continued. "You need to stay closer to the resort."

"Roger that. I didn't realize these paths were…off-limits. We'll head back to our room."

Adams and Fanshawe turned and walked away, Fanshawe humming obnoxious porn music. What an asshole.

We were safe, but I had no doubt Frey and Martinez were gone for the night and would now be much more careful. They wouldn't have any more open meetings like this. Hopefully Callum would be able to make something of what I'd recorded.

I turned to Bethany. She was pale, eyes big from where she still sat on the ground. "Did those guys have guns?"

"Yes, they were security team members." Security for criminals, but that was immaterial for this conversation.

"Why were you even out here?"

I scrubbed my hand down my face. "The party got a little much for me, so I decided to go for a walk. I accidentally stumbled onto these guys and was about to go back the way I'd come when you tapped me on my shoulder."

Her face said she couldn't decide whether to believe me. She looked out toward the cliff edge then back at me. "Did you make out with me because you knew the guards were coming?"

"Bethany—"

"The truth, if you don't mind."

I crouched down beside her so we were eye to eye.

"Earlier tonight when I was at the bar, I saw Vincent Frey had a gun under his blazer. I know you've mentioned your father has had some contact with criminals in the past. I wasn't sure if Frey was one of those criminals. If he was, I didn't want him to think we were spying on him or something."

"So, you did what you had to do."

"Yes, exactly. I wanted to keep you safe."

Her face fell carefully blank. "Well, I'm safe now. So, no need to pretend anymore."

Her tone was as blank as her features. That wasn't good.

"Bethany, look—"

She moved to stand up. I offered her my hand, but she didn't take it.

"Thanks for the rescue. Again. Goodnight, Landon."

Shit. That phrase could've come straight from her mother's mouth it was so dismissive and cold.

I wanted to chase after her, wanted to explain that it had been a cover, but that hadn't been *all* it was.

And then prove it to her in a way that ended with both of us naked and me buried deep inside her.

So I forced myself to stay where I was as she walked away. Because that couldn't happen.

I followed her from a distance back to the resort to make sure she got back to the room safely. *Our* room. For once, I could be thankful for my insomnia. Staying out of the room wouldn't be that difficult.

Once she was inside, I turned back toward the ocean. I needed to get this recording sent to Tristan, then find out what I could about Martinez, including his room number.

Mostly, I needed to figure out a real plan to get these transmitters planted.

I was running out of time in more ways than one.

Chapter 15

Bethany

Landon didn't even try to stop me from walking away. Didn't offer to get me back to the room safely. Didn't attempt to convince me that lying down on top of me and kissing me senseless had any elements of real attraction to it.

I supposed I should be thankful he was so quick-thinking. I knew some of the people Dad associated with were criminals, but I didn't think he would invite them to the wedding. But I believed Landon when he said he saw Vincent Frey carrying a gun.

I don't think he or his men would've shot us over running into him while on a walk, so the whole make-out session was probably overkill.

Did Landon think I was an idiot for the way I had responded?

I thought I was an idiot for the way I had responded.

Worse, my body was still tingly and heated where his

had pressed up against mine when he'd hiked my leg over his hip. I could still feel the phantom touch of his hand on my breast and his lips on my neck.

I *wanted* him.

And once again, it was all just an act for him. Not. Real.

I wasn't sure when he was coming back to the room, and I definitely didn't want to discuss anything that had happened tonight, so I rushed into the shower. He still wasn't here when I got out. Still wasn't here when I got into the bed and turned off the light.

When I finally fell asleep and woke late the next morning after a pretty fitful sleep, it didn't look like he'd been here at all.

I hugged one of the pillows from my big bed and stared at the sofa. There was no folded-up blanket, no pillow. Evidently, Landon had preferred not sleeping at all to being in the same room as me.

I guess that meant our date at the pool was canceled too.

I clamped down on the disappointment trying to well up inside me. Landon had made that offer as part of his act. It all was part of an act he took ever so seriously for whatever reason. There was no need to be disappointed just because we were taking a break from the ruse.

I'd work on business stuff instead. I certainly had enough to do. A small business owner's work was never done, and I was behind on paperwork.

I called to order coffee and breakfast delivered, got dressed, and sat down on the couch to get to work. Concentrating wasn't as easy as it normally was—with my balcony door open, I could hear people laughing and splashing outside in the pool—but I wasn't going to let it derail me.

I'd had to re-add the figures in one column three times to figure out how much I owed one of our vendors when the knock came on the door. Good. Maybe coffee would set me straight.

It was the blessed nectar of the gods at my door. But Landon was holding it. Beside him was a cart with my breakfast plate.

I raised an eyebrow. "You working for the resort now?"

"I told the waiter maybe this could help get me out of the doghouse. And I tipped him twenty dollars." He handed the coffee mug to me.

I took a sip. It had cream but no sugar, just as I preferred it. Landon had been paying attention at some point when I drank coffee and had made note of how I liked it.

That was something, but not enough.

"You didn't sleep in here last night."

"No. I didn't sleep at all."

"Really? Why?"

He took a breath and blew it out. "I actually don't sleep a lot in general. Chronic insomnia since I was a kid."

"Oh." I stepped out of the way so he could come in. He wheeled in the cart. "I'm sorry."

He shrugged one shoulder. "It's been a fact of life for me for so long, I've learned to cope and work my way around it pretty well."

"So, what did you do last night?"

He took the top off the tray of food and gestured for me to sit, then wheeled the cart over in front of me. Eggs, bacon, toast. I grabbed a piece of bacon and nibbled on it as he sat in the armchair.

"I worked out. Sent some emails. Stared up at the moon and pondered...things."

I wanted to ask if what happened between us was one

of the things he pondered but was too chicken. "What causes your insomnia?"

"Navy shrink says a combination of childhood trauma, genetic makeup, and stubbornness. The last mostly because I refuse to take medication."

I placed my bacon back down on the plate. "Childhood trauma. Your dad?"

Landon shrugged. "He was a drunk and he was mean, and I learned from an early age to sleep lightly, or even better, not sleep at all, if I didn't want a fist catching me unawares."

"I'm sorry." The words seemed woefully inadequate.

"Don't be. It's actually helped me some in my adult life. They thought I was a superhero in the Navy—could function on less sleep than everyone else combined. I've learned to cope."

"Do you need to sleep now? I can clear out."

"Nope." Dimples. "I'm hoping I still have a lovely date for the pool."

I grabbed my bacon again. "Landon, there's no need. I get it—it's all an act. And while I'd appreciate it if you'd be willing to keep it up a few more days while we're in public and, of course"—I threw him a forced smile—"if we're about to get shot by bad guys, there's no need to waste your time with me."

Before I could blink, he'd moved from his chair to next to me on the couch. He'd moved that fast last night when I'd come up on him unawares. He was so damned fast when he wanted to be.

"Time spent with you is not a waste." His face was close to mine. I could smell his own coffee on his breath. I just wanted to get closer.

No. I needed to keep my distance. "You don't have to

pretend when it's only us. I shouldn't have gotten upset about what happened last night. I just felt stupid."

"Why?"

Because I'd been willing to have sex with him right then, and he'd merely been putting on a show? I shook my head. "It wasn't real. I get it. You were protecting us."

I leaned back from him and put the bacon back on the plate. The thought of eating now curled my stomach.

He ran a hand through his hair. "I was trying to protect us. And I won't lie, I did kiss you and pull you to the ground so they wouldn't get suspicious."

"I know." My voice was small. I couldn't even look at him. I thought about my moans last night, about grinding up against him.

"But that didn't mean I was unaffected, Wildflower. Don't think that you were the only one aware of the heat between us."

Now I looked at him. "Really?"

He shook his head with a wry grin. "Oh, believe me, yes."

He seemed authentic.

"I don't want to let things get out of hand," he continued. "Or take advantage of an unorthodox situation and make it more complicated. But don't think I wasn't affected by what happened between us last night."

If I told him I wanted him to take advantage of me, or vice versa, would he let me talk him into it? I could hear Michele screaming internally at me to find out, but I was too much of a coward. So I merely nodded.

"But I would very much like to keep our pool date today if you'd agree. You deserve a chance to relax."

He looked like he wanted to say more, and I knew there was a lot more I wanted to say, but both of us stared.

Finally, I nodded. "Pool date sounds great."

"Good. Don't bring your computer. This is an afternoon off."

I couldn't meet his eyes. "I wouldn't do that."

"Tablet either."

Damn it. I definitely would've slipped my tablet into my bag. "Fine."

He grinned and winked at me, and parts of my body flushed all over. "Let's have some fun, Wildflower."

Chapter 16

Bethany

I'd thrown my bathing suit into my suitcase at the last minute. I hadn't expected to be spending much time lounging by the pool or frolicking in the ocean on this trip.

Definitely hadn't planned on having someone who looked like Landon by my side as I did those things.

I put on my bathing suit and looked at myself critically. Definitely wasn't going to be confused with a size two, but overall, I wasn't upset with how I looked. My one-piece was modest but cut out in places that gave it a sexy vibe rather than matronly. At least, I hoped.

I threw on a sheer cover-up and grabbed my beach bag, pre-packed with a book, sunglasses, and sunscreen.

We made it down to the pool early when there weren't many people there, so we snagged two loungers close together under an umbrella. Even though I had no reason to feel any embarrassment about what my body looked like, I felt a twinge of shyness as I pulled off my cover-up and my body was more exposed than it had been.

Hell, the cover-up was sheer to begin with. It wasn't like I'd stripped from a turtleneck and jeans into the buff.

But Landon's eyes went to my body and lingered there a few seconds longer than they had to. Definitely appreciative. I sat quickly and put on my sunglasses to hide my blush.

Then he took off his shirt.

Holy bathing suit gods. His trunks were plain navy blue. Nothing notable. But the sculpted abs he revealed under his shirt were notable and then some.

"Come on, Wildflower." Landon grinned at me. "Let's swim."

He jumped up and ran for the water at full blast. I laughed as he dove in because he totally messed up his dive, belly-flopping with a resounding smack. His glorious abs were going to be super-bright red.

Maybe that would give me an excuse for staring.

I shook my head as I walked at a much more reasonable pace toward the pool.

He swam back to the edge. "Was that funny?"

I crouched down next to him. "Sure was. I wouldn't keep admitting to being former Navy with that dive, *sailor*."

That speed of his again. He reached up and grabbed my upper arms, pushing himself off the pool wall as he yanked. With a screech, I fell face first into the water.

"Still funny?" he asked.

I shrieked and lunged for him. I hadn't planned on getting so far in that I ruined my hair and makeup, but now I was soaked from stem to stern. I laughed. Nothing I could do about it now, except take him down in revenge.

Of course, Mr. Hotbod got away from me easily. We

played a game of cat and mouse for a while as the pool and surrounding chairs filled up with guests.

I came up for air and whirled, looking for Landon. I was ready to splash him as soon as he materialized. Even though the pool was crystal clear, he was so sneaky that he'd startled me several times.

And he managed it one more time as I spotted my mother and Christiana walking toward the pool, both of them looking like swimsuit models on a photo shoot.

Landon burst from the water and tackled me. I barely had time to gulp in a breath to hold before going under.

I did, however, have time to see my mother roll her eyes. Of course. She'd look down on such frivolous behavior. But I didn't care. This was the most fun I'd had in as long as I could remember.

Sinking to the bottom of the pool, I peeked my eyes open and ignored the burn of the chlorine, trying to find Landon.

Bubbles erupted from my mouth when I realized he was underwater too, on the bottom of the pool with me, staring right at me. I squealed and pushed off the bottom to get away from him.

When my head broke the surface of the water and I sucked in a deep breath, I swam for all I was worth, but still, when I grabbed the side of the pool and looked around, he was right beside me.

"You can't beat me," he said smugly. "I'm a seal."

I didn't care what sort of water animal he was. I gave no warning as I pushed off the side of the pool and sprinted my way across the water to the other side. I heard his splashes, but I wiggled my body, kicked my feet, and swung my arms harder than I had before in an attempt to beat him. Even though we were both laughing so hard every time we came up for air I was surprised we didn't drown.

This was what I wanted. To have fun with a man who legitimately seemed to be having fun with me right back.

Water stung my eyes, so I glanced quickly at how much farther I had to go and closed my eyes for the last push. But I'd misjudged the distance or something because instead of slapping my hand on the side of the pool, I slapped it onto the hard muscles of a chest. I gasped and sucked in water.

Sputtering, I came up for air. Landon's strong arms circled me and held me upright as I wiped droplets from my eyes and caught my breath. My feet floated off the bottom of the pool as my legs pressed against his.

Oh my.

The laughter in my chest fizzled out as I raised my eyes to meet his. His gaze was glued to my lips. Then I couldn't help but stare at his.

The sun beat down on our heads as our lips touched. After the way we'd teased each other in the pool, back and forth, racing, tickling, dunking, my body was overly ready to rub against his as his mouth pressed against mine.

I didn't want the moment to end. I wanted to push it further, grind against him or let my legs lift in the water and wrap around his waist. To feel all that muscle and hardness against me again like last night.

Somebody cleared their throat, bringing me back to reality. We were in a public pool. I opened my eyes, easing back from Landon.

He looked just as dazed as I felt.

And that made me smile.

When he saw it, he wrapped his arm back around my waist and pulled me closer. Almost as if he couldn't help himself.

One of my arms resumed its place around his neck, and I slid my other hand up his chest. I looked down as my fingers traced over a scar on his pec I hadn't noticed before. Puffy, round.

"What's that from? Somebody shoot you?" I asked.

It was the wrong thing to say. I watched as the Landon I'd been playing with for the past half hour disappeared and someone else took his place.

Someone with razor focus and almost palpable determination. His features hadn't turned exactly *hard*, but they were crisp in a way they hadn't been a few seconds ago.

Charming, laughing Landon was sexy, but this Landon... He was so much more. He was compelling, dangerous even.

But then dangerous Landon disappeared, and charming Landon was back. He placed his hand over mine. "Yeah, bullet wound. The list of people who want to shoot me is impressively long. Come on, I'll race you to the other side again."

He shot off then spun back around and splashed me, trying to get me to chase him.

Trying to avoid talking about that scar.

I'd been joking when I'd suggested it was from a gun, but now, I honestly wasn't sure.

We raced to the other end again, and I only won by cheating, pulling him back by the leg and using the momentum to propel myself forward. We were both laughing and out of breath as we leaned up against the wall.

"Ready to get out for a while?" he asked.

My stomach growled loud enough to be a reply, and we both burst out laughing. "How about lunch?" I asked.

"Sure," he said. "I'm going to use the restroom first."

"I'll order us some burgers." I floated on my back,

kicking my feet to propel toward the pool stairs as he walked beside me.

"Sounds great." He shoved my head underwater with a grin, and by the time I slung my hair out of the way and wiped my eyes, he was out of the pool and headed toward the outdoor restrooms near the entrance to the gardens.

I grabbed one of the fluffy white towels from a stack and dried my face and arms, so I didn't drip all over the counter at the pool bar.

"What can I get you?" The bartender smiled and cocked her head at me, then typed onto a tablet screen as I rattled off Landon's order, then my own. I spread the towel over the seat of the barstool to keep it from scalding my legs and perched on it. I knew I had a stupid grin on my face, but I couldn't seem to stop.

My grin faded when I sensed someone standing close behind me. Turning to my left, I was blinded by the sun, so I didn't recognize the man at first. When I shaded my eyes and squinted, I realized it was one of the guards from last night. The one who'd been so obnoxious when he found us.

"You looked like you wanted some company," he said. His gaze was glued to my breasts, and I wished I'd wrapped the towel around myself instead of using it on the stool.

The bartender set my iced tea on the counter. I hoped she'd stay, but she walked back to the other side of the bar to take someone's order.

"No, I don't want company. I'm waiting for my fiancé."

His smile was more of a leer than anything else. "Sorry we interrupted you last night. Hope you don't hold that against me."

His pinkie touched my arm on the bar, and I yanked it away. I didn't want to make a scene, especially since this jerk seemed like the type to announce to everyone that he'd stumbled across Landon and me making out.

"I don't hold it against you." Snatching up my tea, I slipped off the stool and walked in the opposite direction, around the side of the bar.

As soon as I got there, I realized I'd made a mistake. The bartender had gone to deliver some food, and of course, slimeball guy followed me. We were secluded.

"Smart. Now, we'll have some privacy. I like it." He stepped closer.

I held up my hand. "No," I said in a firm, strong voice. "I do not want privacy with you. Please leave. Now."

His face changed from suggestive to angry in an instant. "You seemed okay with being pretty public in your affections last night on the beach. Almost like you wanted us to see you."

I gritted my teeth. "I'm the sister of the bride, and if you don't walk away this instant, I'll have you removed from the island."

My words fell on deaf ears as the man closed in on me further. "No need to be like that. I promise I can show you an even better time than your fiancé. You won't have to put on a show if you've got a real man to keep you happy."

I could not believe this was even happening. If I screamed, I could get rid of him, but I knew that would draw everyone's attention at the pool. Patricia and Mina would have a field day.

"Back off, asshole."

He sneered at me. "I don't think so. I think if you really wanted me to back off, you would've let somebody know by now. It's okay to want a man to take it from you. I know how to play that game."

I wasn't going to try to hit him; he was a trained security guard. Creating a scene was going to be my only option. I opened my mouth to yell for help, knowing it was going to cause as many problems as it solved. But I wasn't going to stay here and be molested by this guy.

Landon's voice stopped me. "How about if you and I play a game instead, Fanshawe?"

I spun to look at him, so relieved. But I froze as I saw his face. This wasn't friendly, grinning Landon. This was the man I'd caught a glimpse of a few minutes ago in the pool.

Dangerous Landon was back.

Chapter 17

Landon

I knew something was wrong by the look on Bethany's face as I headed back toward the pool area. She looked scared and pissed at the same time, off to the side of the bar, but I couldn't tell who she was looking at.

I suspected Mina, but when I rounded the bar, it was fucking Fanshawe. I already owed him from his obnoxious shit last night.

As I took in the scene, he stepped forward again, his body language menacing. He was so big next to Bethany.

Neither of them noticed me heading their way. As he got closer, Bethany's eyes darted around, searching for a way to bolt.

I moved faster, catching his words to her. "…it's okay to want a man to take it from you. I know how to play that game."

I could feel fury bubbling up inside me like a goddamn

fountain. I'd thought he'd been propositioning her, which was bad enough. But this was outright threatening.

"How about if you and I play a game instead, Fanshawe?" I closed the rest of the distance as Bethany spun toward me, relief and some sort of surprise evident in those green eyes.

I stepped past him and put my arm around Bethany. She trembled once, her skin cool from the pool water drying on it. I knew she wasn't cold, though. He'd gotten to her. I wanted to rip his face off.

I forced myself to pull back the rage. Fanshawe was still my best shot at getting to Frey. Putting him in a coma wasn't going to help.

He sneered at me. "I was just trying to be friendly with your fiancée here, and she's ordered me to leave and says she's going to have me fired."

Even with me standing in front of him, obviously willing to protect Bethany, he still glared at her and clenched his fists.

This guy was definitely not suited for security work.

"I'm sure it was a misunderstanding," I said. As much as I wanted to break his hands, I didn't touch him, just forced a smile onto my face. And I needed Bethany not to have Fanshawe fired. "Let's all calm down." I turned and squeezed Bethany's shoulder. "I'm sure if we avoid each other the rest of the week, there's no reason for anyone to be fired."

I hated saying the words. He deserved to be fired. Moreover, he deserved to have the shit kicked out of him. But that wasn't a viable option at the moment.

"Yeah, right," Fanshawe drawled. "This bitch is going to go running to Mommy and Daddy the minute my back is turned."

I took my arm off Bethany's shoulders and held up my hands. "Hey, man. I'm trying to say let's let bygones be bygones, whatever happened. There's no need for you to call her names."

Fanshawe laughed in my face. "You're so pussy-whipped you can't see what a slut you're marrying."

And he'd just crossed a line I wasn't going to back down from, mission or not.

"Watch your fucking mouth." My voice dropped in volume, but I had no doubt he heard me.

"Or what?" He stepped forward and squared off his shoulders.

Bethany plucked at my arm. "Come on, Landon. Let's go. This asshole isn't worth it."

She was right. We should walk away and have her father make sure Fanshawe was removed from the island.

"Who are you calling asshole?" Fanshawe lunged at Bethany in that threatening, shoulders-first way that cowards did when they wanted to appear menacing. He wasn't actually trying to grab her. It was nothing more than a dick move to get her to flinch. And it worked.

She flinched.

I'd had enough.

I stepped in front of Bethany so she couldn't see clearly what I was doing. With three jabs of my hand, Fanshawe was laid over the bar, unconscious.

He probably had me on brute strength, but when it came to speed and actual knowledge of how to incapacitate someone, I'd beat someone like him every time. I could've just as easily killed him, so he should consider himself lucky.

"Landon," Bethany gasped. She hadn't seen exactly what I'd done, but she knew I'd done something. "Is–is he dead?"

"No." Sadly.

She had one hand over her mouth and the other on my arm again. "You barely moved. How did you know how to do that?"

She didn't look scared, just shocked. I wasn't sure how I was going to explain this to her. Giving her as much of the truth as possible seemed like the best option. "You know how I was in the Navy?"

"Yeah. They teach you that sort of stuff?"

"They do if you're a SEAL."

She stared at me. "You said seal in the pool, but I thought you meant the animal."

Fanshawe began to stir. I'd known he wouldn't be down long. The blows hadn't been meant to render him completely unconscious, just stop him in his tracks and give him a hell of a headache.

"Adams, get Fanshawe out of here." I grimaced at Vincent Frey's voice behind us.

"With pleasure." Adams walked forward and grabbed Fanshawe by the back of the collar, straightening him as he blinked and moaned.

Frey sighed. "I apologize for my employee's lack of respect, Miss Thornton. It won't happen again."

Bethany gave him a little nod.

I needed to smooth things over if I had any chance of getting near Frey again. "Mr. Frey, I'm sorry I hit your man. He—"

Frey held out his hand. "Fanshawe has been a problem more than once. I don't hold you responsible for doing what you had to do. I'm glad you were here to take care of it."

Fanshawe was fully awake now and livid at being pushed around by Adams. "That bitch came on to me, then when her boyfriend showed up, she changed her tune, tried to act like she hadn't been trying to get some good dick."

That fucker truly didn't know when to keep his mouth shut.

"Fanshawe," Frey said sharply. "I left my phone in my room. Go get it. I'll use it to set up your removal from the island."

Fanshawe—*a total fucking dumbass*—opened his mouth to argue with Frey, completely oblivious that no one was believing his lies and that anything he said would just get him in more trouble.

"Now!" Frey's tone brooked no argument.

With one last nasty look at Bethany, Fanshawe whirled and stalked toward the hotel.

Frey and Adams turned and went back to their cabana by the pool.

Shit. This was the best chance I'd had all week to get my hands on Frey's phone.

But it meant leaving Bethany alone.

I took her arm. "Come on, let's get you back to our loungers until the food comes."

She was a little unsteady as we walked. I was sure adrenaline was playing havoc with her system.

"That was crazy," she whispered.

"It sure was." I helped her into one of the loungers. I grabbed the towel I'd wrapped around my stuff…including the transmitters in my wallet. "Whole thing gave me a bit of a headache. Do you mind if I run up to the room and grab some ibuprofen?"

She didn't want me to go. She didn't say it outright, but I could tell. And rightfully so. After what had just happened to her, what she needed most was for someone to sit with her, let her system settle.

I had to harden myself not to be the person who gave her what she needed. I was tempted to let this opportunity pass and hope for another one. But I was out of time.

"Yeah," she said, voice shaky. "I might need some too."

I shot her a smile, forcing myself not to drown in those green eyes taking up half her pale face. "Be right back."

I walked at regular speed until I was out of sight. As soon as I hit the cool interior of the hotel, I sprinted toward the stairs.

I took them two at a time up to Frey's floor. When the door opened, Fanshawe stood in front of Frey's room with a cell phone in his hand.

We both stared at each other.

Shit. There was only one way for me to play this.

"You need to stay away from her, asshole," I snarled and exited the stairs, advancing on him. He didn't budge. He crossed his arms over his chest and glared at me.

I shoved him. He took the bait and swung at me.

I ducked his fist with ease, but while doing so, I threw my arm out and hit the one holding Frey's phone. It went flying down the hall, landing several feet away. Good.

I slammed my fist into his gut, doubling him over, before cracking him on the side of the head with my elbow.

As he reeled from my blow, I pulled the transmitter out of my pocket. I shoved him back toward the phone on the carpet. He tripped and hit the floor.

He rolled to the side, away from the phone and onto his knees, trying to get up. Before he could see my movements, I pulled the transmitter off the clear backing and, in one swoop, stuck it on the back of the black case. It was tiny, not much bigger than a speck of dust.

It was done.

I got up and backed away from the older man.

"Enough, Fanshawe. Leave Bethany alone, and I'll have no problem with you." I needed him to get that phone back to Frey.

I turned and walked toward the elevator. The muted sound of Fanshawe's footfalls on the thick carpet alerted me to the fact that he was rushing me from behind. I didn't move until the last second, then shifted my weight, stepping to the side and catching his arm as he lunged for me.

With one fast move, I yanked him over my shoulder. He flew through the air and landed with a thud in front of the elevator, just as it opened.

Adams was there, staring at Fanshawe on the floor, in shock. "What the fuck is going on?"

I held up my hands. "I was on my way up for ibuprofen for Bethany when the elevator stopped here. He attacked."

"Bullshit," Fanshawe croaked. "He came to find me."

Adams looked back at me to see if I would refute. All I did was raise my eyebrows and shake my head. Sometimes less was more.

Adams bought it. He turned back to Fanshawe. "Yeah, I don't think so. Mr. Frey sent me up here to find you. Go pack your shit. You'll be on the next flight out."

Adams grabbed the phone and pocketed it without noticing anything amiss.

Couldn't be any more perfect than that.

"Sorry for the drama, man," Adams said to me as he once again grabbed Fanshawe by the collar and hoisted him up. Fanshawe was still whining about his innocence as Adams led him down the hall.

"No worries." I turned and got in the elevator, but I took it up rather than back down to the pool. I needed to get in touch with Tristan right now to make sure the transmitter worked.

I took the elevator all the way up to the rooftop balcony then walked over to a corner away from the few people who were out there.

Original cake is in the oven. Need confirmation that the recipe was good.

Tristan's reply came in seconds. ***Hold.***

I knew he needed to test the transmitter to make sure it was working correctly. And I knew sometimes that wasn't a quick process. But every minute that passed was another minute Bethany was down at that pool, wondering what the hell I was doing.

Cursing down at my phone wasn't going to help, but that was what I did anyway. It was another ten minutes before Tristan finally replied.

Cake looks like it's going to taste wonderful.

The transmitter was working. I bolted toward the elevator without responding, trying to think of what I'd say to Bethany. Should I go get ibuprofen? She had some in the bathroom. But that would take more time.

I would tell her Fanshawe jumped me. That would match what Adams thought had happened and explain my taking so long and not having the painkillers.

She would buy that. My step was lighter as I came out of the elevator. One transmitter down, one to go. Getting close to Martinez would be even more difficult, but at least he was all I needed to focus on now.

And Bethany. I wanted to make sure she was all right after her scare with Fanshawe. At least I could assure her she wouldn't have to worry about him anymore.

I wanted to spend time with her, talk her into swimming some more with me in the pool. I liked having her lush curves pressed up against me in the water. I liked spending time with her on multiple different levels.

I wanted to make her smile. Wanted to confirm she was

okay. I'd get a couple of drinks in her and make sure she could laugh it all off by later this afternoon.

But when I got back to the lounger, it was empty. Bethany had taken her stuff and left.

Chapter 18

Bethany

When Landon didn't return by the time I'd eaten my meal, I got worried. I went to the room to find him, but he wasn't there.

But the ibuprofen was. So, wherever he'd gone, it hadn't been to the room to get the pain medication.

I looked at myself in the mirror. My eyes were still a little too big, my hands shaky. I might not have been in actual danger with that guy Fanshawe at the bar, but evidently, my mind and body hadn't gotten the message.

I'd needed a hug. Specifically, I'd needed Landon's strong arms around me, assuring me everything was okay.

But he'd disappeared, right when I'd needed him most.

Not tonight, honey. I've got a headache.

I'd admit, it stung. As the minutes passed and I tried to sort out my own shaky feelings and body parts, I kept expecting him to return to help me. But he hadn't.

Then I'd had to add crushing disappointment to the list

of emotions coursing through my body. I didn't want to be a diva, but what could possibly be more important to Landon than being with me when I was so shaken?

Because: *not real*. Once again, I didn't seem to be able to understand that simple fact. Although the playing in the pool had felt real. Or at least like we were friends and he cared what happened to me.

But the truth was, I didn't understand anything about my *fiancé*. Didn't understand how he jumped from hot to cold so quickly. Didn't understand how he authentically seemed to care, then disappeared without warning.

Didn't understand how a Navy SEAL was working as a part-time carpenter.

But SEAL explained a lot of things about him. How he sometimes moved so quickly. How he'd been able to take down Fanshawe without hardly moving.

A Navy SEAL. Hell, maybe that really was a bullet wound on his chest.

Despite our kisses, despite our talks, despite the fact that I was desperately attracted to him, I really didn't know Landon Black at all.

I needed to get out of my own head and get my wobbly body under control. The best way to do that was to dive into work and put Landon and what had nearly happened at the bar out of my mind. I changed clothes and headed toward the auxiliary kitchen.

The rehearsal dinner was tomorrow, so it was time to pull out those cake pieces anyway. They needed icing and then decorating, which could be done tomorrow, but starting today would give me the extra peace of mind of knowing I was ahead.

I was still pretty shaky even as I put myself back into the world my mind and body understood. This was a world

I controlled, rather than being thrown around by what others did. I needed to focus on it.

When I pulled the cakes out of the refrigerator, I discovered one had an enormous crack. Normally I'd be irritated, but today, I smiled. Even better that I was prepping a day early. I could've hidden the cake's flaw with icing, but this would give me a chance to rebake it. Maybe that was what I needed.

I put on some soft music on my phone and got busy. My body still didn't feel exactly right as I measured and combined ingredients, but this at least allowed me to push everything else from my mind.

The groom's cake was going to be an absolute masterpiece. Christiana wanted it at the rehearsal gala so it wouldn't detract from the beautiful wedding cake itself at the reception.

The gala tomorrow night was taking the place of a traditional rehearsal dinner. Christiana and Simon had decided not to have any attendants as part of their ceremony—they'd just be saying their vows to each other on the beach—so they didn't need an actual rehearsal. But, of course, they hadn't wanted to miss a chance to include one more party in this week's affairs.

Tomorrow's gala was fashioned after Carnevale in Venice. Everyone would be wearing elaborate ball gowns, tuxedos, and masks. The whole thing was a little over the top for my tastes, but I'd made sure the decadent chocolate groom's cake would fit right in.

The multitiered cake—each layer a different type of chocolate and surrounded by various fruits—would wind up and around a chocolate fountain. It was the most elaborate cake stand of the entire week.

I put the cake mixture in the oven and stared at the stove. Could I trust Landon to get it built?

Yes, he would get the job done. He might run hot and cold when it came to the two of us, but he had yet to be anything but thorough and professional when it came to the stands.

Thinking about Landon had tension pounding through my body again. It was almost as if I was dealing with two people when it came to him—one so considerate and attentive, one distracted and not interested in me.

I cleaned up my working area and got the other cakes out of the walk-in and the decorating materials out of the pantry closet.

No thinking about Landon allowed. No thinking about the kiss two nights ago or our fake make-out session last night. No thinking about what his hands had felt like on me in the pool.

No thinking about Fanshawe at the bar or that Landon had disappeared when I'd really needed him.

The door slammed open behind me, and I spun, heart racing. Two young waitstaff stood there giggling and holding hands.

"Oh crap," the girl muttered. "We're sorry."

The boy was backing out, pulling his girlfriend with him. "We forgot they'd assigned this room for use. Sorry."

They backed the rest of the way out, muttering apologies. Obviously, this was their normal make-out room. At any other time, I would've thought it was cute. But this one last shock to my system had hurled me over some sort of edge.

I couldn't stop my hands from shaking. Couldn't seem to get my pulse down to a normal level. Couldn't get the tears out of my eyes.

I tried to push through. My somewhat-shaky hands hadn't made much difference when I was remaking the cake, but now that I was trying to decorate it, they made a huge difference.

I managed to get the first layer of frosting on, but attempting to add the delicate piping of the royal icing was nearly impossible. More than once, I had to start over completely.

I worked for hours. At some points, my hands were steady; at others, the shakiness returned. I forced myself to keep going even when that happened.

I couldn't let today derail me completely. I couldn't let Landon or Fanshawe or anything steal the joy of what I loved to do.

"You're not supposed to be in here." Landon's sexy, deep voice pulled me from my work. "Today's supposed to be your day off."

I laid down the piping bag without turning to him. Just as well anyway. Once again, my shaky hands had messed up the intricate design I'd been attempting. I rubbed my eyes. Normally, elaborate icing was my forte.

And why was he even here?

"I decided to come in here and get some of tomorrow's work done. Not that it's doing much good."

He walked over to stand next to me, but I still didn't look at him. "Are you okay?"

I didn't want to admit how badly my body and psyche were responding to the past twenty-four hours. It wasn't like anything had actually happened.

"I'm fine." Now I looked at him. "Ever get your ibuprofen?"

He winced. "I ran into Fanshawe as I was on my way back to the room. He was still pretty pissed and tried to start something. Took a while to get it sorted out, and by the time I got back, you were gone."

The fact that he hadn't left me for no reason made me feel a little bit better. "He didn't hurt you, did he?"

"No, he didn't get a hit in. For a guy who works in security, he broadcasts his punches pretty loudly."

I tilted my head as I looked at him. "You being a former member of one of the country's most highly trained military forces helps out too."

He stiffened just slightly. "It does."

"Why didn't you tell me you were a former SEAL?"

"I wasn't trying to keep it from you. I just generally don't mention it unless it comes up. It can have various effects on people. Not always good."

"Like what?"

He shrugged and turned so he was leaning back against the counter, studying me. "Some people are normal. A 'thank you for your service' or generic questions about how long I was in, stuff like that. Some people are nosy, want to know if I ever almost died or killed someone else. I don't generally answer, unless it's someone I know well."

"Yeah, I can see why that would be off-putting for you." I cringed as I thought of me asking about that wound on his chest. I hadn't thought I was overstepping a boundary at the time.

"People are curious. I don't give them details, but I at least understand their reasoning behind asking. They're definitely not the worst."

"What's the worst?"

"There are women—and men—who are SEAL groupies. Bag 'n taggers, we call them. Willing to sleep with anyone who has ever been a SEAL."

"Oh." Mina's face immediately came to mind. She'd been all over Landon and hadn't even known he was a SEAL.

"And then there are the guys who take it as some sort of badge of honor to pick a fight with a SEAL. Hoping for bragging rights or some such shit."

"So, it's easier to keep mum about it from the beginning."

He nodded. "Yes. My service is a big part of who I am, but it's not the only identifying factor about me. Just like being a fabulous baker isn't the only identifying factor about you."

I took a large spatula and scraped icing off the layer of cake I'd been attempting to decorate. It was definitely subpar.

"Being a baker isn't even going to be a single identifying factor about me if I don't get my shit together," I muttered.

"Things not going right?"

I rubbed my eyes again. "I want tomorrow's cakes to be as good and as beautiful as what people have tasted the other nights." And I wanted my body to cooperate with me to get it done.

"If I go ahead and get the cake stand together, would that help?"

"Yeah, sure." Although it probably wouldn't.

We worked for a couple more hours, not necessarily talking much, but not in awkward silence either.

I couldn't worry too much about talking with him. I had to restart what I was doing more than once, but I tried not to let it show.

Though by the time I had to redo the decorations on the same cake for the third time, I was ready to fling it against the wall. I was even more frustrated at the tears leaking out of my eyes. This shouldn't be a problem. I was safe; I was fine. Creating the flowers and geometric shapes was nothing I hadn't done a hundred times before.

I needed to get out of here before Landon realized what a mess I was.

"Hey, what's going on?"

Too late.

He covered my shoulders with his hands, pulling me back against his chest. I couldn't help but lean against his strength.

"I can't seem to get this decorating right, even though I should be able to do it in my sleep. I've been like this all day."

"Is there something wrong with the ingredients or the gear you're using?"

"No, it's me. My hands are shaky. My head is spinning. I feel like I should go run five miles, and I don't even like running."

He tightened his fingers on my shoulders. "It's from what happened earlier with Fanshawe. Your body can't figure out what to do with the stress."

I spun so I was facing him, which I immediately realized was a mistake. We were way too close. I was caught between him and the prep counter.

"That's just it. Nothing happened. You stopped him before he did anything."

He tucked a curl back behind my ear. "Your body recognizes the danger it was in. Combine that with what happened last night—hell, this entire week of having to constantly watch your back? The shakes and spinning head are your body's way of dealing with compiling stress and threats of harm."

"So, I do need to go out and run five miles, that's what you're saying?" Lord, I'd have a heart attack. "Because if I can't get these cakes decorated by the gala tomorrow night, then I'll basically be proving everyone who said I would fail completely ri—"

He kissed me.

His tongue buried itself in my mouth as our bodies melded against each other like he couldn't bear for there to be space between us. I expected him to ease back after a few moments like he had in the room when we kissed.

But he didn't. He moved closer, one hand wrapping around my hip, the other grasping me at the back of the neck. His lips moved from mine, nipping down my jaw.

"I should've come back sooner today." His lips continued to work their way down to my throat, tilting my neck with his hand so he could have the access he wanted. "I could've helped you work through this earlier. Gotten it out of your system and mind before it spiraled. I shouldn't have left you to deal with it alone."

I could barely make sense of his words. I wanted to focus on the apology that meant so much to me, but I was drowning in what his lips were doing to my neck. I strained closer.

He slid his hand up from my hip to cup my breast, rolling my nipple in a motion just short of pain. I moaned and lifted on my tiptoes to get closer. Yes, this was what I wanted.

His lips moved away from me, but before I could let out a moan of disapproval, he dipped down and slipped his arm behind my knees and lifted me into his arms.

"Landon!" My voice came out as a shriek. I wrapped my arms around his neck. "I'm too heavy. Put me down."

He shot those dimples at me full force. "Nothing about you is too heavy. And what I want to do to you can't be done on this food prep table."

I was pretty sure my eyes were bugging out of my head. "Oh," I managed. "And what's that?"

"I want to taste you, Wildflower."

He walked with no problem—honest to God, as if I

weighed no more than a tray of cookies—into the storage closet and set me on the table in there. His lips met mine again as his hands reached down and made their way slowly up the outsides of my thighs, catching the edge of my skirt and hiking it up until it was bunched at my hips.

He was staring at my black panties, the heat in his eyes unmistakable. He'd seen me in less earlier today at the pool, but I still felt exposed.

He gripped the sides of my underwear, easing them over my hips and all the way down one leg until they were hanging off the ankle of my other. Then he started kissing his way back up my calves, moving back and forth between both legs.

When he got to my knees, he wrapped his hands around them and opened me wide.

Maybe I should've been embarrassed at the dimples in my thighs and the looseness in the muscle tone. But I couldn't be with him looking at me like I was the sexiest thing he'd ever seen.

His eyes met mine before sweeping back down my body. "So beautiful."

He kissed his way up my thighs and covered me with his mouth, his tongue moving in a swirling motion that had me sobbing his name in just seconds. He played me, alternating between jabs that teased and long, steady strokes that had me gasping for breath.

I gripped his hair with my fingers and kept him pulled to me, not that he seemed to want to be anywhere but there. I looked down my body at us. This strong, sexy man between my sprawled legs that he held open, my skimpy panties still hanging off my ankle. It was nothing less than decadent.

All I could do was moan. And feel. And dissolve into nothing.

His hazel eyes locked on mine as he thrust his tongue deeper, and new waves of fire rolled up my body. And he didn't stop. Not until ecstasy crashed over me in swells and I sobbed his name.

Only then did he slow, easing me down from the orgasm, my body boneless.

Those dimples were back as he helped slide my panties back up my legs and smoothed my skirt down so I was decent. I was still trying to pull my world back into one coherent whole.

"What about you?" I finally got out. "I—"

He shook his head. "No. This was about you and what you needed." He jumped up onto the table next to me and pulled me into his lap.

And with the beat of his heart against my ear, I realized the extra adrenaline was gone.

No more shaking.

Chapter 19

Landon

The key to undercover work was not to just stand and stare. That drew too much attention. Made people nervous.

Do something and stare instead.

So here I was playing cornhole—the nicest set I'd ever seen—by myself at the edge of the beach.

1. Toss a sparkly silver beanbag. 2. Look for Joaquin Martinez. 3. Repeat.

Actually, it was more like: 1. Toss a sparkly silver beanbag. 2. Look for Joaquin Martinez. 3. Think about how fucking fantastic Bethany had tasted yesterday and how amazing it was to hear her crying out my name. 4. Shift shorts so it wouldn't be so obvious I was becoming aroused. 5. Repeat.

I never should've left her yesterday at the pool. Not that I'd had an option. But she wasn't a warrior, didn't have the mind-set or coping skills to talk her body down from the ledge stress had driven her up.

Unfocused adrenaline was like quicksand. You never knew what step was going to cause you to sink.

There had been times after missions when I'd had to spar or work out for hours in order to get myself to the point where I wasn't buzzing.

I couldn't imagine trying to do something as intricate as decorating cakes with that extra energy coursing through me. She'd attempted it for hours.

No wonder she'd been about to completely fall apart by the time I got there. Even though she'd tried to hide it.

There had been other ways I could've helped her deal with the stress: a run, a swim, even some self-defense moves I could've taught her.

Who the hell was I kidding? As soon as I kissed her, I knew I wasn't leaving there without getting a full taste of her sweet body.

I drew the line at having sex while on an active mission where I was using her as my in. But evidently, draping her gorgeous thighs over my shoulders wasn't over the line.

Adjust shorts.

Toss beanbag.

Afterward, I'd known her crash was coming. I'd helped her get the kitchen into some semblance of clean, then gotten her back to the room.

She was shy, even a little embarrassed at what had happened. That brought out every protective instinct I had. While she'd brushed her teeth, I'd gotten her one of my shirts to sleep in since I didn't know what she normally wore. I'd helped her into it and tucked her in bed, getting in next to her.

She was asleep almost as soon as her head hit the

pillow. I'd planned to move to the couch as soon as she did, but hell if I didn't fall asleep for a few hours holding her.

I threw the beanbag way too hard.

This woman was all up under my skin.

After all the shit I'd given Ian and Sarge for falling so hard and fast for their women, this was karma coming around to bite me in the ass. Here I was, unable to get Bethany off my mind, even in the middle of a critical mission.

This job needed to conclude so that I could move on with my life. But now, I wanted to find some way that my post-mission life could include her.

Shit.

That was going to take some unraveling of a lot of half-truths, and I wasn't sure she was ever going to forgive me.

My phone buzzed in my pocket. Tristan.

"What's up, honey?"

"Had your fill of eating Bethany's sweets yet?"

My eyes bulged out of my head. How did Tristan know that? "*What?*"

"I'm going to laugh when you come home weighing twenty pounds more. I've been reading up on how good Slice of Heaven is."

Bethany's sweets. Not Bethany's *sweets*.

"Right. Yes. She's a very talented baker."

"You lucky bastard."

He didn't know the half of it. "Believe it."

"How's it going with Martinez?"

"Haven't seen him at all since that recording I sent you. He doesn't hang out at the pool like Frey."

"We know he's still on the island, so be ready."

I tossed the beanbag again. "I'm thinking his computer

might be easier. Lifting someone's phone involves getting up close and extremely personal."

"Be careful, brother. Bad guys don't like strangers getting personal."

"Given what's at stake, it's worth the risk. Find out anything more about the *shipments* Martinez and Frey were talking about?"

"Callum is on it. Definitely human trafficking."

Lives were at stake. "Then I'm definitely going to do whatever I need to to get the transmitter on Martinez."

I tossed one more beanbag, not coming anywhere near the hole I was aiming for. But it didn't matter. Martinez and his two guards walked across to the café where breakfast was being served.

There was no chance of getting to his phone but maybe his computer, which would still be in his room.

"Gotta run, T. Going to try a break-in."

"Roger that. Watch your six."

I disconnected the call and walked toward the lobby, being careful not to make any eye contact with Martinez or his guys.

I went to the lobby phone and dialed the front desk.

"Guest services," a polite voice said.

"Yes, Mr. Martinez asked me to have housekeeping come by while he was at breakfast, if you don't mind."

"Of course, sir. I'll send someone up right away."

After thanking her, I headed to the stairs and up to Martinez's floor, watching through the door until the elevator opened and the maid rolled a cart out. As soon as she opened the suite door, I walked out of the stairwell and headed straight for Martinez's door.

"Morning," I said. "Sorry to interrupt, I forgot something. I'll be out of your hair in just a moment." I swiped my keycard in the open door to prove the room was mine but positioned my body so the maid couldn't see the light flash red when it didn't work.

I shot her a smile. She nodded and smiled back. "It's okay, sir. I can start in the bathroom."

As soon as she disappeared through the bathroom door, I rushed over to the desk. No computer. Nothing on the couch or coffee table. I went into the bedroom, but I didn't see one lying around either. I glanced over at the safe. Shit. If he'd put it in there, I wouldn't be able to get to it.

Hell, maybe he hadn't brought one at all.

I grabbed Martinez's suitcase and rifled through it as neatly as I could. I hissed a small sigh of relief as I found the laptop nestled in the back.

A noise behind me had me glancing over my shoulder to find the small woman in the kitchen area, wiping down the counters. Her attention wasn't on me, but I was running out of time.

I peeled the plastic off the back of the transmitter and stuck it to the bottom of the laptop.

"Mr. Martinez?" the maid asked. She looked at a piece of paper in her hands. "Can I help you with anything?"

She was getting suspicious. I needed to get out of here right away. "No, I forgot my hat. Got it." I grabbed the Dodgers cap at the top of the suitcase and put it on my head. "But thank you."

I left without making any more eye contact, pulling the door closed as I went.

The elevator doors opened seconds after I called it. I pressed the button for the lobby and breathed a sigh of relief when the door shut without further incident. I slipped the hat off my head.

I'd done it. The transmitters were both placed. Martinez's computer might not be as ideal as his phone, but hopefully it would get Callum the intel he needed to stop whatever human trafficking plans Frey's and Martinez's organizations had. I needed to let Tristan know so he could get the info to Callum.

I was barely out of the elevator in the lobby when I spotted Martinez walking from the café toward the elevator. Shit. It had taken too long for housekeeping to get to the room, and evidently, Martinez hadn't been enjoying a full breakfast.

If he went up to the room, the housekeeper was going to know there was a problem. It wouldn't take much for her to remember it was me rummaging around in Martinez's room.

I had the hat. It had the slightest bit of suntan lotion smell. It had been used recently out in the sun, which gave me an idea.

It was a Hail Mary, and I prayed it would work.

I plastered a huge grin on my face and brought the hat up in front of my face so I was looking at it as I walked. I stayed in the middle of the foyer so Martinez couldn't help but notice me.

"This is it," I said to the hat as Martinez and his men got closer, heading toward the elevator. "This is a sign that you guys are going all the way this year. Don't let me down."

My eccentric behavior worked. Martinez stopped to talk to me. "You a Dodgers fan?"

"Every year. Win or lose. But this is going to be a winning year. This hat proves it." I blew a kiss toward the hat. "You a fan too?"

"Yeah, although sometimes I'm tempted to give up on them." Martinez shot me an indulgent smile. "I have a hat just like that, and unfortunately, it has never meant that they had a winning season."

"I was sitting out by the pool, thinking about how last year was a rebuilding season and they should reap the benefits this year, and then I found this hat." I grinned over at him. "It's a sign, I tell you."

I didn't follow baseball much. I hoped he didn't start talking about specific players.

But mostly, I hoped he stayed here and talked to me.

"You said you found that hat at the pool?"

When he didn't see the cap in his room, he was going to know right away that I had it. How I answered now would affect whether he believed he'd accidentally left it somewhere.

But if he hadn't been at the pool yesterday and I said I found it there, he'd know I was lying.

I shot Martinez a sheepish look. "Actually, some employee had it. He'd found it somewhere, and I told him it was mine. Do you think it's yours?"

I held it out to him, and he looked inside it before handing it back. "Probably."

I made my face fall. "Sorry, man. I wasn't trying to steal your stuff or anything. I figured it was about to go in a lost and found basket somewhere, and I thought I'd keep it. Put it with my shrine."

"Why don't you go ahead and do that?"

I shook my head and held the hat back out to him. "No, it's yours. Like I said, I wasn't trying to pull anything over on anyone."

Martinez was a few inches shorter than my 6'2". Midfifties, dressed in tailored trousers and a collared white shirt. Nothing about the man screamed *bad guy*. If you didn't know he was terrorist scum who dabbled in human trafficking, you'd probably label him as nonthreatening. Friendly, even.

He was more dangerous because he'd made sure not to make himself look that way.

He gave me a smile. "If you really think you being in possession of that hat will make the Dodgers win this season, then I will gladly donate it to the cause."

His men had been standing to the side, out of the conversation, but as he turned toward the elevator, they took a step forward also.

"Hey, can I buy you"—I looked around like I wasn't quite sure what his security team was—"and your friends a drink? We can talk team stuff. I'm bored with wedding shit."

All three men chuckled.

"While I can understand that boredom, I'm afraid I can't join you right now."

"Are you sure?" I asked. "It's the least I can do for giving me your hat and making sure we have a winning season."

"No, but thanks for the offer."

I couldn't push any more. The last thing I wanted was for Martinez to think I was stalling him. Hopefully, I'd bought enough time for the housekeeper to be finished with his room.

"No problem, another time. When the boys go all the way this year, you remember—we did it together! If you change your mind, I'll be at the bar."

I turned and walked the rest of the way through the foyer, hat in hand. I sat at the bar, choosing a seat where I could see the doors. I crossed my leg casually so I'd have easy reach of my ankle holster and waited to see if Martinez sent one of his men to get me.

I relaxed after twenty minutes. Housekeeping must have already been gone by the time Martinez got to his room. He wasn't coming after me.

I paid for my drink and stood. I shot off a text to Tristan about having gotten the transmitter on the computer.

My steps were lighter than they'd been all week, and I knew very clearly why.

The mission was over. Now there was no reason I couldn't concentrate completely on Bethany.

Chapter 20

Landon

When I made it back to the suite, Bethany was already gone from the bed. My disappointment was tangible. I had wanted nothing more than to wake her up and not leave the bed for the entire day.

The mission was over. If she wanted me and I wanted her, then there was nothing to stop us from enjoying the hell out of each other.

I knew exactly where she was. And when I walked into the auxiliary kitchen, she was back at the counter, working on the decorations she didn't get through yesterday.

The smile she shot me over her shoulder when I came in took my breath away.

"Look, no shaky hands."

I came up behind her and kissed her nape, exposed by the curls tucked up in a messy bun. "Good." I liked how she shuddered and goose bumps broke out on her skin.

"Watch it, buddy. I can't afford to have to start over again on these after the time I lost yesterday."

"How about if we have a repeat of yesterday, but in a bed where I can drive you crazy for hours?"

Those green eyes got big as she looked up at me. "Really?"

"Do you not want to?"

She put down her decorating tools then spun around to face me. "I would very much like to…continue last night's activities. But I wasn't sure you did. Despite yesterday, I wasn't sure that you were interested in me that way."

I shouldn't be surprised she'd picked up on my reluctance, although it had been for an entirely different reason than what she thought.

I wrapped my hands around her soft waist. "Never not interested in you. Only not interested in making a complicated situation more complicated."

Her smile stole my breath once again. "Then let me get everything finished up here."

The next hour was filled with laughs and touches and her feeding me bits of cake and icing. And as good as that tasted, it still wasn't anywhere near as sweet as her.

The air was charged with the knowledge of what was to come.

I should've known it was going too well. The hotel staff had come to get the cakes and we were closing up the auxiliary kitchen with four hours left before we needed to be at the gala, when she got the text. My hands were on her hips once again—since I couldn't seem to keep them off her—and I felt her stiffen.

"Everything okay?"

"It's Christiana. She's having a bride moment. Wants me to come get ready for the gala with her."

Disappointment crashed through my system with

surprising force. It still didn't stop my words. "You should go."

Bethany's face scrunched up into the most adorable little pout. "I don't wanna." She ran her hands up my chest. "I want to stay with you."

I kissed her forehead. "How about if we make up for it later? If you don't go to your sister now when she needs you, you'll regret it."

She muttered something about having the worst luck ever and responded to the text. I cupped her cheeks and kissed her.

"I'll see you tonight."

The only thing that made rich people seem richer was when they dressed up for a masquerade ball. This entire thing reminded me of something out of *Phantom of the Opera*.

The men were in tuxedos, the women in formal dresses. Everyone in masks of some sort, either the kind held by a stick or tied behind their heads. Unlike the luau two nights before, where the DJ had played upbeat and contemporary music, tonight's classical strains were provided by a chamber ensemble orchestra.

Bethany's chocolate decadence fit right in with the feel of the evening.

She and her family hadn't arrived yet, but I'd already spotted both Martinez and Frey. Martinez hadn't bothered with a mask at all, and Frey kept taking his off since it didn't fit perfectly around his pudgy face.

When they started talking with each other, everything inside me itched to get closer and find out what details I could. I had to force myself not to. I'd placed both transmitters, and now the best thing I could do was to keep the hell away from them and not make them suspicious.

I wanted to take them down right here and now, but I couldn't. Law enforcement had to make their move, and what I'd done on this island was probably only the first step. And it would all be out of my hands.

That sucked.

I removed my mask a few minutes later when Frey walked over to my perch at the bar. Adams was just a couple paces behind him.

"Landon, right? That's your name?" Frey asked.

I kept my face as neutral as possible. "That's right."

"I want to thank you again for handling the situation with Fanshawe yesterday. It really could've turned into some unwanted attention, and I appreciate you stopping it before it got to that point."

I relaxed. He wasn't suspicious of me. "That guy is an asshole."

"Agreed. And he's no longer in my employ. No longer around at all."

Shit. I wasn't sure if that meant Fanshawe had been escorted off the island or if they'd buried him somewhere. I made a mental note to have Callum's team check. I hadn't been trying to get the man killed, asshole or not.

"I'm glad to hear that Bethany doesn't have to worry about him harassing her."

Frey nodded. "It was a mistake to bring him here. I apologize."

"Apology accepted."

I shook the man's outstretched hand, even managing to keep a smile on my face. It helped to know that what I'd started here would hopefully rip his organization apart bit by bit.

My eyes were torn away as Bethany entered the ballroom with her family. That dress. Holy hell. Black, sparkly, accentuating her curves in every way that made me glad I was a man. And that I was going to be the one who got to enjoy those curves later tonight.

Yes, both Christiana and Angelique were thinner, more polished, but I couldn't tear my eyes away from Bethany to look at them for more than a few seconds in passing. Bethany had a fire, an authenticity, they didn't.

And that was without knowing how kind she was and her amazing work ethic.

Simon approached Christiana, so I quickly made my way to Bethany. Someone who looked as good as she did shouldn't be standing alone.

Or maybe I was worried that someone looking as good as she did *wouldn't* be standing alone for long.

She had a white mask attached to a thin stick and was looking over at the desserts to make sure everything was as it should be when I came up behind her and gently grasped her elbow. "May I have this dance, milady?"

Her eyes lit up from behind her mask. "Indeed, kind sir."

We flowed out onto the dance floor with the others. I knew enough about a waltz to keep us moving. Having her smile up at me while holding her in my arms was enough to make me feel like we were all alone in the room.

Boy, I had it bad. But I didn't even care.

After a few dances, her father called for everyone's attention from the microphone near the small orchestra. We stood still to listen.

"In less than forty-eight hours, my lovely Christiana will be married to the man who puts a constant smile on her face. I could not be more thrilled at her choice or the chance to celebrate the two of them all week with you. She is the apple of my eye."

"Hear, hear," someone called out, and everyone who had a drink raised their glass in toast.

I slid my hand around Bethany's. Her mask was figuratively and literally in place, but I knew the words had to hurt a little bit. These people didn't realize what a gem they had in her.

Or maybe they did. "I would also be remiss not to mention our other daughter, Bethany," Oliver continued. "If you've gained ten pounds this week, blame her and the delicious treats she's created. We're so glad to have her here with us where she belongs."

It wasn't as poetic as what he'd said about Christiana, but one look at Bethany's face told me it had been perfect for her. The key to Bethany's heart was respecting her hard work and talent, not complimenting her looks or status.

Oliver Thornton knew his daughters well.

Bethany was lit up. For the rest of the night, people were talking to her about her business. A few people had heard it was hers throughout the week, but now, everyone seemed to want to compliment her on her skills. I was happy to stand at her side and let her have the limelight. Would've stood behind her in support all evening.

I was prepared for it to be a long night. She deserved her chance to shine. No matter how much I was longing to get her out of that dress.

My time in the military had taught me discipline and patience, and I could admit it was taking all of that right now not to hoist her over my shoulder and make our way out.

We had a moment alone a couple hours later, and she lowered her mask, then peeked up at me before raising her mask again. She looked like she was going to say something but just blew out a little breath instead.

"You doing okay?"

Mask lowered again. "Would it make me a terrible person if I said I just want to get out of here?"

"What's wrong?"

She shrugged one soft shoulder. "What Dad said was perfect, and I think I'm going to end up with more business than I'd ever thought possible."

I trailed a finger down her cheek. "Well-deserved business. Is that okay?"

"Yeah. It's just…" She trailed off.

"A little overwhelming?" I finished for her. "A little scary to know you'll have to take some big steps? A little hard to be the center of attention?"

She put a finger over my lips. "It's just that I'd like to get out of here and finish what we started this afternoon. I love that my business is growing in front of my eyes, but I can hardly concentrate on it because all I can think about is getting you naked."

I almost swallowed my tongue. "Then by all means, let's get out of here. Do you want to say goodbye to anyone?"

"No," she whispered.

Throwing her over my shoulder would be the most expedient way of getting us out. And I was tempted. Lord, was I tempted.

Especially when Mina stepped in front of us as Bethany and I were making our way, hand in hand, toward the door.

"Not now, Mina," Bethany said. "Whatever snarky thing you have to say can wait until tomorrow."

Mina's eyes narrowed. "Maybe I wasn't going to say anything snarky. Maybe I was going to say congratulations for getting the recognition you deserve."

"Oh." Bethany blinked at her, obviously caught by surprise. "Thank you."

Mina caught Bethany's other hand. "I'm happy for you. You've got a great business, and you two are so hot for each other that you're about to take off for a quickie."

There was going to be nothing quick about it, but the hot part was right.

"Who would've thought you'd be the one to have it all together," Mina continued. "How did you do it?"

Bethany grinned over at me. "Karma, I guess."

I leaned down and whispered in her ear, so softly Mina couldn't possibly hear. "I'm about to show you karma, Wildflower. All night."

God, if I didn't love the way her cheeks burned.

Mina cleared her throat. "I have to admit, you two do seem authentic."

I turned to Mina. "Not everything is for show. Bethany figured that out a long time ago."

"I guess she did." Mina pulled her mask back up to her face. "I'll let you guys get to wherever you're going."

We didn't say anything else, just held on to each other's hands as we darted for the door.

Chapter 21

Landon

We didn't talk as we made it back to the suite. I didn't kiss her either. Because if I stopped to do that, I wasn't sure we were going to make it somewhere private before I had that dress off her and her naked body pressed up against a wall with me buried deep inside her.

Once we were in the room, with the door locked behind us, she took my hand and led us toward the bed, kicking off her shoes as she went. Only then did I pause, my conscience kicking in.

The mission was over, but that didn't mean I'd been honest with her. There was still so much between us that was built on half-truths.

This wasn't my first rodeo. In our work at Zodiac Tactical, we always made sure we were the good guys. Which meant the ends generally justified the means.

Providing half-truths as to who I was and what I did to a few people was an acceptable trade-off for bringing down Frey and Martinez and their associates. In other missions, I'd told a lot more lies for a lot less gain.

But looking into Bethany's green eyes, I hated every fucking lie that was between us right now. It was enough to have me pulling away.

Those eyes clouded over at my movement. "Change your mind?" she whispered.

"No. But..." I scrubbed my hand down my face. "There are things you don't know about me."

Things I had never planned on telling her because I'd never planned on letting things get this far. And even though the mission was over, I couldn't tell her right now. Maybe ever.

She narrowed her eyes. "Are you married?"

I shook my head rapidly. "No, never have been."

"Girlfriend?"

I continued shaking my head. "Not since before getting out of the Navy." I'd had a few flings along the way, but nothing remotely serious.

"Do you live in a bomb shelter and spend all your spare time prepping for the apocalypse?"

I had to laugh at that one. "No. But, I do actually know a couple of people who live that way."

She placed a hand on my chest. Right over that bullet wound. A constant reminder that none of us was guaranteed a tomorrow. "Do you have any plans to hurt me?"

My hand covered hers. "Never."

"Do you want me? Do you want this?"

"Almost more than my next breath."

"Then I think I know everything I need to know about you. The rest can wait for later."

I should've argued more, but she stepped closer, her softness pressing against me, her hand pulling my neck down so she could cover my lips with hers.

And then words didn't matter anymore. She was right; we knew enough. I knew that keeping my hands off her wasn't an option.

I turned her so I could slide the zipper down her dress, my fingers trailing the soft skin of her back as I went. It pooled on the floor at her feet, leaving her in her black bra and panties.

"You're so damned beautiful."

I thought she would get shy and make some sort of token protest, but she looked at me over her shoulder, her smile so full of confidence and heat I was afraid this might be over before we even got started.

I turned her and covered her mouth with mine. I knew how to kiss a woman with finesse and skill, but not now, not with this woman. All I could do was devour her.

Fortunately, she didn't seem to mind. Her tongue matched mine in the duel—her fingers coming up to wrap in my hair, keeping me pinned to her.

As if I was going anywhere.

I eased her back toward the bed, pulling my clothes off as I went. A low sound of need escaped me as she pressed closer. I trailed my lips down her jaw to her neck, sucking gently as she gasped.

I'd have to be careful not to mark her fair skin, surprised that I had to stop myself from doing so. I'd never had that urge before, but now, every part of me wanted to leave marks of my claim all over her body.

Most of those marks would be on places others couldn't see—her breasts, her thighs, her soft belly.

But also on her neck, where people would notice the little love bites and give us sly smiles, knowing what we'd been up to.

Knowing, without a shadow of a doubt, that Bethany and I were together.

I laid her down on the bed and kissed down to her full breasts before I could give in to those base urges to mark her neck. Not that her breasts were any less of a temptation. I teased one breast then the other with my lips and tongue and teeth.

"Mine."

I didn't even recognize my own voice and its Neanderthal traces as I pulled deeply on her nipple. Thank God she didn't seem to care. She moaned and pulled me closer.

I needed her. Needed to be inside her. I removed my lips from her skin, only to strip away the last of our clothes and pull on a condom—one I'd never thought I'd need on this trip.

"I want to be on top." She bit that full bottom lip, and it was all I could do not to reach over and do the same with my teeth.

This was going to be embarrassingly short if I didn't pull it together—especially once she was perched on top of me.

"Yes, ma'am," I managed to bite out. I lay down on the bed, swallowing my moan as she kissed down my chest, then straddled my hips.

"It's been a while," she whispered as she looked down at our bodies, so close to being joined.

"For me too." I ran my hand up her bent leg from her knee to her thigh. "We can go slow."

I watched, sweat breaking out on my forehead, as she lowered herself onto me one miraculously agonizing inch at a time. I closed my eyes at the feel of her soft heat engulfing me.

She worked herself all the way down, breath catching. "That feels so good."

I tried to reassure her that it was more than good, that it was bloody fantastic. But me, the guy with a charming quip always on the tip of his tongue, couldn't find my words.

All I could do was grip her hips as she began to ease her way back up then work her way back down on me, over and over.

"Yes," I finally muttered as she picked up speed. I opened my eyes to find her lush breasts swaying as she rode me, head thrown back, eyes closed.

It was so damned sexy.

"Fucking beautiful." I gripped her hips as she slid back up, holding her there, stopping her progress before I lost all control.

She let out a mewl, like a cranky little kitten, pressing downward, eager for me to impale her. Finally, I let her go, and as I slid into her, she crushed her mouth to mine, pressing her tongue between my lips and swallowing my groan. Then she began to move, drawing herself up over me, then back down.

Slowly again. Excruciatingly slowly.

I fought the urge to grab her hips and drive her movements, wanting to let her have whatever control she wanted. But when she bit my lip as she ground against me, the act savage in its innocence, my good intentions disappeared. I growled before holding her against me and flipping us over, taking her completely.

I thrust into her again and again, relishing how tight her inner walls were as she clamped around me.

I couldn't hold on anymore. I was amazed I'd lasted this long.

"Come for me, Bethany." I was nearing the point of no return. "Come *with* me," I amended, my tone urgent as my breathing rate increased.

She tensed underneath me and pulsed around me, her orgasm taking her with no warning to me, and it was the last straw. I thrust harder until there were no thoughts in my head but her name and the pressure building through my system.

She cried out my name, her hands moving to my shoulders and clinging to me, riding out both of our orgasms. I inhaled sharply and held myself above her as I came with a force that shocked me.

Although, I didn't know why it should. Damned near everything about this woman shocked me.

She reached up and cupped my cheek, and I pressed a soft kiss to her lips as my hips slowed and our breathing crashed into each other.

"That was amazing," she whispered.

"Yes." Once again, I couldn't find any more words than that.

When we could finally both breathe again, I led her to the shower, washing us both off before taking her against the shower wall. We were both limp with exhaustion by the time we were done.

She smiled at me as I dried her off, and I had to close my eyes.

There were so many things I wanted to say to her, explain to her. Because all I knew was that there was no way this week was going to be enough for me.

Maybe when we got back to LA, I could tell her about the mission—but explain that it had been over by the time I'd slept with her. I never wanted her to think that I'd used her body for anything outside of pleasuring us both.

I wouldn't be able to give her specific details, but I could let her know about my true employment with Zodiac Tactical. Because I wanted her to meet everyone there. They were just as much my family as my mother was.

I had to believe that she would understand and forgive me. The alternative gutted me.

But right now, I wanted to hold her in my arms while she slept. That was all that mattered—the rest would wait. I might not sleep, but I didn't care.

She curled up into my arms, reminding me of an exhausted kitten this time, little claws pressing into my arm wrapped around her. I could feel her hair covering my chest, and I didn't ever want to move.

Soon, she was snoring in the most adorable way I'd ever heard.

The sun was coming up when my phone buzzed on the nightstand. I wanted to ignore it but knew I couldn't. I hadn't slept much, but that didn't bother me at all. I reached over and grabbed the buzzing annoyance, careful not to disturb her.

I let out a curse when I saw the message from Tristan.

Computer transmitter you placed is a no-go. It's been wiped.

Chapter 22

Bethany

I slept much later than I normally did. My eyes blinked open, and the bedside clock told me it was already past breakfast hours and deep into brunch.

I stretched, laughing with a groan at the soreness in my body. The best sort of soreness. All over sort of soreness. An *I want it again!* sort of soreness.

I reached out to touch Landon, but the bed was empty. I sat up and looked around, but there was no sign of him. I remembered falling asleep in his arms last night.

I texted him.

Sleeping Beauty has finally awoken.

I waited for a clever comeback, but nothing came. I didn't know why I was texting him looking the way I was anyway. If he burst in the door right now, I'd have to hide under the covers. Morning breath. Morning hair.

I dashed into the shower. He'd get my message and head back, probably with coffee and breakfast. Then I'd convince him to let breakfast get cold while I dragged him back to bed.

Because I wanted round two. Or round five, if you counted how many times we'd made love last night. In the bed, in the shower, on the sink counter.

I truly expected him to be back by the time I got out of the shower. But he wasn't. And there was no response to my text either.

Okay.

I would try one more time.

Hey, you. I'm up and at 'em. Going to grab something to eat then get to work on tomorrow's cakes.

I cringed as I sent it. Was that the right mix of wanting to let him know I wanted to see him without seeming too clingy? I hoped so.

Still no response.

Where was he?

I hung out in the room, taking time to get my hair fixed into a cute bun, putting on some makeup, hoping he'd show up. As noon came and went, I decided to go out to the pool area. Maybe he was working out or swimming— somewhere he didn't have his phone directly on him.

He'd aim those dimples at me when he saw me, and this ridiculous feeling in the pit of my stomach would melt away.

But he wasn't at the pool or the gym. And as time passed and I didn't hear anything more from him, the ugly feeling grew rather than melted until it was a huge ball of ice in my gut.

Landon was avoiding me.

I hadn't seen that one coming. I forced myself to eat lunch—which did not do anything but make my stomach feel worse—then went back to the room. I looked at myself in the mirror, studying the care I'd taken with my hair and makeup. I wanted to scrub it all off and pull my hair down until it was a disaster.

But that was nothing but childish. I had work I needed to do. I had set aside today to finish the final wedding cake decorating. I'd already lost the morning, so there was no point in sitting around here feeling sorry for myself.

And there was definitely no point in sitting here wondering what had made Landon run for his life.

Part of me was still hoping it was all a big misunderstanding. That he'd come rushing in here at any moment with some crazy story about how a hut had collapsed on the beach and he'd had to single-handedly rebuild it using only duct tape and chewing gum. He'd been so busy saving some family's vacation that he'd lost track of time and forgotten to check his phone.

Until I glanced at my phone.

Read.

I had been left on *read*. He'd seen my message but hadn't responded. That told me everything I needed to know.

I stuffed my phone into my pocket and headed toward the auxiliary kitchen. I was here to do a job, and that's what I was going to do. I wasn't going to let Landon derail me from my purpose here.

Even if it was a little bit difficult to breathe around the ball in my throat.

He and I had no promises. Hell, hadn't he tried to talk some sense into me before we'd had sex last night? Maybe he knew about his tendency to lose interest and become a complete jerk the morning after.

It came back to the fact that I really didn't know anything about my *fiancé*.

I channeled my angst into working, blocking everything

from my mind. My hands weren't shaky today. My heart might have taken a hit, but it wasn't going to show in my work.

It was almost dinner by the time I had the cakes exactly how I wanted them. They were ready. They were perfect. They would sit in the cooler until tomorrow when they were moved for the reception.

My job was finished. But as I came out from the cooler, all I could see were the cake stands in pieces over in the corner. Landon was supposed to have put them together this afternoon. Yet here they were, still in pieces.

This entire week, he hadn't given me any reason to believe he wouldn't have these stands set up in time. Until he went AWOL today.

I rubbed at the tension that had settled in the center of my neck. I had worked hard all afternoon, and I was tired. Putting those stands together would take me hours—much longer than it would take Landon.

But I couldn't trust him to do it, and I wouldn't be able to do anything else or get to sleep tonight without knowing they were complete.

I grabbed my phone and pulled up the plans for building the elaborate stands. I'd built this business from the ground up by myself.

I was the only person I could count on. Something I wouldn't be forgetting again.

~

Landon

As soon as I'd snuck out of our suite after getting the text from Tristan, I'd called him. I wasn't sure how bad the situation was, but I didn't want to lead Martinez to Bethany if he suspected I was undercover.

"What the hell happened? Am I compromised? Does Martinez know there was a transmitter placed on his computer?"

"Negative," Tristan responded. "It looks like this was more of a standard wipe. Something may have made him suspicious, but there was nothing to suggest the transmitter was found."

That at least meant my life wasn't in danger. "But we're back to square one when it comes to Martinez. And phone is my only option now."

"You can try again with the computer, but yeah, phone is best. At this point, we'll take whatever you can get." Tristan sounded as tired as I felt.

I rubbed my gritty eyes. "I thought this mission was over."

There was a long moment of silence. "Is your identity still secure?"

I knew what he was asking. Had I told anyone—particularly Bethany—what I was really doing here. "Yes. Mission isn't compromised. I just made some...decisions I wouldn't have if I'd known I was still in the middle of all this shit."

Visions of Bethany reaching for me, her soft smile lighting up her face, danced before my eyes. I never would've drawn her into the middle of an active mission, no matter how much I wanted her.

"Decisions based around a certain lovely baker? That's not your normal MO."

"I know." I rubbed the back of my neck. "I thought the mission was complete, or I never would've let anything happen."

"Does she suspect anything? Will it compromise your chance to get near Martinez?"

"No, she doesn't suspect anything." Because she trusted me. "But I'm down to the last transmitter, so I better make it count. I'm going to have to take some chances."

"Libra, I've got the full file on Joaquin Martinez sitting right here in front of me."

If Tristan was calling me by my Zodiac code name, I knew it was serious. "Not pretty?"

"Dude is the opposite of pretty. Frey may be dipping his toes into the human trafficking waters, but Martinez is up to his neck in it. As soon as Callum figures out the mole in his department, taking Martinez down is going to be his number one priority."

"Even more important for me to get this transmitter on him, then."

Tristan let out a sigh. "If he catches you, you won't make it off that island alive. He's ruthless."

"Then I'll have to make sure not to get caught."

"You don't have any backup. If I show up now to help cover you, it'll be suspicious. This was supposed to be an easy mission."

I rubbed my eyes. "I get it. You're like the rest of them, don't think I can handle it."

"Fuck off. That has nothing to do with it. I've argued to put you back on active missions since before you left the hospital. But that mind-set you've got—that you have something to prove more than anybody else?—that shit will get you killed if you're not careful."

He was right. It was my mind-set, and I hadn't even been aware of it. "I don't like you very much, Pisces."

He chuckled. "You don't have to like me. You do have to stay alive."

"I want to help take this bastard down. After what

happened with Wavy and Bronwyn... I can't stomach a trafficker going free when I can do something about it. But getting near him is fucking tricky."

"How about I send a drone with a benzodiazepine strong enough to help with the job?"

"That's a good option. If I can't get near him today, I could roofie him at the wedding. Everybody's drinking at weddings, so hopefully he won't make too much out of a twelve-hour memory gap."

"It'll be at the drop point by this afternoon."

"Hopefully, I won't even need it." Getting something into Martinez's drink wasn't going to be much easier than getting to his phone.

"You have to be careful."

"What I have to do is get that transmitter on him."

"Listen to me, brother. I know you feel like you should've seen what was going on with Wavy, but it fooled us all. Planting the transmitter—which may or may not work in the long run—is not worth your life. I would be saying the same thing to any other Zodiac team member on this mission. Hell, I hope you'd be saying it to me if the roles were reversed."

"I would." And I would mean it too.

"Survival is always the most important thing. So, do what you can, but no matter what, you come home. We already came too close to losing you once."

Tristan was a good friend and a huge asset to Zodiac. I needed to make sure Ian was reminded of it. "Roger that."

After our call, I spent the entire fucking day trying to get close to Joaquin Martinez. I pushed every other thought—even the fact that I'd left Bethany alone in the bed with no idea where I was—to the back burner.

All that mattered was getting close to Martinez.

Getting back into his suite wasn't an option. He'd come

down for breakfast like he had yesterday, but he had left one of his men guarding the room in the hallway. Using housekeeping to get in there twice wouldn't have worked anyway.

After breakfast, he'd gone back to his room. There was no following him from the inside, so I'd rushed around to the outside of the building, climbing a damned tree so I could see into his balcony.

And I'd waited.

I'd gritted my teeth as I'd received the texts from Bethany wondering where I was. If I opened communication with her, I knew I'd lose any shot I had at getting close to Martinez.

Ended up it hadn't mattered anyway. He'd only left his suite twice throughout the day, and neither time had I been able to get close enough without making it obvious I was up to something. I would have to try tomorrow at the wedding with the roofie.

Shit.

The wedding.

The sun was already going down, and I hadn't put any of the stands together for tomorrow. And I'd been ignoring Bethany's messages all day.

There was only one way this could look to her—like I'd abandoned her completely after our night together in bed. I rushed to the auxiliary kitchen. Whether she was there or not, that was where I needed to be.

She was there.

And she'd put the cake stands together herself. She was putting the finishing touches on now.

Fuck.

She looked up when she saw me come in then concentrated her focus back down on the stands without a word.

"Bethany, I'm sorry." I had no fucking idea how I was

going to explain this to her when the truth wasn't an option.

She didn't look at me. "None of your services—*any* of them—are needed any longer."

I scrubbed a hand down my face. "Bethany, I swear to you, I'm so sorry. I didn't mean for you to have to put this together yourself."

Now she looked at me. "But for clarification, you *did* mean to ghost me all day and not return my texts or talk to me at all?"

There was no good response for that either. "All I can do is offer my sincerest apologies."

She stood tapping the socket wrench in the palm of one hand. I was prepared in case that came flying at my head. "Are you some sort of commitment-phobe, Landon? Is that the big reveal from last night I wouldn't let you get to? You're a *hit and quit it* sort of guy?"

"No." Although I could totally see why she would think so.

She tapped the wrench harder. "Okay, then. Are you on drugs? Battling some sort of addiction?"

This was my easiest way out. She was tapping that wrench in a vaguely threatening manner, but her eyes were soft. She was too kind for her own good and willing to forgive someone who was suffering from some sort of addiction.

All I had to do was say yes. Hell, both my parents had been addicts—she already knew that. If I told her I had the same struggles, she would forgive me for today's silence.

But the line was right here. If I took this option and lied to her, it would mean the end of anything permanent between the two of us.

She might possibly forgive me working undercover and

using her to get criminals, but lying to her to get out of personal trouble would be a trust broken that couldn't be rebuilt.

When Wavy had pointed that gun at me all those months ago, I'd been sure my life was over. There had been no way out and no options. All I could do was be a passive observer in my own demise as the bullet hit me in the chest.

Not this time. This time, I had choices. They weren't good ones, but they were choices.

I would not lie to her about this.

"No. I'm not on drugs."

She studied me silently for a long minute. "But you're not going to tell me, are you? Whatever it is that's going on. And there is something going on."

"It's better if you don't know." I took a step closer. "I'll finish this if you want. I know you have to be tired. I can make sure it's ready for tomorrow."

"No. I'll do it. You go get your things out of the suite. Like I said, your services are no longer required. I'll finish everything here."

Everything in me wanted to stay and fight for her. To explain, with whatever lack of details I could, how much she meant to me. How much last night had meant to me.

But there was more at stake here than my feelings. If I wanted to help take down Martinez, I had to walk away from Bethany right now.

With a nod, and against every instinct I had, I turned and walked out the door.

Chapter 23

Bethany

Watching Landon walk back out the door without a word, I wanted to throw the wrench across the room. Or take it and slam it into the cake stands.

I had no idea how to make any sense out of him. I believed him when he said it wasn't drugs or having some sort of emotional withdrawal. There was something going on here, and I didn't know what it was.

And he wasn't telling.

I looked around me. Everything was finished and ready for tomorrow evening's wedding. The stands were stable and steady, the cakes were finished, decorated beautifully, and resting in the walk-in.

All I had to do was not have a breakdown before the wedding.

Whatever was going on with Landon wasn't my problem. He didn't have to explain himself to me, and obviously, what we'd shared last night wasn't a priority for him.

I needed to let him go and separate myself, and my emotions, from him completely. Whatever secrets he had were none of my business.

But I found myself quickly locking up the kitchen and rushing back to the suite even though I knew Landon would be there.

Who was I kidding? *Because* Landon would be there.

I wanted answers.

The closer I got, the more I thought I had it figured out. The possibility had been running through my mind all day.

Dad had hired him as security for me.

My jaw clenched so tightly it was giving me a headache. I'd known for years that some of Dad's contacts were questionable, criminal even. He wasn't part of that life anymore, but that didn't mean they weren't still around.

I walked faster.

Dad had all but freaked out when he'd found out Joaquin Martinez was on the island. He'd told Mother, Christiana, and me to be sure to stay away from him. Maybe Dad had been afraid that warning me wasn't enough and that I needed someone nearby as a sort of bodyguard.

And who else better to protect me than a former Navy SEAL?

It made way too much sense. Made sense why Harley suddenly had a *family emergency* last week.

God, I was humiliated. My parents had known from the beginning that Landon wasn't my boyfriend, fiancé, or anything. They'd humored me, barely short of patting me on the head.

And Landon had been in on it from the start. It was why he hadn't wanted to sleep with me.

I stopped. Why had he slept with me if he was working for Dad? Because I'd asked him to? Had I been some sort of *pity fuck*?

I started moving again, now almost running. I wasn't sure I'd ever been this angry in my whole life. I burst into the suite, slamming the door behind me.

"Was I a pity fuck?" I yelled.

I screeched to a halt when I found Landon standing in the bedroom naked.

Our eyes met and held for a long moment until mine dropped to the evidence that he was growing, uh, very happy to see me.

He gestured to that mouthwatering hardness. "Considering this happens every time I'm within ten feet of you, or look at you, or think of you...I'm going to go with, no, not a pity fuck."

He stepped into the bathroom and came back out wrapped in a towel. "I didn't expect you here so soon. I wasn't sure where I was going to end up sleeping tonight, so thought I would grab a quick shower in case I didn't have one."

I couldn't stop staring at those abs, that chest. That bullet wound.

"Do you work for my father?"

His eyes narrowed. "Doing what?"

"Guarding me."

"*What?* No. Your father did not hire me for anything."

I took a step closer. "Would you even be allowed to say if he did?"

He blew out a breath. "As a member of his security team? Maybe not, depending on what the contract paperwork stated. But as a member of his security, I would be the first to tell him that *secret guards* are a bad idea."

I crossed my arms over my chest, forcing my eyes to

stay pinned to his. "You mean that me not knowing you were assigned to me as a bodyguard would be a bad idea."

"Yes. In order for someone to be truly protected, they need to be aware of what's going on around them."

"Sounds like you know what you're talking about."

He stilled then relaxed his shoulders in a deliberate move. "Residual knowledge from being a SEAL."

I called bullshit.

"You're not a carpenter by trade."

"I'm good at carpentry."

"This business your friend Ian started. Tell me more about it." Maybe he wouldn't tell me his whole truth, but with enough pieces of it, I could at least figure out the shape of the puzzle.

"Some things I can't discuss with you."

"Is your real name Landon Black?"

He nodded.

"And the other stuff? No wife? No girlfriend?"

"All true."

"Do you work for my father?" I asked again. I still couldn't let it go.

"No, I never met or spoke with Oliver Thornton before I arrived on this island."

"Did you sleep with me to get to something or someone?" I hated how my voice got weaker.

He took a step closer. "No. I promise you, last night was one hundred percent about me not being able to keep my hands off you and your sexy curves. Nothing more or less than that."

That at least made me feel a little bit better. I sat down on the edge of the bed. He was still standing in front of the bathroom door, towel low on his hips.

"I'm not sure what I'm supposed to think."

He scrubbed a hand down his face. "Let me shower,

and we can talk some more. Although there's not a lot I can say. The most important thing is that I never meant to hurt you, and I'm sorry I did."

He disappeared into the bathroom.

I lay back on the bed, bringing both arms up to cross over my face. I was tired. Not much sleep, then the worrying, and finally the work—mine plus his. I had reason to be exhausted.

And I was just as confused as I'd been when I got here. I had no idea what to believe about Landon.

My phone buzzed with a text on the bed beside me, and I grabbed it. With my luck, Christiana had probably decided to call off the wedding.

Martinez is leaving tonight. You've got to make your move now.

What?

It took me a second to realize it was Landon's phone in my hand. Someone named Pisces had texted him.

About Joaquin Martinez.

I dropped the phone like it was on fire and jumped off the bed. Landon needed to make a move with Joaquin Martinez?

Bile pooled in my gut. I'd been asking the wrong questions. I'd assumed that Landon was the hired muscle for Dad, but what if he wasn't on the right side of the law at all?

I stormed over to Landon's duffel. He'd already put his clothes in it, and it was sitting open on the luggage rack. I cringed but didn't stop myself from rooting through it.

I froze as my hand brushed something metal.

A gun.

I jerked away like it burned me, then put my hand back in to grab it and pull it out to study. I didn't know much about weapons, so I held it by the butt so I didn't shoot myself.

This gun was small—my hand wrapped around it easily. I guess it made sense that Landon was going to have a small gun if he was going to try to wear it around here.

I dug back in his bag and found a holster. Not one that fit on a shoulder like on television shows. This one was small—it must go around his ankle. That was how he'd hidden it.

I sat back on the bed with the gun in my lap, trying to figure out what to do.

I should leave. Go get security. And tell them what? It wasn't illegal for Landon to have a weapon.

Why did he need it?

He came out of the shower, that towel wrapped around his waist. He froze when he saw the gun in my lap.

"Wildflower? I need you to set that weapon on the bed next to you."

I kept my hand wrapped around it in my lap. "Why?"

"Because I don't want you to accidentally hurt me or you."

I stood, gun still in my hand. "I found it in your bag."

His eyes were glued to my hands as his weight shifted on the balls of his feet. "Yes, I had it in my bag. Can you please place it on the bed?"

"Why do you have a gun, Landon?"

I brought the weapon up to show him—as if he wasn't familiar with his own gun—and he moved faster than I'd ever seen him. Before I could even figure out what was going on, he had my wrist in his hand, ripping the weapon none too gently away from me. My breath escaped in a little squeak.

"Sorry." He grimaced, stepping away, doing something to the gun so the magazine clip slid out of it. He set both on the dresser. "The last time someone as kind and gentle as you had a gun in her hand in front of me, I took a bullet to the chest."

My eyes fell on that scar. I'd thought it was from something during his Navy SEAL years, but evidently not. I rubbed my wrist from where he'd twisted it to get the weapon from me.

"Are you okay?" he asked.

Was I okay? My wrist was fine, but was I okay? No.

"Why do you have a gun?" I whispered. "If you don't work security for my dad, why do you have a gun?"

"I can't tell you."

"Because you're a criminal? Does my father know? Who do you work for?"

I needed to get out of here. I started backing toward the door.

Landon was studying me with those intelligent hazel eyes. He should scare me much more than he did. Even right now, I wanted to understand what was going on more than I wanted to get away from him.

"I'm not any sort of criminal. I promise." He brought out his smile to attempt to put me at ease. "I have a legal permit for that gun. After my time in the SEALs, I feel naked without having a weapon."

That was probably true, but it wasn't the whole truth. Nothing with Landon this entire week had been the whole truth.

"I can't stay here with you. I have to report this to my father and the security team. I'd be a complete idiot if I didn't."

I turned for the door, tense for him to physically restrain me from doing so. That would tell me if he was a bad guy, wouldn't it?

It would also be too late for me to get away from him.

"Wildflower." The word came out as a sigh. "I'm here undercover for law enforcement."

I froze three steps from the door.

"They sent me under to put a recording device on Vincent Frey's phone. He's a big-name criminal, and getting near him is almost impossible. When they found out he'd be here for the wedding, the Feds decided to make a move."

I turned to face him.

"This island has such strict security, it puts people —*criminals*—at ease. Cops can't just show up here. Invitations were closely guarded and monitored, so law enforcement had to find another way to send someone in."

"Me," I whispered.

"Your handyman Harley had a warrant out for his arrest."

"He did?" This kept getting worse.

Landon shrugged. "Nothing bad—a mistake, actually. A lucky break on our part. He helped me get in with you, and, in turn, we made that warrant go away."

I stood staring at him, trying to get my thoughts under control. "Is anything you told me the truth? Is your name even Landon?"

He took a step closer, and I wasn't sure if I should back away or not. "Yes. Anybody who searches my name will find some general info on me. Things that have been built to make me seem as boring as possible."

"So, you're a cop?"

"No, I work for a security company called Zodiac Tactical. That's the one my friend, and former SEAL teammate, Ian DeRose built. What I said about being a jack-of-all-trades is true. We do all sorts of work. A friend in law enforcement needed someone who could build for you and get the transmitter planted. I fit the bill."

"And I fit the bill as someone pathetic enough to believe everything a stranger would say."

Another step closer. "No. You had needs, and I could fulfill them. It got me on the island."

"And everything since then?" I hated that my voice was weak. Why wasn't I screaming at him?

"Everything with you has been real, Wildflower. Not being able to stay away from you has been completely authentic. You blow my self-control straight to hell, woman."

"I don't know if I can believe you." But God, how I wanted to.

He crossed all the way over to me now, gently touching my arms. "I held out as long as I could. If—*when*—you found out about this, I wanted to be able to tell you that we didn't make love until after my mission was complete. I didn't want you to think I'd used you in that way."

My brow furrowed. What about that text? "Your… mission is done?"

He let out a sigh. "I thought so last night when I made love to you. But there was an extra complication. That's where I've been all day."

"Was that complication Joaquin Martinez?"

His head snapped back. "Why do you say that?"

I shrugged one shoulder. "I didn't just randomly go digging through your duffel. You got a text about Martinez."

He dashed to the bed and lifted his phone. A vile curse fell from his mouth.

"I have to go." He forsook all sense of propriety, dropping the towel and pulling on his clothes. "Nobody knew Martinez was going to be here. He's an even bigger fish to law enforcement than Vincent Frey. I thought I'd gotten a transmitter on Martinez's computer yesterday, but it got wiped. I need to get a transmitter on his phone. I thought I had all day tomorrow."

"But he's leaving." That's what the text had said. "What are you going to do? Martinez isn't going to just hand over his phone."

He sat down to pull on his shoes. "I'll have to figure something out. It's critical. Martinez and Frey are neck-deep into human trafficking. If I don't get that transmitter on him, we'll lose the chance to gather critical intel."

"Martinez is dangerous. Dad didn't want me anywhere around him. He was very clear about that."

"Martinez is definitely fucking dangerous. But I've got to try. Lives are at stake." He grabbed something tiny out of his duffel. "I've got to get this transmitter on his phone." He slipped it into his pocket.

I watched in silence as he grabbed his gun and put it back together, before slipping it into the ankle holster. I wanted to tell him not to go, but I already knew he wasn't going to listen to me.

He was completely focused—more of a Navy SEAL than I'd ever seen him. Ever seen *anyone*.

As he walked by me, he slipped an arm around my waist and placed his lips against mine. "Every kiss was real. Every single one. Don't ever doubt that."

He pulled away and walked out the door.

Chapter 24

Landon

I'd missed eight texts from Tristan. I called him as I dashed out the door.

"Dude, I thought you were dead," he answered without any other greeting.

"What's going on with Martinez?"

"He called for a flight to leave tonight. Don't know why. No indication it has anything to do with you. He'll be wheels up in less than an hour."

I stepped out of the elevator and walked briskly through the hallway—just slow enough not to draw undue attention to myself. "Anything you can do to stall him?"

"I've already done everything I can on my end. We kept his jet on the ground in LA as long as possible. He was trying to leave a few hours ago."

"Let me know if anything changes. I'll keep you posted." I disconnected the call.

Instead of heading left, toward the interior of the hotel

and the back patio, I went right, toward the front doors. I'd need one of the resort shuttles to take me to the island's tiny airfield. The shuttle stand was half a block from the lobby.

I would have no reason to be out at the airfield. Just showing up there was going to put Martinez and his men on high alert. Acting shit-faced drunk was probably my best bet. Hopefully, I could literally stumble into Martinez and get the transmitter on the phone. His security team would probably beat the hell out of me for getting too close, but I'd take it. And hope they didn't shoot me.

But I had to get to the airfield first.

As I exited the lobby doors, my luck turned. Martinez stood outside a limo at the shuttle station, his phone in his hand, waiting to get in. I stumbled in that direction, running my hand through my hair to muss it. It was still damp, but it would have to do.

A member of Martinez's security team walked around the limo and opened the trunk, placing luggage inside.

I half jogged, half stumbled forward. "Hey, you," I called, letting my voice slur. "I remember you. Go Dodgers!"

The security guy slammed the trunk and stepped between Martinez and me, but Martinez put a hand on the guy's back. "It's fine, Clark."

Clark stepped to the side, crossing his arms over his beefy chest, but he didn't move far.

"How's my cap? What's your name again?"

"Landon. I'm Landon. Your cap is fine." I looked around like I couldn't figure out what was going on. "Wait, are you leaving? You can't leave! What about the game tomorrow?"

He chuckled, shaking his head. "The wedding is

tomorrow, so you won't be catching the game. And yes, I have to leave early."

"That sucks. I was looking forward to having someone who could help me sneak off and watch it."

"You're the bride's sister's fiancé. I think your absence would be noted."

He'd looked into me. Fuck. But evidently, my cover had held.

I made a face. "I'm still gonna sneak out. All I did was promise I wouldn't be watching the game during the ceremony. God, everybody is so uptight here."

"Oliver mentioned you and his daughter today at our poker game. He seems to like you."

I scrubbed a hand down my face in an exaggerated fashion, inching closer. "Look, I don't know how well you know Oliver, but I don't think this is gonna work out with me and his daughter. I mean, she's a good baker, but that's about it, you know? I never should've proposed. I got caught up in the moment. She's boring."

I stumbled just the slightest bit closer without touching him, hating what I was saying about Bethany.

He nodded. At least he seemed interested in the conversation. "You're young. You've got a lot to learn. You marry the good girls, Landon, keep that in mind. Marry the good girls and have your fun wherever you need to on the side. But the good girls raise good children for you and keep your home happy."

My fingers itched to ball into a fist and clock him on the jaw right here. Bastard was going to stand here and talk about *good girls* when he was neck-deep in human trafficking?

Taking a chance at touching him with Clarky-boy nearby, I clapped Martinez on the shoulder with one hand and stuck the other in my pocket to work the transmitter off its backing so I'd have it ready to stick on his phone. "Wise words, my friend, but I'm going to have to find myself a different good girl. This one is too damn uptight."

I looked past him, hand still on his shoulder, at the limo. "Are you leaving?"

Bastard slid out from under my hand but at least didn't sic Clark on me. "I already said I was."

"Right. Right-Right-Right. I may have had a few too many. Hey, listen, I know we don't know each other that well, but do you think you could give me a ride off this island? I'm done here. I need off."

He narrowed his eyes and shook his head. "I don't think that will work for me."

Shit, he was getting suspicious and starting to put more distance between us. I stumbled closer.

This wasn't working. Clark stepped forward, and Martinez was beginning to lose his amused demeanor. My drunk act was wearing thin. I was about to stumble directly into him and deal with the aftermath when Bethany's voice interrupted us.

"Mr. Martinez," she called.

What the hell was she doing here? I forced myself not to turn around and give myself away. Instead, I flinched and rolled my eyes.

"Damn it," I whispered to Martinez. "She found me. Help me, man. Get her out of here. Get *me* out of here."

Martinez chuckled.

I turned to see her hurrying toward us with a pastry box in her hands. "My father sent me with these." She beamed at us and held out a pink box in front of her. "He heard you were leaving and asked me to bring them out."

What the hell?

Martinez looked confused. I was sure I did too.

Bethany stepped directly in front of me, opened the cake

box, and shoved it under his nose. "It's some of the desserts you'll be missing out on tomorrow. I'll admit, I insisted on bringing them to you. I think they're the best I've made this week. I'd hate for you not to get an opportunity to taste them. And tell all your friends if they need a baker for any events."

With her free hand, she reached back. It took me a second to realize she wanted me to give her the transmitter.

Oh shit.

I didn't want to do it. I didn't want her anywhere around this situation. If Martinez caught her...

She shook her hand in an obvious instruction that I was to give her the transmitter *now*.

Fuck.

I slipped the transmitter into her hand while Martinez and Clark were distracted by the treats in the box, praying I wasn't about to get both her and myself killed.

As soon as she had the tiny device, she stepped forward. "I'm sorry you couldn't stay." Lifting her chin, she held out her cheek, clearly indicating she wanted him to kiss her. "Please keep me in mind for any future baking needs you have. I put my card in the box."

He leaned in to press his jaw to hers in a polite, high-society kiss, but Bethany lurched forward, and the cake box flew into Martinez's chest. Clark moved with catlike reflexes to catch it, and he probably would have if Bethany hadn't been pushing it forward as she pretended to fall into Martinez.

Neither of them ended up falling, but they both ended up half bent over, near the ground. Clark yanked the bakery box away, and Bethany bent to pick up Martinez's fallen cell phone.

"I'm so sorry," she exclaimed.

"Jesus, Bethany, come on! What's wrong with you? You're so clumsy!" I stumbled over Bethany and hard into Clark, blocking his view of the cell phone. Bethany's body already kept Martinez from seeing it.

"Get it together, man," Clark whispered as I pushed my weight into him. "You're embarrassing yourself."

Martinez, with icing on his shirtfront, snatched the phone from Bethany. "I will keep your bakery in mind."

She nodded. "I'm so sorry! Can I pay to have your shirt laundered? I'm such a klutz."

"Yeah, she'll pay for it." I wavered on my feet to keep up my pretense as I made the obnoxious statement. Anything to keep him focused on me and not on his phone. The transmitter was tiny and wouldn't be noticed, but I only wanted Martinez remembering me.

He pulled a handkerchief out of his pocket and got up all the icing he could. "Don't worry about it. Laundering is not necessary. Let's go, Clark."

Clark jumped back and opened the limo door, the remains of the salvaged box in hand. Martinez slid into the limo, and Clark ignored us as he closed the door, then walked around us to get behind the wheel. They pulled away from the curb without a second's pause, moving quickly down the road toward the airfield.

Bethany and I stood there staring after them.

"I'm pretty sure I got it on the back of the phone. I didn't know if it had to go on a specific place or what." She bit her lip.

"Anywhere. As long as you got the transmitter on the phone, it can do its job from anywhere on it."

She glanced over at me. "Then I got it."

"You shouldn't have done that, you know." I crossed my arms over my chest. Now that Martinez was gone, all I could think about what how much danger Bethany had put herself in.

How much danger *I* had put her in. If Martinez had caught her…

The thought of it almost doubled me over.

"Why? I thought you just said I got the transmitter on the phone okay."

"Because it was dangerous, Bethany!" My voice got deeper with my emotion. "Because Martinez might have killed you if he'd caught you."

"I'm pretty sure he would've done the same to you if you'd been caught, and I had more excuse to be around him than you did."

She didn't get it.

For the first time, I had an inkling of how Ian and Sarge had felt when their women had been taken by criminals over the past year. The helplessness that had nearly drowned them. The bitter fury at the thought of Wavy and Bronwyn being hurt.

I was already feeling the same, and nothing had even happened to Bethany. Just the thought of it happening…

"But that's my job." I grabbed her hand and marched her a little farther into the privacy of the trees heading down toward the beach. "I have training and experience with this. You don't. You should not have put yourself in danger like that."

We went around a couple of trees and then ended up near the beach. No one was around. Good. I still had this yin and yang of icy fury and fear floating around in my veins.

Fuck being the one who always smiled. The one who was good with people. Right now, I could hardly get a handle on this storm blowing through me.

I wanted to throw Bethany over my shoulder and carry her somewhere safe and never let her out of my sight.

"Landon…"

I kept walking, her hand in mine, as she rushed behind me to keep up. I didn't care that I was being unreasonable. I wanted her as far away from Martinez as possible in case he came back.

"You should've stayed in the suite," I bit out. "Do you know what Martinez would've done if he had even suspected you might be planting a transmission device on him?"

I couldn't even stomach it. The thought of it turned me into someone I didn't recognize.

"Landon, stop."

"Do you hear me? He's a human trafficker, and I'm not even sure that's the worst of his sins. Do you think that you being the sister of the bride would've stopped him from—"

She yanked on my hand and before I even knew what she was going to do had me pressed back against a tree and kissed me.

One of my hands immediately wound into her hair, the other wrapped around her hips and yanked her to me. I ravished those sweet lips like I'd been afraid I'd never have another taste of them again. Which wasn't far from the truth.

We were both breathing heavy as we broke apart.

"I think the words you're looking for are, 'Thank you, Bethany,'" she whispered with a smile.

I closed my eyes and pushed down the fear. She was right. I definitely owed her thanks.

"Thank you, Bethany," I repeated before kissing her again. "You saved lives today. My life definitely—because I was about to have to resort to desperate measures to get that tracker on Martinez's phone. But also the lives of the people who are going to be helped by law enforcement because of what you did."

I gripped her hips tighter. "But I still didn't like it."

She shrugged and gave me a gentle smile. "Placing the transmitter was worth the risk. It was more important than me or you."

I stared at her in the moonlight. *She got it.* Without any sort of training or military background, she understood the importance of what had needed to be done.

Even more importantly, she had done it.

I still didn't like it.

She put a finger over my lips. "Is your mission really and truly over now? No other bad guys going to burst through here at any moment, guns blazing?"

I kissed her finger. "Martinez was the last one."

I could see the gleam in her eye. "Good. Then I'd like for you to make love to me. *Here.* I need you inside me, right now."

Chapter 25

Bethany

I didn't know how to explain the adrenaline that was rushing through my blood, but I didn't have to. I could tell Landon already knew what it was all about.

He spun me so I was against the tree, and his lips began working their way down my neck, stealing my breath. One hand slid down my thigh and pulled it up over his hip so he could press against me right where I wanted him to.

Everything was so complicated. I was still confused and more than a little pissed that Landon had used me for this mission. But if he had to lie to me, at least it was for a good reason.

Stopping human traffickers was the best of reasons. It was why I had rushed over to the auxiliary kitchen and dumped some sweets in a box. Because if Landon needed help, I wanted to be able to give it to him.

And because I couldn't stand the thought of what someone like Martinez might do to him. Landon had been trying to get on Martinez's plane, for God's sake. There were so many things that could've gone wrong—all ending with Landon's body being tossed over the Pacific.

So yeah, I wanted him to fuck me hard right up against this tree. For all the things that could've gone wrong but didn't. And most importantly because we'd just saved the day. I was giddy. And hot.

And already wet.

His lips moved against my throat as he lowered my leg and grabbed my panties under my skirt, sliding them down my legs. He unfastened his pants just enough for his hard length to spring free. I couldn't stop myself from wrapping my hand around him.

"Wildflower," he said through gritted teeth. "I don't have any protection with me."

"I'm on the pill," I responded without hesitation. "I'm okay if you are."

He leaned his forehead against mine, jerking as my fist closed harder around him. "Are you sure?"

"Very."

That SEAL speed again. Before I even guessed what he intended, he lifted me off the ground and pressed my back into the tree, fitting himself against me. And then he was inside me, stealing my breath and trapping me between himself and the rough wood.

"Landon." His name came out as a half sob.

I was so full of him. Fuller than I'd felt last night. He was so deep he felt like he was a part of me, and he hadn't moved yet.

He gathered my wrists in one hand and pinned them above my head. Leaning forward, he kissed his way along my jaw to my ear. "You like living dangerously, don't you?"

I couldn't breathe, much less answer, as he moved his hips—a slow, rolling movement that was everything and still not enough.

"Please," I whispered.

"Mmm." He nuzzled his cheek against mine. "I like that. Please, what?"

"Please more."

He rolled his hips again with agonizing slowness. He still held my wrists in one hand, the other supporting me. I was trapped and helpless. Pinned to the tree. He knew I wanted more—rough, fast—and deliberately wasn't giving it to me.

I squeezed down on him, and he groaned, thrusting in response. Two could play at this game.

I squeezed him again and moved my hips against his. But no matter what I did, he kept the smooth, steady pace. Every grinding movement brushed right against where I needed him, and pleasure rose like a tide that threatened to drown me.

Pulling against his hold, I wanted to move. I wanted to drag him against me and force him to move faster. "You're going to kill me," I breathed.

His low laugh sent goose bumps cascading down my whole body. My nipples hardened against his chest. He kissed me, never stopping that infernal, torturous movement that was sending me higher and holding me back all at the same time.

Delicious friction consumed me. Lost in the sensation, I couldn't keep my eyes open. I could barely keep myself from moaning loud enough to bring any passerby into our hidden area.

Out of nowhere, he let go of my hands and gripped my hips with a bruising force. He changed his motion, switching from a smooth roll to a deep stroke that hit my center so perfectly I saw white. He pulled back, almost all the way out, and slammed home.

Whereas the first rhythm wasn't enough, this was almost too much. I let out a sob that he caught with his mouth to keep me quiet.

Yes. This was what I'd wanted. He'd known it all along.

Pleasure splintered through me with each stroke—it felt as if I were breaking, with glorious light shining through the cracks. I was shaking, clenching down on him inside me, trying to hold on through every stroke. Every driving movement of his hips was a new beam of light.

"Yes, yes, yes." The words were a soundless chant as he continued to give me what I wanted over and over, my body meeting his thrust for thrust.

It was a celebration of being alive, of surviving danger, of finally knowing each other on a true equal level.

Landon made no sound as he moved inside me, but I could hear his breathing getting heavier, feel the tension racking his hard body as he got closer to release. He held my weight against the tree as if it was nothing, his hips picking up the pace and driving me over the edge.

My nails scored into his neck as pleasure crashed over me, stealing my breath. He whispered my name like it was a sacred prayer as he found his own release.

My body went limp in the delicious aftermath as he buried his face in the side of my neck, breathing in my scent. He still pinned me to the tree. My blouse was going to be ruined from scraping up against the wood, but I didn't care.

He finally moved back and lowered me to the ground. "That'll teach you not to put yourself in danger."

I laughed. "I don't know. I may not quite have learned my lesson."

He kissed me. "Then we'll have to get some more practice in. As long as it has nothing to do with Joaquin Martinez or Vincent Frey."

"Tomorrow is our last full day on the island. We better make the most of it."

He adjusted his pants then grabbed my underwear where they'd fallen to the ground and handed them to me. I used them to wipe myself off, then stuck them in my pocket.

He brushed my hair back from my face. I couldn't even imagine what sort of mess it was. "Definitely want to make the most of tomorrow. But I'm also hoping you'll be willing to see me once we get back home."

"Really?"

"I've been racking my brain to figure out how I could talk you into seeing me once we got back to real life. I didn't want to lie to you, but I couldn't tell the truth either. Now, that doesn't matter."

"There's still a lot I don't know about you."

He leaned his forehead against mine. "And much I don't know about you either. Difference is, now we've got time to learn each other. And believe me, I want to learn all of you."

By the time we made it back to the suite, my legs were a little shaky. "Look what you've done to me, I can hardly walk."

He grinned over at me as he opened the door. "As much as I'd like to take all the credit, that's your body coming down from the adrenaline."

I loved the feel of his hand at the small of my back as

we entered the room. "I think I might have to try a little more monkey tree sex to see if that's actually the case."

He winked. "I offer myself as tribute. In the name of science, of course."

This man. I thought I'd liked him before. But now that I knew he worked to stop criminals, I could feel my heart doing backflips.

I needed to give my heart a stern talking-to about how it had been less than a week and it was way too soon to be feeling this way.

Somehow I had a feeling my heart would have no interest in listening to reason.

I peeled off my clothes and got in the shower as Landon checked in with…whoever he checked in with. I wanted to ask for more details, and I would. But right now, I just wanted to relax.

Having him join me and pull me close under the steamy spray and hold me—a gentleman who let me have the hot water hitting me in the back—did not make my heart do any fewer gymnastics.

He was staring at me as we dried off.

"What?" I asked him. If he wanted more sex, I was going to have to tell him…*yes, please*. No matter how tired I was.

"Once my team hears how you thought of bringing desserts to get close to Martinez, you're probably going to get hired by law enforcement. It was a great idea. I don't think he suspected a thing."

I gave him a goofy grin. "It was the first thing I thought of that would give me a reason for showing up. Actually, you're lucky…"

Wait. I stopped drying.

"I'm damned well aware I was lucky you're so smart."

"No. I was going to say you're lucky because I ran over to the auxiliary kitchen, but I forgot my keys. The door happened to be unlocked."

He wrapped his towel around his waist. "Sounds like I was doubly lucky, then. If you'd had to come all the way back here then go to the kitchen again, you'd probably have been too late to help with Martinez."

I nodded vaguely, but that wasn't what was bothering me. "I know I locked the kitchen door when I left earlier. I was pissed at you because you hadn't set up the cake stands, and I decided I wanted to have it out with you. I am one hundred percent positive I locked the door."

His brows furrowed. "Okay, maybe the cleaning services came through? I'll still count myself lucky."

"I need to go lock the door. I won't sleep if I don't."

He nodded without argument. "I'll go with you."

I rushed to get dressed. All the good feelings that had been swimming around my belly had switched to dread.

Nobody should've been in that auxiliary kitchen except me. The resort staff had been very well aware of that fact —it was in my contract with them.

Landon was ready to go before me. He waited as I slipped on my shoes then grabbed my hand as we walked out the door.

We didn't talk on the way, but I knew he saw the open door to the kitchen at the same time as I did.

I didn't leave that open. I knew no matter how much of a hurry I'd been in to get to Landon with the treats box, there was no way I'd left that door open.

"You didn't do that," he muttered.

I was thankful I didn't have to explain, but I knew this wasn't good.

The notion was confirmed as I made it to the doorway.

I blinked as I took it all in. The cake stand I'd spent hours building was destroyed.

The door to the walk-in fridge was wide open.

And tomorrow's wedding cake was in pieces all over the floor.

Chapter 26

Bethany

I stood there and stared. I couldn't believe it. The cakes I had carefully crafted back at my shop and then painstakingly decorated earlier were lying in multiple pieces on the floor.

This had been deliberate. An earthquake strong enough to topple the entire resort wouldn't have done as much damage.

"I think I'm going to throw up," I said to Landon.

He was standing next to me, muttering curses. "This was done on purpose. We need to call security."

Security wasn't going to help. They might be able to eventually pinpoint who the culprit was, but it wasn't going to make any difference in the fact that there was now no wedding cake for a wedding taking place in eighteen hours.

"It doesn't matter who did this." My voice came out like a croak. "There's not going to be a wedding cake."

"Hey." He folded his hands around my arms. "It's going to be okay. We're going to figure this out."

I didn't know if he meant figure out who did it or figure out how to keep the wedding from being a disaster.

I gestured over at the cake stands that had been destroyed too. I couldn't even wrap my head around it all. "I don't know what I'm going to—"

A screech cut me off.

"Oh my God, Bethany, what have you done?"

Landon and I both turned to see Mina standing in the doorway. Her eyes were huge.

"You sabotaged the wedding cake, didn't you? I *knew* it. I knew you would do something like this. I tried to tell everyone, but no one would listen to me. Wait until Aunt Patricia sees this. I tried to warn her."

I swallowed a sob. That was what everyone in the family was going to think—that I had deliberately ruined the wedding cake. And I had no way of proving otherwise.

Landon crossed his arms over his chest. "What are you doing here, Mina? It's after midnight."

She didn't falter a bit. "I couldn't sleep. I had a bad feeling about tomorrow, and now I know why." She already had her phone out and was texting somebody. "I can't believe you would do this, Bethany. I just can't believe it."

I wanted to cover my ears so I didn't hear her accusation. I wanted to close my eyes and hide forever at the mess in front of me. I had ruined my sister's wedding even though I hadn't done anything.

"Step outside, Mina," Landon said.

"Why? I didn't do anything wrong. It's your *fiancée*." She spat the word. "Aunt Patricia is on her way. I can't wait to see her face."

"Out," Landon growled and pointed toward the door. Mina was actually laughing as she left.

"She did it," Landon said under his breath. "There's no way in hell she just happened to be walking by right when we discovered this. She's been waiting."

I rubbed my hands up and down my arms to ward off a chill even though it wasn't cold. "Probably."

It didn't matter even if she had. It didn't change the fact that there was no cake for tomorrow.

Landon gently cupped my elbow. "Come outside. There's nothing you can do in here right at this second. We'll call somebody, get it cleaned up, and then we're going to come up with a game plan."

I blinked up at him. "There's no way I can recreate that cake in eighteen hours."

"But you can do something. It may not be the cake you've been envisioning, but I have no doubt you can make something beautiful for your sister."

Not that would feed hundreds of people and wouldn't look like it hadn't been bought at the local supermarket. I could only hope Mother hadn't actually canceled the reservation she had with the resort catering. They would have a team who could make it happen. I only had me.

I was still in a daze as Landon led me outside. A resort employee had come by to see what all Mina's screeching was about, and Landon requested that they send someone to clean up the mess and to help us figure out what was going on.

A few minutes later, Patricia arrived. Right behind her was my mother.

Mina shook her head slowly. "Aunt Patricia, Mrs. Thompson, look at what Bethany did. She sabotaged the wedding cakes just like I said she would."

I looked at Mother. "I didn't do this."

"Where were you?" Landon asked Mina. "Where have you been for the past few hours?"

She crossed her arms over her chest, and her smile got smug. "I was with five of my friends and surrounded by multiple people on the dance floor at the oceanside gazebo. I'm pretty sure you can't blame this on me. Where was Bethany?"

"She was with me," Landon said.

"Ah." Mina nodded in a dramatic fashion. "She was with *you*, the surprise fiancé who happened to show up at the last minute, that none of us had ever heard of or seen. What a coincidence."

I looked at my mother again. "I didn't do this, Mother. I promise."

I couldn't believe the words that came out of her mouth. "I believe you."

Neither could Mina.

"What?" she screeched. "I've been telling you this might happen all week, and now it has, and you're not even going to believe that she did it to herself?"

Mother turned to Mina. "My daughter has spent all week providing impeccable desserts for the guests and building up the name of her business. It would be counterproductive for her to destroy the wedding cake right as she is at the pinnacle of making such a name for herself. Bethany may be many things, but stupid is not one of them. She didn't do this."

I finally felt like some of the weight that had been on my chest was lifted. Mother believed me. She *believed* me.

"Thank you," I whispered.

"No need to thank me." She raised an eyebrow. "There's still no wedding cake, but I know you didn't do this to yourself."

Faint praise, but I would take it. The important thing was she knew I hadn't done this.

"Aunt Patricia." Mina turned to the other woman.

"You can't be as blind as Mrs. Thompson, can you? Surely you can see what's happening here—"

Before Patricia could answer, a wild sound came out from the darkness. We all watched as Mina was tackled to the ground by some screaming banshee.

Christiana.

"You destroyed my wedding cake!" Christiana grabbed Mina by the collar and rolled her over.

"Christiana!" Mother, Patricia, and I all yelled at the same time. I couldn't even believe my eyes.

"You destroyed my wedding cake!" My tiny little sister was on top of Mina, pulling her hair. "I'm about to show you Bridezilla, bitch."

"Christiana, what are you doing?" If my mother had had her pearls on, she would've been clutching them. "Mina didn't destroy your cake. We don't know who did. She has an alibi. Stop this right now!"

Christiana was still straddling Mina. She grabbed her shirt by the collar and pulled Mina's face so that they were only inches apart.

"You shouldn't have sent that video, moron. Your little posse is not smart enough to keep things a secret."

Mina's face went pale.

"That's right," Christiana continued. "Whoever you paid to destroy the cake sent you proof, right? And then you couldn't keep it to yourself, so you sent it to your friends. And guess who got a hold of it?"

Christiana grabbed Mina's hair at the back of the head and slammed her head back. Mina was sputtering and trying to get a word in edgewise, but Christiana wasn't letting her.

Beside me, Landon chuckled. "And I thought the danger had left the island already."

"We should do something," I whispered. "I don't want Christiana to go to jail for killing Mina."

Landon walked over much more slowly than I knew he was capable of, allowing Christiana to get a couple more hits in, before he picked her up by the waist and hauled her off Mina.

"That's enough, slugger. We don't want you to get arrested."

Simon came running in, along with my dad and his. Then resort security showed up, resulting in mass chaos. Everyone was talking at once. Christiana was still screaming at Mina, and Simon was having to hold her back from doing further physical damage.

I just stood there trying to figure out what I was going to do. Because no matter how much of a bitch Mina was, or how impressive my sister was when she really got angry, it didn't alter the fact that we still didn't have a wedding cake.

The cacophony got louder. Mina was protesting her innocence, now blaming Landon. Nobody cared. Security was trying to figure out what was going on, and both the bride's and groom's parents were looking about as dazed as I felt.

This was going to take a while to sort out. And more importantly, it wasn't my problem.

Mina's plan had backfired. No one believed that I had destroyed my own work. Their faith in me gave me the focus and adrenaline I needed.

I turned to Landon. "It's time for me to get to work."

I had a cake to make and a very limited number of hours to make it.

∾

It took a couple of hours, but we finally got the kitchen cleaned up with the help of the resort staff. The manager had offered to wake some of the catering team members to help me make the cakes, but I declined.

We still weren't sure exactly who Mina had hired to do her dirty work. There could still be someone she was paying off. The last thing I wanted was the entire guest list coming down with food poisoning from the cakes.

By the time the kitchen was cleaned up, I still didn't have much of a game plan. The multitiered fairy-tale castle design with geode towers was no longer an option. Neither were the six different flavors the cake was originally supposed to be.

So the guests would be getting my most unique flavor: vanilla chai cake. Even people not normally a fan of chai raved about it. And it was a tribute to Landon. His eyes had already lit up when he saw the cinnamon.

I needed to get the cakes made and in the oven as soon as possible. Cake for three hundred people was a huge undertaking.

Outside was still mayhem as I began to gather ingredients. Everyone was talking about whether to arrest Mina or just get her off the island, but I didn't stick around to figure out what happened. Landon didn't either; he stayed by my side and helped me pull ingredients from the main kitchen.

Landon was going to be working all night too, trying to make a stand out of all the broken pieces currently lying outside. Even with both of us working at full speed, I wasn't holding out much hope.

Christiana came in and grabbed an apron.

"What are you doing?" I asked her.

"I'm going to help. I don't want to be any part of that circus out there, and I think you could use all the help you can get."

Simon walked in behind her. "Me too."

I was going to argue, but the fact was, I did need all the help I could get.

I turned to my sister and cupped her cheeks. "No way, hulk bride. You're getting married in just over sixteen hours. You don't need to stay here and help. You need to go back and rest."

Christiana didn't back down. "I'm not going to be able to rest. Adrenaline. If you only knew what it was like to do something dangerous and crazy."

Yeah, if I only knew. I wondered what she would say if I told her having fantastic sex against a tree might help her work that adrenaline out of her system.

"Okay. Just for a little while." I put them to work measuring ingredients for the cake batter, as I attempted to formulate a plan for decorating based on what we had available.

I wasn't surprised to find Christiana wavering on her feet after an hour. I caught Simon's eye and gestured toward her. He nodded. She needed to be in bed.

I took the spatula out of her hand. "Time for bed. It's the night before your wedding, and I can't be responsible for you looking like a zombie tomorrow."

"But…"

I cupped her cheeks. "I promise I will handle this for you, my sister."

"I know you will." She kissed me softly on the lips. "You're the best sister ever."

Simon stepped closer and wrapped an arm around her shoulders. "Thank you, Bethany, for everything. For understanding, and for going well above and beyond the call of duty. Whatever cake we have tomorrow, we'll be thankful for."

Christiana smiled up at him. "The important thing is that we'll be married."

"Out of here, you two." I pointed at the door with my spatula. Simon led her out with a protective arm wrapped around her waist.

"Those two are going to make it," Landon said from behind me.

"I think so. The love is real. That's the most important thing."

"Yes, it is."

I turned to face him, running an exhausted hand down my face. Christiana wasn't the only one who was crashing. "Whether they have a cake for their wedding big enough for everyone remains to be seen."

Multiple layers were already in the oven, but there was still so much that needed to be done.

"We'll get it done." He kissed me softly.

I didn't even have the energy to plaster a smile on my face and lie all chirpily to him. Sure, we would have something done. But I didn't want it to be too small or too plain.

I wanted the wedding cake to be reflective of what Christiana and Simon felt for each other.

And while I didn't regret sending them to get rest, the fact was, I couldn't get this done on my own. Even with Landon's help. And he'd already turned back to the stands he needed to piece together.

I stared at the mess all around me. This wasn't how I normally worked. My shop was neat and orderly.

I sucked in a deep breath. I wasn't going to fall apart now. There wasn't time.

I'd built Slice of Heaven by myself, and I'd do this by myself too. Even if the prognosis was grim.

The main set of cakes was out of the oven and in the

chiller, and I was in the process of making the frosting when I heard a timid knock on the kitchen door.

"Come in!" I yelled, not stopping my work. No more breaks.

"Is there some way that I could be of assistance?"

I turned, eyes wide, to find Patricia standing in the kitchen doorway. She was wearing plain black trousers, a white sweater, and low heels. It was as informally dressed as I had ever seen her.

Patricia was wearing *work clothes*.

"I don't really have anything glamorous for you to do. At this point, it's tedious, messy, and hard work."

She walked farther into the room. "Believe it or not, I can do hard work and tedious. I would like to help if you'll allow me to, especially since it was my family member who got us into this predicament to begin with."

For the first time in hours, a little bit of hope trickled through my system. Patricia was nothing if not methodical. She could be trusted to make the frosting, which would allow me to start decorating.

"It's not your fault, but yes, I'll take the help if you can give it. Thank you."

She smiled, and it seemed quite genuine. "Thank *you*."

It was hard to believe how efficiently Patricia worked. She listened to my instructions and didn't complain at all, just went to it.

Landon had left to go find needed cake stand parts from the resort maintenance team. I worked side by side with Patricia for hours. We both worked hard.

The sun was starting to rise, and I could feel fatigue plaguing my entire body when more unexpected help arrived.

"I have double espresso for everyone, and we're here to work." My mother and father walked in.

I blinked, then took the steaming cup with gratitude. "Thank you."

"Thank *you*." Mom echoed Patricia's earlier statement with the same emotion, then reached over and kissed my forehead. "I'm proud to be your mother."

Tears filled my eyes, and one leaked out. My mother caught it with her finger. "Save those for the wedding. Right now, put us to work."

I did. And for the first time, I had hope we were going to get it done to the level of beauty I'd envisioned. There were too many people in this tiny kitchen determined to make it so.

A few minutes later, I looked up to find Landon standing in the doorway with the tools he needed, smiling at the little workforce that had been created here in the auxiliary kitchen.

My family had shown up when I needed them most.

Chapter 27

Bethany

My sister might have made a pretty remarkable MMA fighter last night, but today, she made a truly breathtaking bride.

The wedding went off without a hitch. Landon and I finished the cakes and the stands and had them in place at the reception about an hour before I needed to go get ready. It wasn't as fancy—would never be the elaborate cake I'd originally had planned—but it still tasted great.

And even more, it was made with love. Not just love from me, but from the family members who'd come together to make it happen. Without them, there would've been no cake. Mother, Patricia, and I had all shot smiles at one another as the cake had been served. Everyone loved it, including the bride and groom. What could have been a disaster ended up being a triumph.

Mina was gone. She'd been taken off the island, and I already felt less stress knowing she was nowhere around.

Nobody was going to press charges, but I had a feeling Patricia would go out of her way to make Mina's life miserable. Probably worse than being arrested, and Mina deserved every bit of it.

Exhaustion was catching up with me. What a crazy thirty-six-hour window it had been. First, making love with Landon, then thinking he wasn't interested in me, then dealing with the Martinez situation, and working all night on the cake. I was ready to fall where I stood, but instead, I was in my gold dress and heels, watching my sister dance with her new husband.

Landon showed up at my elbow and extended the flute of champagne. I'd been enjoying his company all night—he'd been by my side almost every minute.

"Thank you." I smiled up at him, trying not to be completely overcome by how he looked in his tuxedo. "I'll only have a couple of sips so you won't have to catch me as I fall on my face."

He trailed a finger down my cheek. "If you fell on your face right now, you'd still be the superhero who saved the day twice in the last twenty-four hours."

I shrugged. "I had help, especially with the cakes. Nobody wanted to see the wedding ruined but Mina."

"The help showed up because they believed in *you*. You'd already won your parents and the Carters over with your hard work and talent all week. Their helping was a response to that."

"I'm just glad everything went smoothly tonight. I'd half convinced myself there would be a problem. Don't they say bad things come in threes?"

He gave a wry smile. "With as many times as I've seen bad things come in way more than threes, let's just happily accept two this time."

I clinked my glass of champagne against his. "Deal. I'm too tired to borrow trouble."

"Are you too tired to dance with me?"

I cupped his granite jaw with my free hand. "Never."

He took our flutes and set them on a tray, and then he led me out onto the floor, pulling me close for a slow dance even though the music was more upbeat.

I looked up at him, my heart flipping over itself as he smiled at me—the most authentic one I'd seen from him since we'd met. Those dimples were out in full force, but this smile was different. Warm and tender.

"What?" he asked.

"I like this smile. Your megawatt grin is a sight to behold, but this one is…different."

He brought my fingers to his lips. "That's because this one is real. And just for you."

He danced with me every dance for the rest of the evening, keeping me in his arms like he couldn't stand for me not to be there.

In a lot of ways, this was our new start, a chance to get to know each other. The *real* each other, without any lies or secrets between us. I hated that we had to leave the island tomorrow, but I believed him when he said that he wanted this to continue once we got home. I did too.

About an hour later, we sent Christiana and Simon off with a wave of sparklers. I knew my parents would leave the party open for as long as anybody wanted to stay, but I'd had enough.

"Do you want to walk with me on the beach since it's our last night?" Landon asked. "I know you're tired, so I understand if you just want to get to bed."

I could sleep once I got home. There was nothing more I wanted than a stroll with him on our beach.

"That sounds great," I said, then spoiled it by letting out a huge yawn.

He laughed. "I don't think you're going to make it. How about if I go get us both a cup of coffee?"

"Perfect." Even coffee wouldn't keep me awake for long, but it would keep me awake long enough to steal some kisses—maybe more—with him. "I'll meet you down on the beach."

I kicked off my heels as I walked from the outdoor reception venue into the sand with a sigh of relief. I walked until my feet touched the water, and I looked out at the moon, shining down on the Pacific.

In some ways, this week had been the hardest of my life. I was looking forward to getting back to my bakery and normalcy. But no matter what, my *normal* had changed. I was leaving here with a lot more people in my life. Not just Landon, but my parents and sister.

I saw the slight shadow move behind me. Landon had been quicker than I thought. I turned to smile, but a hand reached and covered my mouth and yanked me to the side.

Before I could figure out what was going on, I was being dragged down toward the isolated part of the beach, near the cliffs. It took a second for panic to set in, but once it did, I began to fight—clawing at the hand covering my face and jerking my weight from side to side.

The person had to be a man. He was much bigger and stronger than me. I tried to bite his hand. I needed to get a scream out, but he clocked me in the head with his fist, and everything started to spin.

"Shut the fuck up, or I'll kill you right here."

Through the haze, I recognized the voice. *Who was it?*

He continued dragging me down toward the empty part of the beach. I fought harder to get away. If he planned to kill me, I couldn't let him get me any more isolated.

I kicked back as hard as I could, but my bare feet didn't do much damage. I tried to headbutt him, but that got me a fist in the gut. All the air flew out of my body, and pain took its place. My weight sagged as I stopped trying to fight and started just trying to survive.

By the time I could get in enough oxygen to start fighting again, he had me right where I hadn't wanted to let him get me—in the isolated, cliff section of the beach.

No one would come this way. Even Landon would assume if I'd started walking without him, I'd gone the other way.

The man punched me in the gut again, right before throwing me to the ground. I was too busy trying to breathe to scramble away. He ripped me up by my hair, stuffed a gag in my mouth, and tied my hands in behind me.

Through the pain, I blinked up at him and finally got a good look.

Fanshawe. That asshole from the bar.

He got right up in my face. "I bet you're wondering what I'm doing here, aren't you, bitch? Your *friend* got me back on the island and paid me to destroy your precious cakes. She said it would be the perfect way to get revenge on both you and your boyfriend, who got me fired."

I tried to scramble away, but he yanked me back by my hair. "But it didn't work, did it? Everybody still loves you, and the wedding was a success. Mina will roll over on me the first chance she gets."

I looked around, but no one was nearby. It was just the rocky beach at our back and copses of trees all around us. No one would come here. Was Landon back from the coffee yet? Even if he was, he wouldn't know which direction I'd gone.

Fanshawe saw me looking around. "You like this place? Pretty secluded, isn't it? We're hidden from sight from everyone. The trees give us cover almost all the way to the water, but I can see if anybody's coming."

He bent close to me, and I scooted back, making him laugh. "I'm sure your boyfriend's going to try to save you, but it's not going to work this time. As a matter of fact, I'm done playing by everyone else's rules. Time to do *me*. I'll prove to Mr. Frey that he should've kept me around."

I let out a sob behind my gag as Fanshawe pulled out a gun with a silencer on the end.

He was going to kill Landon.

I had to warn him. I had to do *something* besides stay here trussed up like a fucking turkey.

I fell over to the side and Fanshawe laughed again, but I used the ground to get the gag out of my mouth far enough that I could scream.

And I did, as loud and as long as I could.

Fanshawe let out a curse, and the next thing I knew, his fist crashed into my face. Agony exploded, and everything faded to black.

Chapter 28

Landon

I grinned as I got the coffee from the elaborate machine in the resort lobby. Bethany was so exhausted she was about to fall down on her face, but she was willing to keep on trooping despite it.

The amount of grit I'd seen from her in the past twenty-four hours would put many of my Special Forces brothers to shame. She'd rolled up her sleeves—literally and figuratively—and worked the problem. Solved the problem.

Saved the day.

I'd only been half kidding when I'd told her law enforcement might try to recruit her. They'd probably try to get her to do double duty, baker and undercover operative.

I chuckled as I filled the second cup. Actually, that wasn't a terrible idea. She could probably get into places a normal agent couldn't, just by waving a box of her sweets under the bad guys' noses.

Not that I was letting her near any more bad guys.

As much as I enjoyed this tropical paradise, I was looking forward to getting back to the mainland and courting Bethany properly. Flowers and dates and long, long sessions in bed learning every inch of that beautiful body.

I got the coffees, adding sugar to mine and cream to hers, and headed out to the beach, but I didn't see her. I turned back and looked around the patio. I wouldn't have been surprised if she'd curled up on one of the chaise loungers and fallen asleep.

Going all night without sleeping was par for the course for me, but not for her.

And if she was asleep, I'd be happy to dump the coffee and carry her back to our room for the remaining hours we had here. Even if it was just to hold her while she slept.

But she wasn't there or back at the wedding celebrations that were winding down. I looked at my phone in case I'd missed a message from her, but there was nothing.

Now I was getting a little worried.

I hurried to the other side of the patio to look in the gardens, in case in both our exhaustion we'd misunderstood where we were meeting. None of the people strolling among the beautiful plants and flowers was Bethany.

I set down the coffee, my senses going on high alert. Something wasn't right. My gut had been nagging me about a problem through the whole wedding, but I'd ignored it, blaming the malevolent feeling on exhaustion and adrenaline from last night. There wasn't anyone left on the island who meant anyone harm.

I wasn't sure about that at all anymore. And every second I couldn't find Bethany had me more concerned.

I ran back to the beach, looking left and right. There were tracks going in both directions. I started off left, toward the main drag with soft sands and calmer waters, but that instinct in my gut had me turning back in the direction of the copse of trees.

That instinct had saved my life more than once when I was in the SEALs. I'd ignored it the day Wavy had shot me, arguing nothing bad could happen with her, and I'd ended up with a hole in my chest.

I wasn't ignoring that feeling anymore. Something wasn't right here.

A little farther ahead, I saw some sand that had been disturbed. My sense of unease intensified. Two dark spots on the beach made me rush forward to make sure I was seeing what I thought I was.

Bethany's heels. *Shit*. She wouldn't have left her shoes in the middle of the sand.

I peered toward the group of trees in the gathering darkness. I couldn't see that far ahead, but every instinct was pulling me that way. If I was taking someone from the beach, that's where I would head. The person in the trees had the tactical advantage—they could see someone approaching and pick them off. I was far enough away right now. But if I moved around the bend in the sand, I'd be in view.

A muffled scream from the direction of the trees proved my gut correct at the same time it drove a spike of terror straight through my heart.

That was Bethany.

I froze, taking in my options. I couldn't run toward her without getting myself, and maybe her, killed. The only options were to circle around from the trees, which would take time I didn't have or...

I looked out toward the rough waves of the Pacific in

the dim light of the moon. My SEAL training had been in this very ocean. I knew how to swim these waters, had done it many times throughout my extensive training, even if that had been years ago.

Hell, even if I'd never dipped a toe in these waters, I'd still do it. Bethany needed me.

Within seconds, I had stripped out of my tuxedo. In my boxers, I ran for the water, pushing as far as I could on foot, then swimming even farther out, gritting my teeth against the icy bite. Once I was far enough that the waves hid me, I turned so I was parallel to the shore and swam with sure, even strokes, coming up for air every few moments to check how far I'd gone and to see if the trees had neared yet.

It wasn't long before I saw them. A man stood over a dark shape on the ground, presumably Bethany. He looked toward the sand—the direction I would've been coming from if I'd stayed on the beach. I kept swimming, going farther than I needed to, checking the man often. He didn't turn or even consider the fact that I could come up behind him in the water.

I pivoted toward the shore, easing back my strokes so I was more hidden in the ocean but still giving me as much speed as possible. I stayed low until the water was at knee-depth then slowly rose up out of it, my eyes on the man the entire time. I moved quickly to the tree line, ignoring the cold and lack of covering for my feet. The sound of the beach obscured any noise I made walking over the large leaves.

It didn't matter anyway; he obviously wasn't expecting me from this direction. When he turned his head, I saw who it was. *Fanshawe.*

I had no idea how he'd gotten back on the island. I guess Frey hadn't killed him as I'd half suspected.

As I got closer, Bethany wiggled on the ground. Relief spread through me to know she was alive. Until I saw she had blood all over her face.

Rage thrummed through my whole body. He'd *hurt* Bethany. Sweet, kind, gentlehearted Bethany.

Now *I* wanted to kill the fucker. He sure as hell wasn't going to get the chance to hurt her again.

I strode out of the trees and up behind Fanshawe silently. Bethany's eyes widened slightly when she saw me, and unfortunately, he picked up on it. He whirled around, gun in hand.

For a second, I froze, hurled back into the past, as I stared at the barrel pointed right at my chest.

Fanshawe was completely different from Wavy. This beach was different from the penthouse apartment where she'd shot me. Everything about this situation was different.

But that bullet would feel the same as it ripped through my flesh and bone and organs. I didn't have to imagine the agony of the burn, the pain that swallowed you whole. I lived with the memory every day.

And right now, that memory threatened to drown everything else.

"I'm going to enjoy killing you and making her watch."

The rubber band of reality snapped back into place at his words. Instead of monologuing, Fanshawe should've killed me while he'd had the chance.

He wouldn't get another.

Taking advantage of the fact that he expected me to mutter some response to his asinine comment, I instead moved a step to the diagonal. Mostly to confuse him but also so that muzzle wasn't pointed right at me.

He swung toward me, as I expected, but this time, I was ready. Using his momentum, I pulled him toward me, yanking the weapon from his grip. I unloaded it in a split second, dropping the cartridge case into the sand and tossing the unloaded gun several yards away.

He used the opportunity to swing at my face and got in a hit hard enough to jerk my head around to the side, but I stayed on my feet. He smirked at me as I spat out blood, obviously thinking he had the upper hand.

"You're not catching me off guard in a hotel hallway this time, motherfucker," he muttered. "You got me fired. Nobody believed you attacked me first. Now you'll really see what I'm capable of."

I shifted my stance so I was lighter on my feet. There was no way in hell I was going down when Bethany was injured in the sand. I would not leave her unprotected against him.

Fanshawe was bigger than me, but that didn't stop me or worry me at all. I knew exactly how to handle him—he'd already shown me his weaknesses this week.

I let him get in another punch to my gut—doubling myself over at the blow. My response wasn't fake, but it wasn't the full truth either.

He grabbed me by the hair and ripped my head up so we were eye to eye. "Not so tough now, are you?"

"Tough enough to take an asshole who can't even keep a two-bit security job because he runs his mouth so much." I headbutted him.

I watched fury light his eyes, exactly what I wanted. I dodged his next set of blows easily. The angrier he got, the more he telegraphed what move he was about to make. I was easily able to avoid each hit.

"What's the matter, Fanshawe? Standing in the unemployment line zap all your energy?"

He dove for me, and all I had to do was step out of the way, let him get up, and do the exact same thing again. He was too angry to make any sort of smart blows at this point. I was careful to stay clear of his fists—his blows might be wild, but they would have the overwhelming power of his anger behind them.

I didn't have to beat Fanshawe. As he'd done all week, he was beating himself.

Bethany's whimper from over to the side jerked me back into the fight. I didn't know how injured she was.

It was time to stop playing. This time when he came at me, I attacked instead of defended. Three blows sent him to his knees, dazed.

I dropped beside Bethany and untied her hands and removed the gag from her mouth. "Hey, Wildflower. You okay?"

"Yeah." She was coherent but had obviously taken a couple of hits to the face from Fanshawe. Behind us, he was staggering to his feet again, fists raised in the air.

I stroked a finger down her swollen cheek. "Stay right here."

The gun and bullets were within reach, and never had I been more tempted to use them on an unarmed man. But that wasn't who I was and, more importantly, wasn't who I wanted Bethany to see me as.

That didn't mean I wasn't going to beat the shit out of Fanshawe for daring to hurt her.

I didn't say another word to him, didn't antagonize him, or wait for him to try to hit me.

And I didn't fight fair.

I got in two hits to his kidneys I knew would be particularly painful, followed by a jab that broke his nose. His head rocked back, and I spun, bringing my foot around in a quick roundhouse kick that had him flying through the air and landing unconscious on the ground. I had to tamp down the need to continue pummeling the unconscious man.

Me, the person known for getting along with others so well.

Not someone who hurt Bethany.

I let out a breath and reeled in my anger—even though it took every bit of my training and focus. I took the rope he'd used on Bethany and tied his hands together, then tied his hands to his feet.

Gathering Bethany in my arms, I checked her over carefully. Her right eye was beginning to swell, and up close, I saw the blood had come from her nose.

"I'm so sorry," I whispered. "I should've been here for you."

She gave me a tremulous grin. "It's okay," she whispered. "You're here now, and that's all that matters."

She was right. I was here now, and I'd be damned if I was going anywhere any time soon.

We lay back, wrapped together. We'd have to get up in a minute, go find my clothes, call security, do all the stuff.

But for right now, I just wanted to hold her. The woman who would always be sweeter than anything she could ever bake.

"I think I might need a vacation from my vacation," she whispered.

"Wherever that ends up being, I hope I'm invited."

"As long as you don't bring any undercover work."

I kissed her forehead gently. "Deal."

Chapter 29

Landon
    One Year Later

"Holy hell. You have got to marry Bethany." Tristan stuffed another of the individual cakes into his mouth. "Or, on second thought, don't. Then maybe I'll have a chance with her."

I looked over at Bethany, who was standing by Bronwyn Rourke, former Zodiac Tactical employee, both of them calmly supervising the distribution of the desserts throughout tonight's events.

"I wonder if Bethany will let us have a secret wedding like this one if I do." I said it as if I wasn't planning to marry Bethany no matter what type of wedding we had. I'd settle for anything from a Vegas quickie to a grandiose affair like Christiana's. As long as Bethany said yes.

Tristan grinned at me over yet another tiny cake, each of which had been painstakingly crafted with edible paint on the top to resemble one of Wavy Bollinger's colorful abstract paintings.

We'd all been brought here tonight in Denver to celebrate the anniversary of Wavy's first art show eighteen months ago. It had been in this very same building. Since then, she'd become famous, her art selling for more than I could comfortably afford.

She deserved it. She'd taken a tragedy that would've broken other people and turned it into compelling pieces of creative genius.

She now had shows all over the world, but she hadn't had one back here in Denver since the first. Hadn't been back in this building at all, as far as I knew. The building where she'd shot me.

So, I'd been thrilled she was having another art show here.

Except it had all been a ruse.

I should've known something was up with this *show* when every person who arrived was all friends and family. Zodiac teammates from all over the world, plus damn near the entire town of Oak Creek, Wyoming, where Wavy's two brothers—Finn and Baby—both had ties to Linear Tactical.

Tonight's show had contained no press, no strangers, no art critics. Just the people Ian and Wavy held most dear.

Ian had grabbed me the second I'd set foot inside the door. "I need you, Libra. Emergency."

If I'd had a weapon on me, I would've reached for it. But instead, my friend dragged me into a side room, set up with rows of chairs and an exquisite arch made of flowers at the front. The room was surrounded on all sides by pieces of Wavy's riveting art.

"Whoa, who's getting married?" I joked.

"Wavy and I are." He clapped me on the shoulder. "Need you to be the best man."

"What?" I knew my eyes were bugging out of my head, but I couldn't stop them. I pulled Ian in for a hard hug. "You son of a bitch. Good for you."

Ian was beaming. "I didn't want a big wedding. Neither did Wavy. And when she agreed to finally stop running and marry me a few months ago, we decided something like this would be perfect. We just had to get the details in place."

I couldn't even be mad at him. "Damn well is perfect. And I'm glad this building was where you chose to make it happen."

"We thought about Oak Creek, but this building was the start of everything—good and bad—for Wavy and me as a couple. We wanted to rewrite what happened here as something joyful and beautiful. That's if you're okay with it. If not, we'll shut this room off and just have a party."

I pulled him in for a second hug. "I couldn't be happier you're making your start as husband and wife here."

"I told Wavy you would feel that way."

I grinned at him. "You be sure to tell her that if it weren't for this building and getting shot, I wouldn't have been the one who got sent to that island a year ago. I would never have met Bethany. Damn well worth the bullet."

Thirty minutes later, to the surprise of all the guests, I stood beside Ian as he married the love of his life.

And then the party had really gotten started and was still going now.

I'd meant what I'd said to him about getting shot being worth it. It now seemed like a small price to pay for the privilege of being able to call Bethany mine.

As soon as we'd gotten back from Santa Catalina, I'd

started making up for the false start in our relationship. First thing I'd done was relocate myself permanently to Zodiac's LA office. Tristan had gotten to see more of me than he'd ever wanted to.

But living there had enabled me to court Bethany in the way I wanted to: slowly and with determination. Proving to her that she was worth it. Because she damned sure was.

In those early days, we'd gone on dates with lots of romance and no sex because I'd wanted to make sure she understood I was in this for much more than just her luscious body.

That had lasted for about two weeks.

By that point, I almost hadn't recognized myself. I was so desperate for her I'd dragged her out of a movie halfway through and taken her back to her house. I'd barely gotten her inside before taking her hard and fast on the kitchen table. Then another half dozen times the rest of the night. Neither of us could walk properly the next day.

I'd spent every night with her since.

I'd gotten worried about eight months ago when it became obvious I needed to return to Denver to run the Zodiac office here. Ian was spending more and more time in New York with Wavy, and I was needed. But I didn't want to be away from Bethany.

Her parents had stepped in and helped save the day. Oliver had invested in a second bakery for Bethany. So for the past six months, she'd alternated her time between two successful bakeries—the original Slice of Heaven in California, and the new Slice of Bliss here in Denver.

To Bethany's delight, Angelique had also gotten involved with the business and helped Bethany find the staff she needed to keep each bakery running smoothly.

Michele managed the California shop, along with two full-time bakers Bethany had found and then Angelique had persuaded to join the team.

And here in Denver, another surprising professional ally had popped up: former Zodiac employee Bronwyn Rourke. Like Wavy, Bronwyn had had her life nearly destroyed by Mosaic, and she'd been slowly putting it back together. She was no longer capable of active duties for Zodiac and was taking literature classes at a local college.

Ended up, part-time work at Slice of Bliss was perfect for her. And I hadn't been surprised for a second when Bethany's gentle presence and kind spirit meant the two women had become friends.

Sarge McEwan, as always, had quietly supported Bronwyn in what she wanted to do—encouraging her to branch out in her activities, but right there to sweep her up when she needed him. The love between the two of them was almost tangible.

I'd like to think the same was true for Bethany and me. She didn't need my overt protection like Bronwyn did from Sarge. But in all the other ways, we needed each other just as much. And more every day.

I caught her eye and smiled.

But she didn't smile back. In fact, she looked away, almost guilty.

What was that about? Everyone was enjoying her desserts—no surprise—and Bethany had rolled with the punches when the art show had turned into a wedding.

Or at least I thought she had. I'd been so busy with best man duties, I hadn't had a chance to talk to her since the nuptials had occurred.

She and Bronwyn had been working hard all week on those individualized cakes mimicking Wavy's paintings. Angelique had even come in to help, and I could've sworn

I'd seen Sarge with a paintbrush in his hand when I'd stopped by the bakery a couple nights ago to drag Bethany home to bed.

The cakes worked perfectly, even if it was for a wedding rather than a show. But once again when I caught Bethany's eye, she looked away.

What the hell?

I ran through our recent conversations in my head. We hadn't had any fights or disagreements. But now that I thought about it, she had been a little distant all week. I thought it had been the pressure for this event—Bethany was still building a name for herself.

But maybe it was something else entirely.

Tristan was still standing next to me making near-sex noises about the cakes as I studied Bethany. While I understood the sentiment, my mind was now focused on other things—like what the hell was going on with her.

I needed to find out what that was.

I glanced over at Tristan. "Don't gain thirty pounds tonight before you take over bodyguard duty of whatever movie star you're guarding next." I knew Zodiac had been contracted for bodyguard work of a well-known actress.

Tristan rolled his eyes. "Don't remind me. I've found that actresses are great with their public personas but tend to be much less likable when you get to know them in reality."

I chuckled. "Then hopefully you don't have to talk to her much and can just stop her stalker."

"That's the plan. Although I'd rather be undercover with Callum."

Callum had infiltrated Joaquin Martinez's organization in Vegas. We were both worried about him since the mole situation in his department had never been completely eradicated. He was having to do a lot of dangerous work without good backup.

"I wish someone had his back," I said. "Although you need to watch yours too with this stalker situation."

Tristan shot me a half grin. "Not my first day, boss."

"I know, asshole. Be careful all the same."

Tristan was shoving another mini-cake into his mouth as I headed off toward Bethany. She was now standing over to the side of the room by herself.

When she saw me, she rushed back into the catering setup room. She was actually avoiding me.

Oh, hell no.

I knew this building much better than she did and ducked around the other side of the coat check room and headed her off at the pass. She was looking over her shoulder the other way and ran straight into my chest.

"Running away from me, Wildflower?"

"Landon!" Her laugh was anything but natural. "No, of course not. I just... I just needed to do some things for the bakery. For the art show." Her face blanched. "For the wedding."

I narrowed my eyes and ran a hand down her arm. At least she didn't pull away from my touch. That was a good sign, right?

"You want to tell me what's going on?"

"Nothing," she whispered, eyes dropping to the floor.

"Hey." I tried to pull her close to me, but she stiffened. "Bethany, what's wrong? Is it something with your desserts?"

"No." She shook her head. "Everyone is enjoying those."

"Of course they are." As expected.

"I didn't like it." Her voice was so low I could barely hear it.

"You didn't like what? The sweets you made?"

"No."

My heart squeezed into a knot in my chest. She didn't like what? Us? Is that why she'd been distant the last few days? Had she changed her mind about us and didn't know how to tell me?

I tilted her chin up with my finger. The tears in her eyes had fear clutching my heart even more. "Talk to me, Wildflower."

"I can't do it anymore." She turned and ran into the coat check closet behind me.

I stared at the door. The tiny jewelry bag in my pocket —the one I'd been carrying around for days as I tried to decide the perfect way to ask Bethany to marry me —mocked me.

She couldn't do this anymore.

No. I wasn't going to accept that.

Eighteen months ago, doctors thought I wouldn't live after I was shot in the chest, and I'd fought my way back to life.

I'd fight for Bethany too, wear her down if I had to. Make sure she understood that whatever she needed, I would do my damnedest to make it happen.

She had given me another chance after how we'd started on the island. We'd come way too far to end it all now.

Not to mention, I couldn't live without her.

I followed her into the coat check room and closed the door behind us.

"I'm not letting you do this," I said to her back. "I love you, and whatever you need…whatever you think you can't do? We can work through this together."

She turned, face now pale. "Oh my God, Landon, no I—"

I couldn't stand the word *no* coming out of her mouth. I crossed over to her and pulled her against my chest. "Not no. *Yes.* We can figure it out. Don't do this to me, Wildflower. Don't do this to us. What we have is too good to give up on."

I was only a half step up from begging, but I didn't care. I would beg.

"Landon." She pulled away from me. I closed my eyes and sucked in a breath. I had to focus. I had survived a bullet to the chest.

I wasn't sure I would survive this.

"I lied to you."

My eyes popped open. "When?"

She shrugged one shoulder. "Well, I didn't really lie to you, I just didn't tell you the whole truth. I thought I would like it. Get back at you for what happened on the island."

For the life of me, I couldn't figure out what she was talking about. "Just tell me how to fix this. Whatever you lied about, we'll work it out."

"I didn't like it," she whispered. "I don't want to do it again. I'm not you."

At first, I thought she meant she'd cheated on me. But that didn't make sense either.

I cupped her face. "I need you to tell me straight up what we're talking about. Because I don't understand. All I know is that I don't want to lose you."

"I knew this was going to be Ian and Wavy's wedding all week. They said I could tell you, but I didn't because I wanted to have the secret for once." Her big green eyes filled up with tears. "I'm sorry. I didn't like it. I should've told you."

This woman. Her big heart and her sweet spirit. She was feeling guilty because she hadn't told me this would be a wedding.

There was no way anyone could love another person more than I did her at this moment.

I brought my lips to hers gently. "I love you."

"You're not mad?"

"You're a naughty girl, and I might have to tie you to the bed later tonight to teach you not to keep secrets from me. But no, I'm not mad."

But I was relieved.

And determined.

And done waiting for the perfect time to tie her to me forever.

I stepped back from her. "If it helps, I've had a secret this week also. And I don't want to keep it to myself anymore."

She raised an eyebrow. "Looks like I'm not the only one who's going to get tied to the bed to be taught a lesson. What's your secret?"

I dropped to one knee in front of her and pulled the ring out of the bag. It was an emerald. I'd gotten it because it reminded me of her eyes.

"Marry me, Wildflower. I'll do this again in a grand gesture befitting someone as beautiful as you. But right now, with just the two of us, promise me forever."

Her smile was breathtaking. "Yes. I love you, and I want forever with you."

I kissed her hand then slipped the ring on her finger. Hell, if my ring on her finger wasn't the rightest thing I'd ever seen.

I stood and pulled her in for a kiss. "You're mine officially now. No take-backs."

I felt her lips smile against mine. "And no more secrets."

•••

Acknowledgments

A very special thanks to the Calamittie Jane Publishing editing and proofreading team:

> Denise Hendrickson
> Susan Greenbank
> Chasidy Brooks
> Marci Mathers
> Tesh Elborne
> Marilize Roos
> Lisa at Silently Correcting Your Grammar
> Elizabeth at Razor Sharp Editing

Thank you for your ongoing dedication for making these romantic suspense books the best they can be.

And to the creative minds at Deranged Doctor Designs who fashioned all the covers for this series and made the books so beautiful—thank you!

Also by Janie Crouch

Ghost

Shadow

Echo

Phoenix

Baby

Storm

Redwood

Scout

Blaze

Forever

INSTINCT SERIES (series complete)

Primal Instinct

Critical Instinct

Survival Instinct

THE RISK SERIES (series complete)

Calculated Risk

Security Risk

Constant Risk

Risk Everything

OMEGA SECTOR SERIES (series complete)

Stealth

Covert

Conceal

Secret

OMEGA SECTOR: CRITICAL RESPONSE (series complete)

About the Author

"Passion that leaps right off the page." - Romantic Times Book Reviews

USA Today and Publishers Weekly bestselling author Janie Crouch writes what she loves to read: passionate romantic suspense featuring protective heroes. Her books have won multiple awards, including the Romance Writers of America's coveted Vivian® Award, the National Readers Choice Award, and the Booksellers' Best.

After a lifetime on the East Coast, and a six-year stint in Germany due to her husband's job as support for the U.S. Military, Janie has settled into her dream home in Front Range of the Colorado Rockies.

When she's not listening to the voices in her head—and even when she is—she enjoys engaging in all sorts of crazy adventures (200-mile relay races; Ironman Triathlons, treks to Mt. Everest Base Camp...), traveling, and hanging out with her four kids.

Her favorite quote: "Life is a daring adventure or nothing." ~ Helen Keller.

facebook.com/janiecrouch

amazon.com/author/janiecrouch

instagram.com/janiecrouch

bookbub.com/authors/janie-crouch

Printed in the USA
CPSIA information can be obtained
at www.ICGtesting.com
LVHW040808100823
754633LV00007B/536